THE BUTCHER'S DAUGHTER

The past can hurt you...

SARAH GOODWIN

Copyright © Sarah Goodwin
All Rights Reserved

Author's Note
and Content Warnings

Thank you for reading 'The Butcher's Daughter'.

This novel was conceived and written between my debut, 'Stranded' and my second traditionally published novel 'The 13th Girl'. Sadly it was not picked up for traditional publication but I have chosen to make it available as I still love the story and hope you will too.

All efforts have been made to ensure a smooth reading experience, but there may be the odd error that has been missed, for which I apologise. Hopefully you will enjoy the novel regardless.

Reader discretion is advised.

Spoilers follow:

I'd like to warn readers of sensitive content including – Sexual assault, murder, gas-lighting, graphic violence/descriptions of crime scenes, child neglect, grooming and gore.

TABLE OF CONTENTS

Prologue 7
Chapter One 13
Chapter Two 24
Chapter Three 32
Chapter Four 43
Chapter Five 52
Chapter Six 61
Chapter Seven 70
Chapter Eight 76
Chapter Nine 85
Chapter Ten 94
Chapter Eleven 103
Chapter Twelve 111
Chapter Thirteen 120
Chapter Fourteen 127
Chapter Fifteen 138
Chapter Sixteen 150
Chapter Seventeen 158
Chapter Eighteen 166
Chapter Nineteen 173
Chapter Twenty 181
Chapter Twenty-One 189
Chapter Twenty-Two 197
Chapter Twenty-Three 206

Chapter Twenty-Four 219

Chapter Twenty-Five 230

Chapter Twenty-Six 242

Chapter Twenty-Seven 252

Chapter Twenty-Eight 260

Chapter Twenty-Nine 267

Chapter Thirty 274

Chapter Thirty-One 288

Other books by Sarah Goodwin 295

Acknowledgements 299

PROLOGUE

The lights in the tube carriage fizzed on and off. I felt the swaying of the whole train as it trailed sluggishly around another corner. It was a struggle to keep my eyes open; I hadn't slept properly in days and had to fight to stay awake. The train was warm and quiet, mostly empty at that time of night. Too late for the commuters and those heading out for the evening, too early for chucking-out time at pubs and clubs.

The cardboard box in my lap held the last of my Mum's things. After yet another snippy phone call from her landlord, I'd spent the day finally clearing the rest of the flat. Her clothes, a few books, CDs and domestic clutter were all in a bin behind the Indian takeaway under the flat. The box contained documents, her few valuables and a collection of notebooks turned yellow with age. My mother's diaries dating back to the late eighties. It wasn't much of a legacy, that half-filled box. But it was heavy, weighted with decades of silence and secrets.

When I arrived home to our pokey, rented flat, the diaries were the first thing I dealt with. After a fashion. They went straight into the wardrobe, buried at the bottom of a box of magazines. Adam wouldn't find them there. He was as likely to dig through my true crime mags as he was to borrow my tights. I didn't even look at those magazines anymore. They were just a hangover from my old obsession. A morbid fascination with murder, with psychopaths and monsters. Just more junk I'd be better off throwing away. Only I couldn't.

It was like picking a scab, worrying a sore tooth. That old impulse to take out the magazines and force myself to look. To see the pictures of broken china and bloodstained walls. The tightly packed text detailing the lives and crimes of a thousand murderers. It was a kind of punishment, but also a poisonous release. Like smoking, or downing a few glasses of vodka. A habit that promised to release some of the awful tension in my body by causing a tiny amount of harm. But the anxiety, the creeping dread, always came back, stronger and worse than before.

Perhaps the diaries would change that. I had no idea what my mother had written in them, certainly nothing I'd ever want Adam to see. If he knew where I came from he'd never be able to look at me again. But, if I read the diaries, perhaps I'd finally fully unearth my rotten roots. The secret that had hung over me all my life but gone unmentioned by my mother. She had only ever assured me of my 'father's' innocence. Of her love for him. I wanted the truth she could admit only to herself, within her diaries. If she'd even been able to face it there.

I would read them, but not today. I was too exhausted to start digging up the past. I shut the bedroom door firmly and went to the kitchen.

I was so lost in my thoughts on the diaries that I barely noticed the new addition to the sign outside. It wasn't until I looked out the window while filling the kettle that I saw it. The sign had been there for a few months, '1st Floor Flat For Sale' reminding us every day that we had to find another place to live. Not easy, with my recent redundancy. No one wanted to rent to a couple where only one person was bringing in a wage. My redundancy pay-out was so low, as a fairly new hire, that it'd barely cover a deposit.

Only, in the orange light of the streetlamp. The sign no longer said, '1st Floor Flat For Sale'. Across it, on a bright new sticker, it said 'Sold'.

I stood there, kettle forgotten. Sold. Just like that. No more time. We'd had the viewings of course. Known that there was interest. But we'd never seen the same people twice. Hadn't thought it would be so soon. Adam wouldn't be home until early morning. They must have slapped the sticker on after he'd gone in for his shift. That or he hadn't noticed it. He would have texted me otherwise. To warn me. I took out my phone and sent him a single line, 'Flat sold', that was all I could manage before tears started to blur my vision.

I sat down on the sofa, hard, sending up a waft of stale cigarette smoke. Although the landlord had ruled the flat a pet-free and no-smoking zone, the provided furniture all stank of fags and cat piss. Or what we hoped was cat piss. No amount of air freshener or airing could get rid of the smell, which was only ever covered when the drains backed up or when the full summer sun hit the oily river. I hated it. The stink of the city, the cramped flat with its patches of mould and inadequate, expensive heaters. But it was the only home we had. I couldn't honestly say I thought I deserved better. Adam did though. Ever since we'd been given notice I'd been waiting for him to call it quits. That he wanted to live somewhere without me and my financial baggage weighing him down. Ever since we'd gotten together I'd been waiting for him to wise up about me, and leave.

Casting a despairing look about me, I caught sight of the open box on the floor. I'd left it there after grabbing the diaries. A pile of letters and bills stuck out of the top. I'd scooped them up off the mat at

Mum's. They'd have to be gone through, paid or notified. Another task I had no energy for. Then I noticed the top envelope had my name on it. My real name, not Judith Broch but Julie Pike.

My mother had long since stopped using that name for me. She'd lived under an assumed name herself. The only person who'd be writing to me with that name, at that address was him. Or more likely, someone working for him.

Raymond Wayfield; serial rapist and murderer. My father.

I stared at that letter for a long time. The light shifted in the flat as cars went by outside. Blue whirling lights and sirens went past, setting off a series of thumps and a baby's cries in the flat above. Still I couldn't bring myself to reach out and open that envelope. As if by doing so I'd be letting that man back into my life. Into my reality.

As if he'd ever left.

I forced myself to do it, tore the envelope apart with shaking hands. When I could bring myself to understand the words inside, I felt a stab of disappointment tinged relief, followed by shock. The letter was not from him, but from his solicitor. An official letter, telling me that my father wanted to see me. Then I saw the rest of the envelope contents and went still. There were papers enclosed for me to sign. Papers that would transfer the deed of a property into my name. His house. The house where Raymond Wayfield had lived when he met my mother. The house where he had hidden the bodies of his victims.

The air outside hit me like a cold slap to the face. I hadn't even realised what I was doing, but found myself walking up the street. It was a cloudless night and all the fragile heat of the early spring day had been sucked into the black void of the sky. I wasn't wearing my jacket and the night wind cut through me. I barely registered anyone around me as I went into the corner shop and pulled a scrunched up tenner from my bag.

I shivered my way home, clasping a bottle of red wine and a packet of cheap cigarettes. I lit my first cigarette in four years from the gas ring of the cooker and smoked it to nothing. My hand shook. I lit another at once and read the letter again.

It was the first I'd heard from Wayfield in years. Why was he getting in touch now? To offer me a house of all things? I felt sickly paranoid, as if he knew the bind we were in. As if he'd somehow orchestrated it, which was patently ridiculous. He was an old man, stuck in prison. He couldn't do anything to me. Yet my hands kept shaking and I slugged back the wine to try and quell the fear that was turning my skin to ice. The letter said he wanted me to visit him. Was that what the house was - a bribe? Trying to get me to come back and see him after so long? Did he want something from me? Forgiveness? Never. A kidney? I'd rather cut it out and feed it to a dog myself.

I had a vague memory of him from when I was a child. A normal looking man with my dark eyes and pasty skin. His hairline receding further with each visit. His face sharper, the eyes more sunken. Wilder. Mum made me go but I was never really sure why, aside from the fact that it got her in to see him. But the way he looked at me, like she wasn't even there. I never understood. What was I to him after all? What did it matter to him that I was his daughter?

My phone chimed and I jumped, dropping ash all over myself. It was Adam. A text that said simply 'what do we do now?'. I looked back at the letter. Well, that was the question, wasn't it? What was I going to do now?

I'd thought, naively, that with Mum's death the secret would fade away. Only I would know and I was never going to tell a soul. No matter how good Adam was to me, or how much I loved him. That was all the more reason to swallow back the bitter truth whenever I had the urge to confess. But the past was catching up to me; in diaries and letters and a house I desperately needed. It wouldn't let me be.

I had a choice. Either I could lie to Adam about the house, convince him to move there or we could struggle and beg and exhaust our bank account, to find a place only slightly worse than the shithole we were being forced out of.

A braver person would've turned it down. Someone more principled than me, who was prepared to struggle on. But I've never been brave. I have a rat's instinct for survival. Building nests of lies to keep myself safe.

Of course I knew I'd have to tell Adam something. Anything other than the truth. It meant another lie, but for a good reason, I told myself. To protect him from the truth about who I was, to give us a chance at a life together. I'd never been to that place before and I did my best to look nothing like my mother, nothing like him. No one was going to know me. It was just a house and it had been so long. What were the odds of anyone there remembering?

So I chose. In my head I concocted my lie; that Mum had inherited a house from an old family friend just before her death, and it had now passed on to me. As to the rest, any questions, I'd have to plead ignorance. But I knew Adam wouldn't look at this particular gift horse too closely. We needed it too badly.

I signed the papers.

Given all that came after, I might as well have done so in blood.

CHAPTER ONE

"Do you actually want whatever's in this?" Adam puffed, struggling to heft the box out of our rented van. On the side, scrawled in his schoolboy handwriting were the words 'More of Jude's Crap'. Not exactly a fool proof method for identifying the contents. But we'd been rushing to move. Most of the boxes said something like 'Kitchen stuff and DVDs' or 'Clothes and Tupperware'. It was a mess.

We were moving into the house, or more accurately, derelict bungalow, on an unusually warm day. Despite the fact that it was only April, I was already dripping with sweat and we had half a van to unload yet. It had all been a bit of a rush job. I'd signed the papers and our landlord had dropped the bomb on us that the sale was already mostly finalised. We needed to leave by the end of the month. Not much chance for me to reconsider.

"What's in it?" I asked, not really paying attention as I forced myself to grab another box. If I kept moving the guilt and fear couldn't swallow me whole. I couldn't think what an awful mistake I was making.

Adam dumped the box on the ground and looked inside. "Magazines."

I nearly tripped over my own feet getting to him. Dropping my own box I snatched his up and slapped the top down.

"Steady," Adam said, giving me an odd look.

"Sorry, they're just...private," I said, lamely, thinking of the diaries hidden underneath them. What if the bottom split and they fell out?

"Do you care about that sort of thing though? I've never seen you read them, or watch any of those documentaries. You know, 'Matchbox Boy - Birth of a Serial Arsonist'. That sort of rubbish."

I laughed uneasily. "Not for ages. It was something I got into at uni, just...one of those things. You know, when you've got too much time."

Not that I'd been bored of the magazines when I put them away. Quite the opposite. I'd collected them meticulously, along with books and even VHS tapes with news coverage recorded on them, all old and wavery. Back then it was an obsession, I was looking for my past, looking for a way in to the mind of a killer. I'd stayed up all night, smoking my lungs raw, trying to understand the two sides of my makeup. The serial killer and the girl who'd fallen for him. I wanted to know what neither of them would tell me; the truth.

I'd only stopped searching when I was given an ultimatum – my housemates threatened to kick me out. All the drinking, the constant stream of smoke from under my door, the way my room started to look like a weird shrine. It gave them the creeps. It was give it up, or move out and I didn't have the cash to go it alone. So I went cold turkey on cold cases, boxed up my stuff and made myself leave it alone. I couldn't forget though. It was always there, like an ulcer in my mouth, raw and filled with poison. I could never quite bring myself to throw it all away for good.

I took the box inside, where the cold clamminess of the house remained untouched by the heat outside. The bungalow was cookie cutter 1930s, but with pretentions: red brick, wood floors, and stained glass over the door. Most of the windows were broken and boarded up but one panel of stained glass remained. The bright sunlight shone red through the panes and onto the gleaming floor, like a puddle of blood. I stepped over it.

I dumped the box in the living room. While Adam was busy with unloading his gaming PC I extracted the diaries and went to find somewhere to hide them. In one of the bedrooms a vent cover hung askew. I'd noticed it on our first visit. Behind it the vent was dark and just about big enough. I wrapped the bundle of notebooks in a plastic bag and shoved them in, then reattached the cover and tightened the screws with my fingers. It'd do for now.

Adam came in just as I was dusting my jeans off. He looked around the room and I could see his enthusiasm waning.

"Place is in really bad shape, isn't it?" he said. "I don't think I was taking it in when we came before. I was just so glad to have this drop into our laps, but...fuck. It needs a lot of work. Every time I look around I see something else about to fall off, cave in or turn to dust."

"We'll make it work," I said, trying to exude a confidence I didn't feel. "There's my redundancy money, what's left of it. I'll find another job here, and now you're transferred we'll have more coming in."

Adam nodded, but still looked worried. I couldn't really blame him. The bungalow had been vacant for decades. Damp and rot seeped out of every corner, fixtures and fittings were missing or broken beyond repair. Though we'd been assured by a rushed survey that the place was structurally sound, it wasn't in the least bit liveable. We needed new electrics, plumbing and double glazing to replace the shattered, rotting windows. The wooden floors needed re-finishing, but there were still old, wet carpets that needed removing. All that and the smashed tiling, rusted taps, mottled plaster and peeling wallpaper would have to be put right.

"Everything's out of the van and out front – except the valuables in here," he gestured to the PC, my laptop and several boxes of games, blu-rays and appliances. "I'm going to go pick up moisture traps and a camp stove, glazier's coming in about an hour to properly board everything up. At least we'll have the place secure by tonight."

After he'd gone I started moving boxes in from outside. Our things were all in a jumble; rubbish bags of clothes and bedding already splitting open, boxes looted from behind a shop, taped back together and falling apart. As I dragged a heavy crate of crockery towards the door I realised I was being watched.

An elderly woman had come out of the house next door with a small dog on a lead. I raised a hand to wave, but she glared and turned her back on me. I watched as she strode away, feeling uneasy. Maybe she was just a mean old bag. Nothing to do with me personally. With the house. I hoped it was just me being paranoid. No one had any reason to suspect I was connected to anything that happened back then. Although I looked quite a bit like my mother I'd been dying my hair black for years and hadn't inherited her blue eyes. I'd hoped to pass unnoticed.

I carried on with the unpacking but ten minutes later, disaster struck. One of the bulging black bags caught on something in the overgrown lawn; a stick or piece of rusted metal. The plastic ripped like wet tissue and underwear went everywhere. I threw down the scrap of empty bag.

"Shit," I hissed, glancing around as I dove to scoop up the embarrassing heap of old and knackered pants. There were empty boxes stacked outside and I began to fill one. The hot, gritty wind flipped a silky pair of knickers away and into the overgrown rosebushes under the front window. Just what I needed if that cow from next door came back.

I jumped when two pairs of hands appeared beside me, scrambling to help me collect the spilled underwear. Once it was piled into the box I straightened up and found myself face to face with two women. One was a teenager, maybe just edging into her twenties. Her white-blonde hair and ghostly foundation making her look like a Victorian orphan. Only Oliver Twist never carried a black lace parasol or wore a bat-print tea dress.

The second woman was perhaps my age, warily eyeing thirty like it was a dog that might bite. She had dark brown curls all around her shoulders and had on an olive coloured jumpsuit. She was the first to smile and introduce herself, graciously ignoring my red sweating face and shocked silence.

"This is awkward, isn't it?" She said, handing me the pair of knickers from the rosebush. "Just moving in? I'm Marianna by the way, this is Katrine." The gothic waif bobbed her head shyly.

"Judith. Jude," I managed, still clutching a holey sock in one hand. "Thanks, for the help."

"Not from around here, are you?" she said.

"Yes. I mean, no. We're from London."

"Do you know whose house it was?" Katrine piped up, eyes wide and eager. I felt my stomach flip.

"Raymond Wayfield's," I said. "Yeah, I know who he was…is."

"You bought it then? We never thought anyone would," Katrine said.

"Looks like your kind of thing. Done some research on it?" Marianna asked, glancing down at one of the open topped boxes, containing books and DVDs on serial killers. More of my old collection.

"A bit," I said. I was starting to feel distinctly interrogated and wanted to get away. Judging from Katrine's goth getup these two were probably no strangers to a morbid fascination with the strange and unusual. If they were locals they'd know all about the town 'murder house'. I didn't want to be another thing for them to pick over and analyse.

"You should come to our book club," Katrine said, giving me a smile that went some way to reassuring me that they were just being friendly. "We read anything and everything, so long as it's true crime. What's your specialty?"

"Oh…I don't really have one. I just have a sort of…casual interest."

Katrine nodded. "Me too, at first. It's something that really speaks to the real heart of humanity, isn't it? Murder. I mostly read up on the occult crimes nowadays; sacrificial killings, vampires, lycanthropy."

"Lycan…" I repeated, sure she couldn't be talking about what I thought she was.

"Werewolves," Marianna interjected, widening her eyes in a 'don't get her started' way. "The rest of us have our own special interests. Personally I'm partial to assassinations. JFK, John Lennon, Versace. Takes all kinds."

"You should come," Katrine reiterated. "Hang on, let me get your email, I'll send over an invite."

I didn't have to give it of course. I could have just said I wasn't interested. That would have been a lie though; I was interested. Because the box of magazines was open, the scab was off and I was surrounded by sharp reminders of Wayfield, ready to draw blood. What else had I imagined would happen when I came back here? Maybe this was what I'd wanted – the diaries and his home, the perfect place to unravel my history.

I wanted to know what these local crime connoisseurs might know about their neighbourhood serial killer. Perhaps they could help me with the details of his crimes. The pathology behind them. Perhaps they could explain who he'd been on the surface, how my mother had fallen for him so blindly and completely that she'd never once admitted that he was guilty. Maybe they could help me to piece together enough of my history that it would fill the void in my chest.

As Katrine took down my email address, I couldn't help but hope.

*

My first book club meeting was a week and a half later.

We were settling in at the house, as best we could. The windows were slowly being replaced, the camp beds were up and we were officially out of money until Adam got paid. The electrics, water and everything else would have to wait a while. The warehousing company he worked for had transferred him down to Bricknell's nearest depot, so we wouldn't have too long to wait. Still, time dragged without showers, hot tea and a proper bed. Our old place had been furnished and we'd not got much in the way of homeware. At night we ate dinner sitting on an inflatable mattress beside plates covered in tea lights. It looked like a drug den.

In the ten days I'd had to think about it, I'd considered ghosting the book club meeting. As much as I wanted to hold the facts of my life, my parents' lives, up to the light. To know exactly who they had been before me. I knew that was like trying to catch a moving blade. Dangerous and like as not to leave scars. It would mean more secrets to be kept from Adam. More difficult truths to keep close to my heart, prinking it with every move I made.

In the end though I couldn't stay away. I had the same instinct for self-preservation as my mother: none whatsoever. I'd been drawn to those magazines, those books, for a reason. Perhaps this time, if I delved down far enough, I'd find enough truth to sate my curiosity for good. To move on.

The meeting was at Katrine's. The email she'd sent had mentioned that her housemates were off with their caravan for the weekend. It felt safe enough, away from London, to trust that she wasn't planning anything insidious. Adam made some half-serious comments about finding my body in a bin bag, but he didn't seem that worried. He dropped me off in Newston, the larger town just outside of Bricknell. It was a normal looking street of post-war brick houses, though I saw Katrine's touch in the gargoyle by the front step.

When she answered the door she looked surprised and happy that I'd come. Within seconds she'd grabbed my hand and pulled me through to the living room. It was a pinky beige, with a floral velour sofa and terracotta orange carpet. Katrine saw me give it the once over.

"Awful isn't it? I swear my Mum's colour-blind. That or the seventies sucked away her good taste."

"You said you had housemates?"

"Same difference," She muttered, going a bit pink under her white as plaster foundation. I realised she was probably desperate to fit in with everyone else, who were all clearly older than she was. Housemates sounded a lot cooler than 'Mum and Dad'.

"This is everyone by the way – say hello everyone."

I recognised Marianna and gave her a wave. Everyone else was eclectic to say the least. They ranged from a professorial man in his sixties to an acne scarred guy in his twenties who looked like he ought to have been selling single ciggies to kids at the school gates. Aside from those two there was a kind of cute guy my age, whose expert fade saved his cords and jumper look from total nerdiness. Beside him was a woman in a hoodie with a dragon on it, scrolling her phone. The case was falling apart but read 'World's Best Mummy' on the front.

"This is Judith," Katrine said, taking a seat by the cigarette-flogger.

"Jude," I corrected, smiling so as not to look standoffish.

"David," the professor said, reaching to shake my hand. His palm was dry as chalk but his smile was genuine, warm as his tweed jacket.

"I'm Finn," the guy in the retro jumper said, giving me a nod.

"This is Siobhan," Marianna said, when it became clear the 'world's best mummy' was too engrossed in her phone to introduce herself. She did glance up quickly and flash a rueful smile before going back to texting rapidly.

"And I'm Ricky," the lad smirked, revealing gappy teeth. "You're the one who flashed her knickers all over the crescent then?"

Katrine elbowed him, but it did nothing to subdue his grin. Neither did David's withering look. I didn't mind too much. I'd dealt with worse at my old job, you couldn't drive a bus route in London without developing a thick skin. It seemed like he was trying to be funny, which was welcome in the awkwardness of meeting so many new people.

"Marianna told us you're a true crime fanatic," Finn said, moving over on the velour loveseat so I could stop hovering awkwardly. "You've just moved into the Butcher's house, is that right?"

"Yeah, that is, me and my partner, Adam."

"Must've been cheap, it's nearly falling down," Ricky sniffed. "Been in there a few times myself."

"Oh really? Jude, did you find any leftover ketamine – only, Ricky'll be wanting it back," Katrine teased.

"Piss off," Ricky muttered, but still the grin remained. Looked like he had a bit of a crush on Katrine.

I let the moment for revealing the truth, or some of it, pass. They didn't have to know that I hadn't bought the house at all. Katrine hopped up and fetched out some drinks; tinned G&Ts and a few beers.

"How much do you know about him, the Butcher?" Finn asked, passing me a can.

"Just what's public record" I said, truthfully. I'd read the press coverage, the discovery of the bodies, the manhunt, the trial. I knew the dates and names, the dry facts. But a lot of what I'd read was sanitized, even for the tabloids. The descriptions were short and perfunctory 'disarticulated remains' didn't capture the essence of what he'd done. What my father had done. Aside from the murders he'd been convicted for, I knew there had to be others. Crimes only hinted at between the lines of newsprint. Unsubstantiated and undiscovered. Mum had never told me what she knew of what he'd done. I only hoped she'd written it down rather than taken it to her grave.

"Not the really juicy shit then," Ricky said. "The stuff about what he got up to when he was on the road? All those assaults and rapes where the girls mentioned a man that looked just like Wayfield."

"Or his girlfriend," Siobhan put in, abandoning her phone with a final tap at the screen. "The accusations that she was in on it, that she knew and tried to defend him when he got found out."

I nodded, feeling a weight settle in my stomach. This was what I was here to find out.

CHAPTER TWO

"If you go back far enough most places have a killer or two to their name," David said, clearly about to give a well-rehearsed lecture. "London obviously has many, most famously the Ripper. Smaller cities might have an arsonist, a shooter or a family annihilator that made the national news. For the market towns like this one, barely more than villages, the stories tend to be old; like the Highwayman."

He cast a pedagogical eye over us and must have noticed my nonplussed expression. He smiled benignly, forgiving my ignorance.

"There's a pub named for him in town. He was a local legend, a sort of Robin Hood figure."

"Only he robbed from the rich and gave it to his poor wives," Ricky quipped. "Had three of them all in difference parishes." He passed me a tube of Pringles and David shook off the interruption.

"Bricknell has a second, more contemporary claim to fame. The Butcher, aka Raymond Wayfield. A serial killer active in the early nineties who lived and killed on the cobbled streets of the sleepy market town you now call home, Judith."

He reminded me of the tour guides I'd often seen around London. Deerstalker hat and pipe in hand, tales of beheaded Queens and slaughtered prostitutes falling from their lips in ghoulish detail. Twenty pounds please, no cards, no refunds.

"Wayfield was charged for killing four women in total. Though he is suspected of many more crimes. He became known when bodies were discovered in his back garden by a curious neighbour. A manhunt followed, though once captured he was quickly forgotten in the wake of a terror attack in Belfast. Most media coverage of his trial was local with few stories managing to make the national news. He remains internationally insignificant."

I knew the bare facts of this already. Wayfield had buried the bodies in a hole under his shed. Covered in lime, the disarticulated bodies had been found by a local do-gooder. Wayfield's shed blew over in a storm and the poor bastard went to straighten it up for him. At the time, Wayfield was away, working as a driver for a haulage firm. A manhunt began, but he wasn't found for several weeks. Where and how he'd hidden was something I didn't know. They'd cornered him when he broke into a house in Newston, so he'd probably been hiding locally. Where though, I'd be interested to find out.

I was about to ask when Marianna checked her phone and started to gather her bag and coat. I saw Finn and David exchange a glance. Ricky only sighed and opened another beer.

"Off already?" David asked, pleasantly enough but with just a touch of weary disapproval.

"Yes, sorry. Didn't realise how tired I was. I've not been getting much sleep," Marianna said apologetically. "But, do carry on."

"Oh thanks ever so," Ricky muttered.

"We haven't discussed the last book yet, and what about the book for the next meeting?" David asked, puffing up like an irritated robin.

"I only skimmed it. Not sure I'll have much to say. It's Finn's pick for next time, isn't it?" Marianna asked.

"Mine actually," David said.

"Oh, well, email me the title and I'll get on it," she said. "The Ripper again, I assume?"

David sighed, but nodded. Katrine smothered a snort of laughter. Clearly David's specialty was well known. I wondered where everyone else's interests lay. Marianna said goodbye and saw herself out. Once the front door clicked behind her Siobhan sniffed.

"I would have thought she'd be bothered to stick around the night we get a new member," she said.

"Oh you know what she's like," Finn sighed. "Don't worry, Jude. It's not personal, Marianna's just a bit…well, insubstantial."

"Flaky as fuck," Ricky translated. "I'm amazed she was here on time for once. Normally she's twenty minutes late and leaves within the hour."

"And it's not like she has kids to worry about," Siobhan said.

"I'm sure she's very busy," David muttered, clearly attempting to be diplomatic.

It was sort of nice to hear their grumbling. I felt like I belonged, like they weren't on their best behaviour anymore. When Ricky offered me another drink I took the can happily and started to relax.

I stayed for a couple of hours while they discussed their last book pick. Siobhan had suggested it, the memoir of one of the FBI agents who'd pursued the Zodiac Killer. I'd not read it but it did sound interesting. From her comments I guessed that her interests ran to the popular serial killers of America. She talked at length about Bundy and Manson. I suspected she and my mother had a common interest in charismatic psychopaths. Though, Mum had been strictly monogamous in her affection.

By the time things had wound down and Adam arrived to pick me up, I was a little bit pissed. I'd not had the chance for a night out in a while. Adam was a homebody and most of my old mates had settled down, they didn't have time for late nights in the pub anymore. It was nice to have a couple of drinks and a laugh. Even more so because these people shared a shred of my strangeness. I didn't feel so lonely in their midst. By the time Adam poured me into bed I'd decided I quite liked the book club lot.

Of course when I woke up with a belting hangover and a mouth like old underlay I felt a little less friendly. Adam wisely let me acclimatize slowly, feeding me coffee until I could form sentences. In the end he went out on his own to collect some Facebook bargains for the house. But by the time he returned with a beanbag and coffee table I was up and dressed.

"She lives!" Adam exclaimed on finding me in the master bedroom, shovelling debris into doubled-up bin liners.

"So funny," I muttered. "You know what sucks? Not being able to have a goddamn shower in my own house. I feel like I stink of gin."

"You do. It's one of your most alluring qualities."

I threw an old, wet, sock at him. Adam disappeared for a moment and returned with a paper bag.

"Would a slightly squashed McMuffin make up for the lack of amenities?"

It did, sort of. I felt a bit better with warmish food in my belly. Adam had already eaten his but had saved me his hash brown because he knew I loved them. We sat on an offcut of carpet he'd found going free, spread over the wonky floor, like we were having a picnic.

"So, did you have a good time last night? All I got out of you on the ride home were some very slurred demands for fish and chips, and my very sexy body. I bought you a fishcake, which was your lot."

I snorted. "Thanks. Last night was OK. I liked them actually. Bit of a bunch of misfits but, you know, that's sort of where I fall."

"Were they all goths, like those first two?"

"No. Anyway, only one of them was goth-ish. Katrine. Everyone else was…well, different. All different. David's a retired teacher. Siobhan's a stay at home mum. Finn's a frustrated poet, loves his vintage clothes and Ricky's just a bit of a lad."

"What like, lager in the park, broken nose, designer trainers?"

"I guess. Nice though. They all were."

"Well that's good." Adam put on an indulgent, fatherly air. "My baby's all grown up and off making friends."

I threw a scrunched up wrapper at him. "What about you, nerd? Any friends at work yet?"

He shrugged. "Early days. Can't say I've been invited to any parties yet."

He was trying to be light, but it came off a bit hollow. I felt bad. Back in London Adam had his whole family just a tube ride away, not to mention his D&D friends and weirdly serious bowling team. He'd left all that behind to live together in our own place, in Bricknell. A place he still didn't know the history of. Eventually I knew I'd have to tell him something. I didn't want him to find out we lived in a murder house from some randomer at work, or in the corner shop. Still, I hadn't yet worked out how to tell him even half the truth.

"Hey, what's up?" He asked, looking suddenly serious.

"Nothing, just worried. About this place, getting it ready," I said, trying to smile.

"Big job, isn't it?" Adam scooted over and pulled me into a hug that made me feel worse, if anything. He was so understanding, so positive, and I knew I didn't deserve any of it.

"We'll manage, together," he said.

I nodded, but couldn't bring myself to say anything.

*

I went to the next meeting of the book club, and the one after that. It wasn't just about getting information on Wayfield, it became more a matter of escaping the bungalow for a while. On book club nights I could get away from all the work that needed doing and finally relax. I could also avoid Adam and his boundless optimism. It was draining to keep up with; the pretence that everything would be fine, when I knew it couldn't possibly last.

The book club guys were less stressful to be around. Although I couldn't tell them about my past, they also didn't need to know. So it felt less untoward, lying to them by omission. I got to know their quirks and interests; Finn's forensic science obsession, Katrine's passion for Victorian fashion and Ricky's interest in guns, militias and mass shootings. I began to get their in-jokes about David's prudishness, Ricky's lack of attention span and preference for films over books and Marianna's chronic lateness. In fact of the next three meetings I attended she was absent for one and late for the others. Leaving early on both occasions to catch up on sleep. She apparently commuted to London for work and was always exhausted.

I also began to find out more details about my father's history. I started keeping a notebook of names and dates, possible assaults where the victim identified someone who looked like him, or was a driver as he had been. I kept track on a small map, marking each attack with a black cross.

There wasn't much public info on my mother, at least not after Wayfield was arrested. She'd covered her tracks well; changing her name and mine, keeping a low profile, working cash in hand and never applying for a passport or driver's licence. My birth certificate had the wrong name on it, registered after the trial. The group even debated the sex of her child, as the only time I'd appeared with her in print I was just a lump in a blanket. It was odd to hear these people discussing me, while I sat in the room with them. It gave me an odd sense of detachment. In those moments I didn't feel like Wayfield's bastard child; I felt like just another woman in a book club, talking about someone else's life.

Away from the book club, things were progressing at the house. Adam got paid and we hired a sander to refinish the floors, had the living room plastered. Though we still had no oven, the electrics had been tested and repaired so we at least had proper lighting. We even got a little hardship loan and had a new boiler put in. At least we could wash up and have a scrub down, even though we still had to shower elsewhere; Adam at work and me at the gym.

It started to feel like it might one day be our house. I even bit the bullet and told Adam it had once belonged to a local serial killer, though I played it off as having only just found out from David. Adam found it a bit creepy, but mostly seemed unbothered. It was our house now. That was all that mattered to him. Every time we picked out a paint colour or made plans for the fitted kitchen, I felt our future together becoming more secure. More real. Maybe, just maybe, this would be the relationship that lasted. The one that could weather all my bad luck and awful secrets. Maybe this time, I could hold onto something good without it catching the rot from my past.

I should have known better than to hope.

CHAPTER THREE

Six Months Later

I pounded on Marianna's door for the third time in ten minutes. Still no response.

My fingers were turning red in the icy air. Already the warmth from the walk up the hill to her flat was fading and I shivered inside my too-thin coat. I'd always thought myself a sensible dresser. Moving to the country from London had proved that I was delusional. As it turned out, nothing I owned was suitable for more than a dash from overheated tube to overheated shop. In the six months since our move I'd not once thought to buy a better coat. Not that I could have afforded it. I was still looking for a job.

"Marianna!" I called out, by now thoroughly annoyed. Overhead I heard someone yell for me to shut up. Marianna's was the ground floor flat of three in a Georgian house. I stepped away from the door, nearly tripping over someone's premature jack-o-lantern, and looked up. There was only one light on, in the top flat, probably belonging to the solitary yeller.

Overhead the sky was dark and hung heavily across the rooftops like a wet sheet. It was a sky that threatened heavy rain and as I tried to force my cold fingers to tap at my phone, the first fat drops began to fall.

I had a text from Adam, asking when I'd be home. I texted back to say it'd be around ten. It was a rare evening off for him and I felt bad for missing it, but I was in need of outside company.

I tried Marianna's mobile for the third time but she didn't pick up. As I was about to ring again another call came through. It was David. I sighed as I lifted the phone to my ear, already knowing what was coming.

"She forgot she was hosting again, didn't she?" I said, by way of 'hello'.

David tutted. "Seems so. Sorry Judith, I should have called sooner. I tried to get hold of her because we'd been waiting a while, but there was no answer so we've decamped to the pub."

"We? Is everyone else already there?"

"Only missing Marianna and Ricky."

Privately I thought this wasn't much of a loss. I'd gone off Marianna a bit since first meeting her. She was a bit aloof, always busy with something or someone else. I already had a lifetime of being my mother's second choice, I wasn't looking to be someone else's. Ricky on the other hand was just a bit of a dick. Still, he at least turned up and usually brought snacks. Besides, he could be a laugh.

"I'll be there in twenty. Order me in a cider will you?"

David agreed and I rang off. He was a sweetie. I think he was the reason everyone else put up with Ricky and Marianna's less than ideal attributes. David hated to give up on anyone and was always making excuses for them. I suppose that was the retired teacher in him.

The rain was coming down heavier now, starting to make the leaf covered pavement slippery. Raindrops peppered my face as I slithered my way downhill. My boots were not made for weather of any kind, cheap pleather things with studs and shiny soles, already falling apart. It was the countryside, too wet and rugged. The damp got into everything. I knew I ought to be like everyone else and wear walking boots or at least boots from a proper shoe shop. Though even if I'd been able to afford them I wasn't sure I'd want to ditch my biker boots, or my leather jacket. I'd look like someone else without them, not me at all. Sometimes looking like myself was all I had to remind me to *be* myself. Since coming to Bricknell I often felt in danger of forgetting who that was. Like my links to my father were taking over my entire identity.

The Highwayman's Haunt was a pub on a street that branched from the main square of the little market town. I'd been there twice before. Unlike the chain pub down the end of the high-street, the Highwayman was small, intimate and never busy. The perfect place for our little book club to meet on nights when for whatever reason, our host was suddenly unable to accommodate us.

I arrived and quickly removed my drenched jacket. Inside the pub it was warm and almost empty, only a few dour locals at the wooden tables, nursing pints. It was the kind of pub that offered only three things on tap, where Coke comes in cans from a mini fridge and tomato juice is as exotic as drink orders get. Coming from a city of clubs and trendy pubs, it was almost insufferably quaint. There were no gigs at The Highwayman, not even a radio interrupted the morose, beer swilling silence.

"Alright?" I said, nodding to the landlord where he sat at a corner table, reading the paper. He nodded in acknowledgement. I slipped past a ratty velvet curtain and climbed the creaking stairs to the second floor.

Upstairs was the 'function room'. Though it's only clear function was storing broken or disused furniture and wholesale boxes of crisps. Still, it was free to use and had a fireplace which was great given the current cold. A handful of other local clubs used the space as well but mostly on weekends. We met on Monday nights.

I let myself in and dumped my wet jacket over a chair. Ricky had arrived since David's call, so I was the last one there, discounting Marianna. The fire was burning away and David looked up, smiling and gesturing to a pint of cider that sat, sweating, by an empty chair. I sat down and took a grateful swig.

"Hey Jude," singsonged Ricky, the same tired old joke.

Katrine and Siobhan were chatting but caught my eye as I came in, nodding hello. Likely they were discussing one of the many TV shows about vampires or sexy guys in armour that they were both addicted to. Aside from the book club it was the only interest they had in common. Sitting together Katrine could have easily been Siobhan's gloomy goth daughter. Siobhan conversely, in her oversized hoodie, messy ponytail and Uggs looked as ready for the school run as usual.

Finn was making notes and didn't react to my arrival. He always had a moleskin notebook in his coat pocket. I suspected he distressed the covers at home to look more bohemian. David was at the table with the book out in front of him, a neat page of notes written out. Top marks for him.

"Alright," I said, to the room at large. "Sorry I'm late. I stupidly thought Marianna might remember we were all going to hers this week."

"A foolish mistake." Finn said, his deep voice and cool tone reminding me of Jedi masters and documentary voiceovers.

Ricky was more direct, letting out a cloud of vape mist. "If she had a brain she'd be dangerous that one. Can we get a shift on? There's NFL on at quarter past eleven."

We all took our copies of the book out of our bags. Finn had his crammed in a pocket of his coat. Artfully careless. Ricky had his on his phone or so he said. I suspected that quite often he didn't bother actually reading the book, unless it was his pick. He just showed up to talk shit based on the blurb or whatever he'd seen online. He had brought hot wings from his work at the pizza place though, which made up for it.

It was very likely Ricky wasn't the only one to have not read the book. It was David's turn to pick again and so it was about Jack the Ripper. I'd quickly learned that everything David chose was about the Ripper, though sometimes he peppered in the Embankment Murders for variety. If it wasn't unsolved serial killings in 1800s London, David wasn't interested. I didn't mind so much. We all had our special interests after all; Ricky was always recommending things on Sandy Hook, Dunblane, or the Port Ray Massacres. Finn had his bungled convictions, miscarriages of justice and counter theories on famous crimes. His coat covered in badges from Amnesty International campaigns. And Siobhan kept her shelves stuffed with Bundy, Dahmer and the Zodiac killer, all fighting for space with softcore bondage romances – three for eight quid.

They thought I was the weird one, with my attachment to the Butcher. Though I read about other cases my few picks for the group had been books with at least a chapter on Wayfield. There'd been a very awkward evening when Ricky had called Wayfield 'my boyfriend' and I had to cover my revulsion with a coughing fit.

"Before we start, let's decide on the next meet up," David said. "A fortnight from now...I've got you down to host, Katrine?"

"I can't, my housemates are both home that Monday," she said, picking at her frayed lace gloves. I suspected she couldn't wait to move out. Having seen her parents in pictures and having sat in their nausea inducing living room I couldn't imagine they really 'got' Katrine.

"I can host," Siobhan put in, flipping open her new 'Mrs. Cullen' phone case to check her calendar. "I'll get Tom to take the kids to his Mum's for the evening."

"Great, and it's...oh, it's actually Marianna's turn to pick the book," David said ruefully, as if announcing an upcoming exam to the bottom set.

Ricky snorted. "'Course it is."

"That's not very fair, is it?" Siobhan put in. "I mean, if she's not even going to turn up to discuss your book, why should we read what she wants?"

As much as I didn't want to agree with Siobhan when she was getting puffed up about something, she had a point. Marianna wasn't the best at sticking around to actually discuss the book. Usually she was late, left early and sometimes didn't attend without warning; it was getting a bit annoying for me and I was the newest member. God only knew how long the others had been putting up with it.

David sighed. "I suggest we defer Marianna's turn until she's at a meeting to tell us about her pick. In the meantime we can skip to you Finn, if that's alright?"

"No worries. I've got something bookmarked already, about Louisa Masset. First woman hanged in the 20th century. I'll pop the link in the chat."

Ricky sighed. "Can we not get something a little bit more up-to-date?"

"You're after Finn," David said, "so you can dazzle us with one of your contemporary crimes then."

"Good, 'cause I've got something in mind that's proper gruesome. Colour pics and everything, none of this 'newspaper sketch' rubbish."

I noticed David's wince. He wasn't a fan of 'low crime' as he called it. I think he thought the vintage of the Ripper lent the crimes a class and dignity that your average hooker slaying lacked. Though, travel back in time and I expected there'd be a lot of Rickys milling around, trying to gawp at poor Annie Chapman's bloodstained petticoats.

We discussed David's book for the rest of the meeting. It was quite a good one actually, laying down the myths and truths of the Ripper against popular films and novelizations. Some entries into the cinematic lore got quite a paddling, which was a pleasant change of pace to hearing about Mary Kelly's stomach contents for the billionth time.

Ricky kept talking about his favourite Ripper film, 'From Hell' which I thought owed more to the gratuitous nudity than any historical interest. He and Katrine got talking about the costumes for the film. She'd done a project on them for college and was wearing a bodice she'd made herself. I thought she looked like an extra from Sweeny Todd, but in a fun way; lots of lace, fingerless gloves and eye makeup like twin punches to the face. Sort of like a burlesque 'little match girl'.

I was always a little envious of her confidence. My go-to uniform of jeans, retro t-shirts and leather jacket wasn't exactly glamorous. It was more 'grungy' and I felt a waterproof coat would take me over the edge into 'frumpy'. Even my once funky hairstyle had betrayed me; the jet black dye having faded, starting to grow out with my choppy layers. I had blonde roots now which just looked terrible. Money was too tight for a dye job and cut. My last tango with box-dye had left my hair greenish and my neck grey. Sometimes I felt Adam was showing me up with his bright high tops, skinny jeans and vintage button downs. He looked like a cross between a kids TV presenter and a popstar's up and coming boy toy.

As usual our chatter devolved towards the end of the night. We were all a little tipsy after several trips down to the tiny bar to get pints and crisps. It was usually around this time that I directed the conversation to what I was really interested in; what they could tell me about Wayfield. Though I'd let it slip for the past couple of meetings. It'd just been nice to meet up with everyone, chat about normal stuff: roadworks, TV, a local music festival. It'd been less about pumping them for information and more about spending time with friends. It couldn't carry on that way though, I wanted to know everything about Wayfield. Everything about what he'd done and what that said about him. About my mother and me.

That night I got Finn started on the Butcher's less well known crimes. In his twenties he'd crisscrossed the country making deliveries for a multitude of different companies. The few sources devoted to his crimes estimated that he was responsible for many unsolved sexual assaults across the UK and Ireland but could give no real details. There was even speculation that he'd committed offences in mainland Europe. While I had been looking at cases and trying to relate them to Wayfield, Finn had been going the other way; identifying his routes and then looking for matching cases.

"Where did you get those dates from?" I asked, once he'd reeled a couple off.

"There's a haulage company, Franklyn's? It went under in the mid-nineties and they sold off all their assets. Most of the paperwork obviously went straight in the bin but some of the records got sold off with old filing cabinets, which got sent straight to storage. I follow a bunch of people that post paper ephemera and when I saw 'R. Wayfield' on one of the pages they put on Instagram I asked how much they wanted. Obviously he worked for more than one firm and this is only some of the information about his routes, but I've been able to match him up with three assaults so far. Though that's obviously not conclusive. It just means he was there when it happened and they fit his M.O."

"Could I get a copy of the list? Or see the originals?" I asked, eagerly. "I'm still putting together my file on him; where he went, what he was up to leading up to when he started killing, that sort of thing. This would be a great addition."

Finn suppressed a smile, but I could tell he was pleased with himself. "Sure. I'll run off some scans and send them over to you."

"Thanks," I said, already itching to start running down those dates and connect them to possible crimes. I wanted a complete picture of the man Wayfield had been. How had he gotten away with it? What were his patterns? What did he do to these women? I wanted to know if there was any way my mother could have known. I wanted to know if she'd ever gone with him.

I'd had another letter from his solicitor only the week before. That made five since we'd moved into the house. Another reason to regret my rash decision of accepting that 'gift' from him. It appeared there had been strings attached. Strings I'd been too desperate to notice. Each letter said the same thing, only in more insistent terms;

"Your father would like to see you…"

"...urge you to pay a visit to..."

"...of the greatest importance..."

"...without delay..."

I'd managed to get my hands on each letter before Adam, simply because he was asleep after his shift. I lived in a state of anxious desperation, afraid that one day a letter would come on his day off. I didn't want him to see the solicitor's logo on the envelope and start asking questions. Worse, I didn't want him opening it by accident and seeing the truth there in black and white; Raymond Wayfield, 'your father'.

I'd thought about just calling the solicitors and telling them to stop sending the letters. That I would never want to speak to Wayfield, so it was a waste of time. But they were his solicitors. If he wanted them to send the letters, they would. No, it was a problem that had to be dealt with at the source. Wayfield himself.

Whatever it was he was so desperate to see me about, I knew it wouldn't wait forever. One thing I was learning about Wayfield was that he'd go to great lengths to get what he wanted. Soon there would be phone calls, people showing up on the doorstep. If I wanted it to stop I'd have to pay Wayfield a visit. If I could go in there armed with the facts; everything he could use to shock me, every secret about myself and my mother that he could dangle to control me, then I'd be able to make him stop contacting me. Or so I hoped. I just had to find a way to turn it all against him. A secret weapon he wouldn't be expecting. Only I had no idea what it was, yet, or if it even existed.

I felt a bit guilty, using my new friends as a means to an end. I felt sometimes that it made me just like him. A user, not caring what front I had to put on to get what I was after. But I had to know, and it wasn't like I could tell them the truth. If I did that I'd either be hated as a part of Wayfield's dark history, or looked at like a specimen is some exhibit. A gory crime scene picture or bloody axe. Worse, they might think me a victim. Feel sorry for me. I couldn't bear that.

I didn't dare even contemplate telling them. I couldn't let it get out, any of it. I wouldn't be known as a victim or a monster. Couldn't stand to have that knowledge out there for Adam to get hold of. He didn't know the truth about me, and if I had my way, he never would.

CHAPTER FOUR

I got home just after eleven and Adam was waiting up for me. I felt even guiltier then. Not only had I left him on his own for the whole evening, he was losing out on sleep to make sure I was OK. I felt a stab of irritation too. I hadn't asked him to do that after all. I shook it off, more and more often lately I was letting my own guilt make me snappy. It wasn't his fault. I was the one lying. He was just a great guy, trying to be everything I needed. I knew I didn't deserve him and it made me feel worse every time he showed me how much he cared.

I stumbled as I tried to take off my boots. Clearly I'd overdone it on the cider. It was unusual for me. I wasn't much for drinking. When out at a venue I'd happily nurse the same plastic cup all night. I think it was the pressure of lying to my new friends that had me hitting the bar so hard lately. The closer I got to them, the worse I felt.

Inside, the bungalow was chilly. After six months we were still struggling to afford the renovations necessary to get the place up to a liveable standard. The house had sat empty for almost thirty years after all, bringing it back was never going to be easy. It was like trying to resuscitate a mummified corpse.

"Jude? That you?" Adam called out.

"Yeah." I shook off my morbid imaginings and padded down the hallway to the living room.

"You're back late," Adam called, as I slid my socked feet over the newly refinished floor and came to a stop behind him. His desk was in a corner of the living room, the only room we had managed to finish since moving in. He often joked that it really was a living room; we slept, ate, relaxed and cooked there. Every other room still cried out for new plaster, flooring and fittings.

"Sorry, we were having a laugh, lost track of time." I watched him hammer away at his keyboard and mouse for a moment. On the screen a spray of blood signified a successful headshot. The speakers babbled with a mixture of cheers and swearing as the other players took possession of the enemy base, picking off the survivors.

"You could always come along you know," I said. "You'd like it, we have a good time."

"Sitting around talking about flensing and decomposition rates doesn't strike me as being a 'good time'," Adam said, not looking up as he ripped open a door and tossed in a grenade. "That sounds like white people nonsense, which I refuse to be part of. You already convinced me to move into a haunted house, which is bad enough."

"Not haunted, historic. And Finn's not white."

"You don't have to be white to believe white people nonsense, don't be racist," he said archly. The grenade went off and severed limbs bounced unrealistically from the obliterated door. I patted him on the shoulder.

"Yes, I can see you're diametrically opposed to violence. You pacifist you."

Adam glanced up from the screen, which was now flecked in the blood that had sprayed over his character's visor. He grinned at me, gappy teeth making him look, as always, like a cute chipmunk.

"There's a difference between getting my jollies blowing up pixels, and getting them talking about some poor woman getting her very real throat cut."

Since I'd started going to the book club Adam often took the moral high ground over my 'bloody hobby'. It was always mostly a joke, but sometimes I got the idea that it actually disturbed him. I'd find him looking at the cover of one of my true crime books with a slight wince of distaste. I didn't know how to explain to him that, for me at least, I wasn't poking into other people's lives for amusement. I was looking for something else. Understanding. Solace.

"You're missing out. I'm making tea, do you want one? Wash away the taste of cordite and plasma?" I said, eager to change the subject.

"Sure, there's always time for tea in war. We are British, are we not, old chum?"

I laughed, took the kettle from our camping stove and went to the kitchen, separated from the main room by French doors with no glass in them. We'd had a new sink installed only recently. The rest of the kitchen remained a disaster. We'd cleared out the half rotten chipboard cupboards and the smashed tiles. Unfortunately we still had nothing to replace them with and no oven, fridge or washing machine. I was getting royally sick of the laundrette and the one pizza place in Bricknell.

After making tea on the stove I took it over to Adam. He was sniping now, peering at the screen as his crosshairs panned around.

"Oh, I forgot to say. Kelly blew out her back so I'm on for an extra shift day after tomorrow," he said.

I threw myself down on the tatty beanbag. "So you'll be sleeping on Thursday, rather than helping to clear the garden?"

The front garden was still a tangle of brambles with only a beaten track to the door. Out back the state of things was even worse as people had been using the place as a dump; a rusted out washing machine and an old mattress were the principle decorations, lording it over piles of masonry and smashed up furniture. Nothing we could make use of unfortunately, I'd actually been desperate enough to look.

"I know, we can put it off if you like? Present a united front against the rats and tetanus?"

"No, it's OK. I'll get on with it. Might as well, since no one's calling back about any of my sodding applications."

"You'll find something. Don't worry. In the meantime I'm putting in for all the overtime I can. We could get a shower put in when I get paid for this month. I'm really getting sick of using the one at work. You don't want to know what sharing a shower with five hundred warehouse guys looks like."

"Probably still better than the gym. The sheer amount of hair is mindboggling. Our own shower does sound good." I said, wistfully. I was in desperate need of a long hot shower in the comfort of my own home. We had the old bath and a functioning boiler, but the sunken tub was twice the size of an average bath. Exorbitant to fill. I'd even tried washing my hair over the side with a plastic hose, but that didn't exactly leave me feeling relaxed and fresh.

"We're keeping the bath though, right? You did agree," I said.

"I thought you were joking. We can't even afford to fill it. Never mind the other stuff." He looked up incredulously at the wrong moment, and an RPG blew him out of his snipers nest. Adam didn't seem to notice that his body was rag-dolling in a pool of blood.

"It's aspirational. Just think, one day we might be able to afford to fill that bath. And besides, why would I be joking? It's an original feature."

"Of the murder house," Adam said slowly, like I was mad.

I realised belatedly that this was another one of those occasions where I'd become desensitized to something that normal people found strange. It had started happening more often since the move. Like proximity to my parent's past was warping me. I didn't like to think about it, so I tried to style it out by appealing to Adam's logical side.

"If we want a chance of selling this place once it's refurbished, we need to get it looking so fabulous that no one will care who lived here."

"Or who they cut up in the bath tub?" Adam said pointedly. "I mean, where else would he have done it? On the hall carpet?"

"Well if you came to the meetings you might find out," I said, already sorry to have brought it up. "Watch your back, you're about to get shot in it."

Adam swore, whirling on his computer chair and scrabbling for the mouse. He didn't get to it in time. With a heavy sigh he left the game and came to share the beanbag with me.

"Bloody kids and their twitchy trigger fingers. No sense of sportsmanship. But seriously, that bath is a nightmare. Even if we could use it I don't think I'd want to."

"It'll make putting in a shower cheaper though, if we can just install it over the bath. A bath which will hold the two of us."

"You make a good point," he muttered, reluctantly. I cuddled up to him and he squeeze my shoulders, planting a kiss on the top of my head.

We were cuddling quite a lot recently, both out of affection and necessity. The house had no central heating, just a bunch of nonfunctional storage heaters. We'd not had the money to get the one chimney swept either, so a fire was out of the question. Adam was layered in jumpers, his dark curly hair escaping from a knitted hat. The tip of his nose was cold. I kissed it and he grinned, tickling chilly fingers under my sweatshirt.

Later, when Adam was asleep, I got up and went to poke around in the bedroom. I was doing this a lot lately, haunting the house at night. Unable to sleep. It was especially common on book club nights. My thoughts would just keep racing, trying to fit pieces of the past together.

During clearing and cleaning I'd shoved anything salvageable into boxes to sort later. We'd cleared out the broken glass, rubbish and fallen plaster in the first week we were there. What remained now were the things left behind when Wayfield was imprisoned. I'd insisted we keep them on the pretext that they might be worth selling – which Adam had gone along with. The place had been frozen in time while everyone tried to forget who had lived in it. Not even the local council had dared make a move on the house itself. They'd stopped short at compulsory purchasing half the garden as if held back by the wall of gloom that surrounded the place.

There had been break-ins over the years of course; teenagers were second only to true crime fans in terms of ghoulishness. What better place to take your latest conquest but a haunted house? In the years of neglect, furniture had been smashed or stolen. Still, there was plenty left to go through. The things Wayfield had surrounded himself with.

I perched on the windowsill and started to sift through a cardboard box. So far I'd not found anything worthwhile. I'd even had the book club over for a look around in the hope that they'd spot something revelatory. They hadn't. Though David had been the one to point out that the bath was an 'original feature'. It was huge, square and enamelled in seafoam green, with the outside tiled in dark green. It reminded me of the walls of the tube tunnels. Katrine had taken some photographs. Even Marianna had shown up for the tour, late as usual and had complimented the work we'd done.

I picked through the box's contents; a boot, a knitted football scarf rotting to holes in the middle, loose buttons, a comb. I squinted at the mouldering scarf; a West Ham supporter. Not a local team. Had he gone to matches while on the road for work? Were there crimes out there that corresponded to their victories or failures? Something to look in to.

I picked out a cracked glass bottle. It was heavy and slightly green. The brand was worn off the gold label, underneath it said 'aftershave for the discerning gentleman'. The contents had long since evaporated but I sniffed the stopper. Sharp as pine sap and vodka. It seemed to billow into the room like a long held breath.

More items. A plastic alarm clock with a cracked face, the cable for an electric razor, nail scissors, a shoe horn. Bedside table detritus. I discarded the lot into a black plastic sack. There was however a silver compact, hallmarked and everything, though black with tarnish. A trophy? Probably not. Who would carry such a thing in the eighties? It might have belonged to Wayfield's mother. It felt odd to call her my grandmother. She'd been dead long before I was born. What had she been like to have a son turn out like him? I put the compact in the 'sell' box with a shudder.

With the aftershave bottle in hand I picked my way through the darkened bungalow. Stopping at the kitchen window I looked out over the garden.

The original gravesite was at the bottom of the garden. Someone at the council had acquired half the land and incorporated it into a carpark behind our row of houses. That was how the rubbish had been dumped; straight over the fence and into our half of the garden. The burial site was lost underneath concrete and pay-and-display machines.

I opened the aftershave bottle, wondering if this was what the house had smelled like when he'd lived in it. If my mother had bought him the cologne as a present or if he'd chosen it for her benefit. I'd read that scent was a powerful memory trigger, but if I'd ever smelled it before I couldn't remember.

I wondered if Adam was right. If Wayfield had dismembered his victims in our bathtub? If he had he'd have swilled it out with something, bleach maybe, or alcohol. Perhaps he'd splashed the aftershave around to get rid of the smell. I shuddered, trying to imagine him living in this house after that. Bathing where their blood had run. I felt slightly sick, the smell of the aftershave turning coppery in my nostrils.

I drifted back to the bathroom and looked into the deep, green tub. Water dripped from the corroded taps incessantly. We couldn't get them to turn off completely. Drip. Drip. Drip. I pressed my lips together, finding them dry. Perhaps Wayfield had stood where I was, in the doorway, surveying his handiwork. I shivered, surrounded by the sharpness of pine needles.

Had my mother been in that bath? Soaking away her cares, perhaps with Wayfield beside her? Had she not known or just not cared what had gone on here? Maybe Adam was right, we should get rid of it.

The phone ringing made me jump, the bottle nearly slipping from my fingers. I crammed the stopper in, then hurried to the living room, stepping over Adam as he stirred, bothered by the noise. It was my phone. I dug through my handbag until it shuddered into my hand. The screen showed it was almost one in the morning and David was calling.

"Hello? David?"

"Does he realize what time it is?" Adam slurred, struggling to sit up on the unsteady camp bed. I waved a hand at him, David's words not making any sense under Adam's griping and the static of poor reception.

"Say that again," I said, thinking I'd misheard.

"It's Marianna. She's dead."

CHAPTER FIVE

We met at David's the next morning. I hadn't had more than an hour of sleep since he called. The others looked as unusually drained and pale as I felt. It was the first time I'd seen Katrine without makeup on, she looked so much younger, a scared little girl. Siobhan, fresh from the school run, didn't hesitate to hug her. Even Ricky was unusually silent. I hovered on the edges of their grief, not sure what to say or do. I hadn't known Marianna like they had. I wasn't sure what was appropriate.

I let my eyes wander while I waited for someone else to speak. David's place was as meticulously clean as always. Decorated in shades of brown from the hardwearing carpet to the reproduction 'antique' furniture and watercolours of spindly winter trees, all of it was shades of sepia and coffee. Floor to ceiling bookcases dominated the living room. I noticed that most of the more modern stuff was hidden away at the bottom, behind the sofa. Up top were his Ripper books, some turned cover outwards like in a shop. A special hardback Conan Doyle compendium had pride of place on the 1970s mantelpiece.

We gathered around the coffee table, sipping tea from dark brown mugs. Katrine was bunking off college to be there and Finn had phoned in sick to work. David had phoned me first off purely by chance. He hadn't known what to do and my number was the most recent in his history. I'd told him to get to bed, then messaged the chat to let everyone know what had happened to Marianna. That she was dead.

She'd been dead when I was standing in the cold, trying to rouse her. Dead as we sat in the pub taking the piss out of her lateness. Dead as we skipped over her turn to pick the book for us. Three days her sister had told David. Three days she'd been dead in her flat, unnoticed.

"What do they think happened?" Finn asked, the first to break the silence. He was always the one to bring up the hard stuff – naturally curious for all the facts and details. I often thought he was wasted at the sorting office; he should have been a forensic scientist.

David cleared his throat. "Her sister, Diana, said they thought it was a gas leak – carbon monoxide from the boiler."

"How the fuck does that happen?" Riley said. "How didn't anyone realise?"

"The upstairs neighbours had been away. They didn't come back until yesterday and rang up about their boiler not working. The fumes must have found a way down to her flat. By the time the repair guys arrived and went to tell her, it was too late," David said, watery eyes fixed firmly on the brown carpet. "Her sister thought I was her boyfriend – I suppose because I'd phoned so much when she was late for the meet up."

Ordinarily the idea of David being anyone's boyfriend, let alone Marianna's would have had Ricky in fits. Now though he just nodded, preoccupied. I'd already told Adam about the gas leak and he'd promised to get a CO detector on his way to work. The idea of dying in my sleep had always seemed peaceful to me, now not so much.

"I didn't ask about a funeral or anything, it was too much of a shock. I'll call back though...offer our condolences," David was saying.

"Do you think we ought to go?" Siobhan asked. "We did know her. Only, if we are going I'm going to need to organize the childminder."

"Isn't her family all back in Lithuania?" Katrine said. "They might decide not to have a service here."

"I'll find out, in a few days," David said. "I don't want to upset her sister, she sounded distraught on the phone. Besides, there might be an autopsy or an inquest even, to determine fault, if she died due to negligence."

"I don't get how this happened," Finn said. "I mean, carbon monoxide poisoning gets old people, babies – people who can't react in time to the symptoms and get out."

"She was probably asleep," Katrine said.

Finn shrugged. "I'm just saying, it's weird. I'd need to check the studies."

"This isn't a cold case, Finn," David said gently.

"We should do something," I said, surprising myself. "Have like a memorial meet up or something. If we find out there's not going to be a funeral." I felt instantly awkward, but David nodded.

"That's a good idea. I'll find out about the funeral but we could do something special as well. Something she would have liked. Perhaps a visit to St. Julien's Woods?"

"You mean Wayfield Wood?" Katrine said.

I was almost ashamed at how fast I looked up on hearing that name. Another piece of information for me to grab hold of and examine.

"Officially, it's called St. Julien's Woods," David corrected patiently.

"Well yeah, but it was Wayfield's hiding place, wasn't it? When the police were looking for him he hid out there for weeks. Wasn't there a hunting shack or something?"

"A hide," David said patiently, ever the teacher. "For watching badgers."

"Yeah," Katrine said. "We could go on like a...pilgrimage. We wouldn't have met Marianna if it wasn't for the Butcher."

"I didn't know that," I said. They'd never really said how the group had come to be. I'd assumed that they'd just met each other over time and discovered they shared an interest. Like how Katrine and Marianna had stumbled on me. Though, Katrine had confessed after my second meeting that they'd come by on purpose to see who was moving in to the 'Wayfield House'.

"David was the one who started it," Katrine explained. "He was going to write this book on local history, mostly about the Butcher and other local criminals."

"It never came to anything," David said quickly, blushing.

"But he started going around looking at different sites, ordering lots of books for research" Katrine said, brushing his words aside. "And he got talking to Finn at the sorting office."

"He was coming in three, four times a week," Finn said, smiling a little. "We got talking about all the packages he was picking up."

"I was still working in those days. Teaching's terrible for it. I was only in for the post on Saturdays." David nodded at Ricky. "We met in the Highwayman, when I was in there getting a feel for the place. It used to be the old jail, for drunks and the like."

"Still is," Ricky smirked. "Anyway, we got chatting because there was this local ale on tap for a bit – The Butcher. And David asked me if I knew why it was called that, because he had no one else to bore with it…"

David sighed.

"…and I said, I do, as it happens. Because when I was in school the one project I actually liked doing was one on 'local history'. Only my teacher didn't think my subject was 'appropriate' so I had to change it to the workhouse they made into the new ASDA. We already knew each other then, didn't we Kat?"

"You wish," she said, rolling her eyes. "Ricky and I went to school together, before I left to go to college."

"And I left to get a job," Ricky said, smartly. "Anyway, that was when David was all like 'let's start a club for history and crime and stuff' so I remembered Kat liked all that gory stuff and found her on Facebook."

"I mentioned it to Finn when I saw him," David said.

"And I got to know Siobhan's better half because he and the lads all came in to the pizza place every Saturday after football. We got talking and he mentioned she was in to all those serial killer biopics," Ricky said.

"Too many late nights, up feeding the baby," Siobhan said. "We only had a basic TV package then. They were the only thing worth watching that late. And I was looking for something to get me out of the house occasionally. Have a drink and a chat about something other than Paw Patrol."

"And how did you meet Marianna?" I asked.

The buzz of chatter died immediately and I cringed. Stupid to ask, once everyone was feeling a bit better. It was Finn who answered.

"I met her at a bus stop. It was late coming so we did that thing where you start off complaining about the bus, then the weather, then we started talking properly. She had this book she'd been reading about the JFK assassination. I invited her to the club. Didn't think she'd come but she did."

There was a silence and this time I let it lie unbroken. As much as I was desperate to know where this hiding place of Wayfield's had been, it would wait. Everyone was upset over Marianna's sudden death. I was too, but, it was clear the others had known her better than me, and longer too. I felt bad for them. It wasn't long before I made my excuses and left.

I didn't go straight home from David's. Instead I went for a walk along the canal. The quick growing weeds of summer were turning brown and rotting away, making the air stagnant. The canal itself was beautiful however, a mosaic of fallen leaves floating in the dark water. I took a breath of leaf-spiced air and let it out slowly, decompressing. I kept thinking about Marianna, dead in her flat while I banged on the door. It was so sad. She'd been there for days and no one had thought anything of it. Not even her own sister. I walked along the towpath, trying to outpace the image of her, stiff and cold under her duvet.

At the far end of the path, where the canal passed into a red-brick tunnel, there was a shuttered workshop. Half fallen down, it must once have been something to do with the network of boats that had hauled coal and other goods around before the railway was properly established. I clutched my jacket tighter around me and supressed a shiver. I hadn't meant to end up there. Not yet. Although it was one of the places I'd decided to visit, eventually. Today was not the day to be poking around in the past. Still, I couldn't help myself. I picked my way around to the back of it.

The brambles rose in a tangle, almost a wall with the rotting leaves and nettles caught in them. The gap between them and the rear of the building was full of empty cans and condom wrappers. A wet, mouldering towel lay in the mud under the blackberry bushes. Clearly a favourite haunt of horny teenagers. I tried to imagine what it would look like at night. No longer a charming relic of the industrial past but a spooky lair that might conceal an axe murderer or slathering beast. The orange glow of a single streetlight barely reaching behind the workshop. The cries and screeches of nocturnal animals coming out to hunt, or be hunted.

This was where the first girl had been killed. Wayfield's first confirmed murder. The twelfth of January, 1992. Pippa Grey, a sixth former at the nearby college. Her mates had left her with her boyfriend, but after an argument over his supposed infidelity, he'd also gone off, leaving her alone at the far end of the canal. This had been relayed to the police by her tearful friends after her body was found, but not released to the papers. David had told me, about it. He'd found out from a retired officer whose son he used to teach.

Had Wayfield been watching, stalking her in preparation for such an opportunity? Or had he simply been out late, walking, when he came across her? Perhaps he had been looking for someone, not her exactly, but she had been there when he passed by. Bad luck pushing her into his path. Why had he decided to make the leap to murder on that day? With that girl? Had he thought about it, worked himself up to it? Or was it just an urge that overtook him when he saw her alone, in the dark?

There was still so many things I didn't know. Didn't know how to discover without giving Wayfield the visit he still wanted. I wasn't ready for that yet.

I knew from the papers that her body was found in the water, naked, the next morning. She had been strangled. In the early hours of a wintry morning, a narrowboat struck her in the darkness of the tunnel. The two men on board saw her and summoned the police. They had to wake her parents, who were unaware she wasn't in bed, asleep.

I'd seen her picture, the standard school photo. She had blonde hair and light eyes. Just like my mum. Her clothes were not recovered. There was speculation that Wayfield had kept them as a trophy, but they were not found in his home. I wondered what he'd done with them. Relived the murder through them until he moved on to the next girl, then burned them?

Finn had issues with the theory that the canal murder was Wayfield's first. He liked to theorise that someone else was responsible for it, someone too impulsive to bother with disposing of the body in secret. Of the women he'd killed, only the body in the canal had been dumped somewhere other than the gravesite at Wayfield's home. My home. Neither was it dismembered. According to Finn, the canal murder was the event that had sparked Wayfield's killings, inspiring him to kill. It was only irony that Wayfield had been convicted of the murder.

Personally I didn't see the Butcher as being controlled or careful, as Finn categorised him. I did, after all, have insider information. I'd met Wayfield, albeit a long time ago. I'd seen how he was with the prison staff and with my mother. With me. He was manipulative, calculating, yes, but not above fits of rage or impulsive violence. I remembered several occasions when visits had been cancelled because he'd attacked someone. He didn't strike me as someone to consider the consequences of an action, in the moment.

If anything I suppose I ought to have hoped he was a calculated man in complete control of his actions. Rather than someone suffering the kind of bloodlust that might be part of a diagnosable psychosis. One he might have passed on to me.

But still, I believed the girl in the canal was his first. He'd lost control, hunted too close to home in a moment of weakness and then overcorrected – killing the girl to ensure her silence. I saw in her death a man out of control. As to why, I had a theory, but only the diaries would confirm it.

CHAPTER SIX

I got up the next morning, leaving Adam to catch up on sleep after working yesterday with a another shift that night. Living on top of each other in one room wasn't ideal with him working nights. Adam was a light sleeper, especially during the day. To get out of the way I decided to get a head start on the garden.

It needed the time. Aside from years' worth of dumped rubbish there were thick tangles of brambles and towering nettles. Generations of weeds had lived and died on what was once the lawn. Small trees had even started to spring up; thin but numerous. Not to mention buddleia with their brown, crumbling flowers and thick, far reaching roots. The resultant thicket was so dense that the only way in would be with shears. Looking at it I wished for an axe. The kind of wickedly sharp blade used to fell full-grown trees and cut helpless damsels out of wolves.

With a pair of wellies and some heavy duty gloves in case of broken glass, I dug out the rusty gardening tools we'd bought on Facebook marketplace. The shears were stiff even after a dousing with a rusty can of WD40, but the blades were sharp, if jagged. On my way out I snagged Adam's phone. We shared one audiobook account and mine had logged out. I couldn't remember the password and I wanted something to pass the time as I tried to tame the wilderness around our home. Might as well get a head start on Finn's pick.

I was standing in the front garden, searching up the book, when someone walked past. It was our neighbour from the left-hand bungalow. Number twelve. The one with the ratty little dog who'd blanked me on our first day in Bricknell. As she'd continued to do ever since.

"Morning," I called, raising one hand in a wave, more to draw attention to her rudeness than out of hope she'd respond.

She hurried past, ignoring me completely.

Bitch.

I had the urge to follow after her and snip the cauliflower curls off the top of her head with the shears. I went back to the app, scrolling angrily without taking in any of the titles that flashed past. If it had only been one person I could have ignored it. But it wasn't. We'd been living on Julien's Crescent for six months and still not one neighbour had shown the tiniest bit of welcome. No one popping round to say hello. The one time I'd gone to knock on number eight's door they'd not answered, despite the lights being on and someone moving around inside. I was only trying to take a stray parcel round.

It wasn't just the silent treatment either. I'd seen twelve looking out her window at us on more than one occasion, spying. It was such a cliché; twitching net curtains, two little eyes appearing over the fence. Adam cracked me up impersonating her, creeping about like a Disney crone. At that moment though it didn't seem so funny. I actually felt hurt by it all.

I'd hoped there would be more recent transplants, but it seemed many of our neighbours were long-term residents, with long-held grudges. They remembered. They knew and they recognised me.

Word was spreading to the younger residents. I could only selfishly hope that if they were avoiding me, they'd also avoid Adam. I didn't want them telling him anything. That was for me to do, someday. If I could ever face it.

With my headphones in I started listening to the story of Louisa Masset. As crimes went it wasn't particularly inventive or clever. She'd tried to beat her son to death with a brick and finally smothered him in the bathroom of a train station. It was a classic Finn pick though. He loved anything pre-forensics, anything he could try to apply modern methods to.

I made my start on the back garden. I didn't feel like encountering any more of my neighbours. With the shears in hand I started chopping down clumps of nettles and brambles. It was satisfying, forcing the blades through woody stems, watching the piles of greenery fall. The plants gave off a sharp grassy scent as they bled sap. After a while I became lost in the audiobook, chopping rhythmically. I only stopped when my arms began to ache and I realised I was out of breath.

Looking back I saw the ragged path I'd cleared, straight to the centre of the garden. On the way I'd uncovered more debris; broken bottles, a smashed lamp, supermarket basket and beer cans. After all that effort the garden looked worse, if anything. Every mess I tried to clear up had another one underneath.

I was raking the weeds into a pile when Adam's phone went off, interrupting the tale of Louisa. It was his work. I answered.

"Adam's phone, Jude speaking."

"Oh hi...uh, Jude, this is Adam's manager. Is he there? I wanted to see if he could work tonight."

"Sorry he's asleep...wait, he's not already working tonight?"

"No. Unless there's a mistake on the rota." He sounded irritated, I wasn't sure if it was with me or life in general.

"Sorry," I said, propping the rake against the old washing machine that marked the centre of the garden. "My mistake. We're actually going out tonight."

"Right," he sighed. "I'll see him tomorrow then. Tell him to get here on time."

He rang off without waiting for an answer. Rude. I stood there, holding Adam's phone and frowning. I had no idea where the lie had come from; just an instinct to get out of the awkward situation of Adam having clearly lied to me. If he wasn't on to work like he'd told me only last night, where was he going? And why was his manager demanding he show up on time? Was Adam late a lot?

Instantly the worst case scenario was running through my head. He was finally sick of me and seeing someone else. That was what it usually came down to wasn't it? When your partner lied about being somewhere else, overnight, they were cheating…right? I couldn't even really blame him. Hadn't I known that he was too good for me? That it could never last, just like always?

Yet if he was cheating, he was doing a terrible job at hiding it. There was no lock on his phone for fuck's sake. I was constantly borrowing it to listen to books and shop using his work discount. Was it intentional? Did he want to get caught so he could end it with me? Adam wouldn't do that. He'd come right out and tell me, wouldn't he? He was honest, kind. He wouldn't want to hurt me more than necessary.

I stood there, frozen. Did I confront him about it? Casually mention the call and wait for his reaction? Did I squirrel that bit of 'evidence' away and look out for other clues he might have left lying around? I thought irrationally of Louisa Masset, the evidence piling up against her; her shawl at the murder scene, the brick from her garden, the little breadcrumbs of guilt left behind. People could be so stupid in their hope for secrecy. Convinced they would never be caught. But there was always a trail. Always some piece of evidence they forgot about and left behind.

"Jude!"

I whirled around and saw Adam hanging out of the kitchen window, waving at me.

"Finally, you were miles away. Have you seen my phone?"

I raised my hand and held it up.

"Oh, right. Can I use it a sec?"

I picked my way over the weeds and passed the phone in through the window.

"Did you sleep alright?" I asked.

"Mmm? Yeah, fine."

"Ready for your shift then," I said, watching him closely.

"Right...about that." He chewed at his lip, eyes refusing to meet mine. My heart bumped hard against my ribs.

"What about it?"

"Don't get pissed off but...I don't actually have a shift booked tonight. I know we could use the money and, you're going think this was such a stupid idea but..."

"But what?" I asked, waiting for the killing blow, my heart tensed.

"I booked us a last minute hotel yesterday, before what happened to your friend. I wasn't sure if you'd still want to go. I didn't mean to sleep in this late – the whole shift thing was just me trying to surprise you."

"A hotel," I echoed.

"It's not a fancy one or anything. Just one of those places with rooms to fill last minute. I didn't plan on spending much but, it'd be nice, wouldn't it? To sleep in a proper bed, have a long, hot bath without worrying about the electric, watch some telly, be in the warm for once. I thought we could do with a treat."

I nearly laughed. I was such an idiot, jumping to conclusions, forgetting that Adam was the sweetest guy I'd ever been with. He looked so cute, struggling to keep his secret. I leant up and kissed him through the window.

"That sounds perfect."

He came out to help in the garden and between us we made a lot of progress. The promise of a good night's sleep and a bath spurred me on. By late afternoon we'd cut down the weeds and piled them up to be burned later. There were bulging black bags along the front path, stuffed with rubbish. Our recycling bin overflowed with cans and bottles dug out of the garden. That would really endear us to the neighbours; they'd think we were alcoholics. Though perhaps if our garden wasn't such a rat-harbouring eyesore they'd begin to warm to us. Fat chance. As if anything could make up for what my father had done.

After chucking some stuff in an overnight bag Adam drove us out of town and to the hotel. It was one of those chains, a huge building plunked on an industrial estate for business types to use. I didn't care. Our room had a king-size bed, a bathtub and a smart TV. It was bliss.

Adam ordered a Chinese, then trekked down to the lobby to collect it. From the overnight bag he produced a bottle of screw-top wine. We sat up late watching TV in the warmth of the bed, sipping wine from mugs. He seemed distracted, shoulders set in a hard line. I guessed that now we were at the hotel he was worried about spending the money on it. When I caught his eye I smiled to let him know I appreciated the night away from the bungalow. He smiled back, but still seemed far away.

I'd brought along some bath stuff so I could relax with a long soak. Irritatingly I'd left my charger behind, so my phone died just as I was running the water.

"Babe, can I borrow your phone? I was into a book on there," I called.

He appeared at the doorway. "You want me to sign you in on your phone? Or you know, write the password down for you – again."

"Mine's dead."

A pinch appeared between his eyebrows. He handed his phone over. "I'll sign you in when we get back home then."

I left Adam to watch TV and climbed into the bath. Luxuriating in hot water, bath bomb fizzing away in a purple haze, I listened as Louisa Masset was tried and hanged for her son's murder. I suspected it was the child out of wedlock that had done it for her, rather than the murder of said child. That and the foreign boyfriend, younger than her. The public hated a woman alone, loose women even more so, especially a single mother. It likely wouldn't have mattered if she hadn't killed the boy, they'd have hanged her regardless.

After my soak I was too tired to do anything in the big bed but sleep. Adam was of the same mind, already snoring by the time I'd towelled off. I cuddled up to him and let the pillowy mattress soothe away my aching muscles.

It was our first good night's sleep in months. Predictably we overslept and almost missed breakfast. As it was included in the room we loaded up, preparing for another day at war with the garden. I'd never appreciated cheap, school dinner sausages so much. Anything I didn't have to cook on a Primus was Michelin star to me. Adam demolished some Coco-Pops like he was still a kid, then wolfed down a bacon and toast sandwich. We both pinched some mini-jams and I snaffled a croissant for later.

It was almost depressing to arrive back home to our decrepit bungalow. It was cold inside and the air felt a little damp. It was as if while we'd been gone it had started to regress back to its abandoned state. After six months of work we'd managed very little in terms of visible change. I promised myself I'd find any kind of work as soon as possible. The redundancy money was long gone and if we wanted to get the house fixed up in good time, we'd need a second wage coming in.

I plugged my phone in and hurried into the garden. We had a lot to get done.

By that evening the hotel was like a distant memory. Both of us were aching, sweaty and exhausted. The garden was clear, not necessarily a benefit to us but at least it was a job that cost us next to nothing to get done, unlike the rest of the house. Having the outdoor space would help when it came to getting the more serious work done. I'd also stacked chunks of wood from the debris against the house. Once the chimney was swept we'd have free firewood to keep us warm. If we could afford to have the chimney swept.

That night couldn't have been more different than the one before. A tepid shower using the tap hose, then dinner of pot noodle and half a Kit-Kat. Nothing to do but watch badly streamed telly on the tiny laptop screen.

It was dark by the time I switched my phone back on to do some job applications. Since being made redundant from London transport I'd had no luck finding vacancies with the local bus company. All their routes were covered and many were being cut. Now I was looking at coach hire companies. Surely someone needed a driver? Anyone. I was days away from making enquiries into dustbin lorries.

A string of chat notifications sprung up. I went to check, expecting to see news of Marianna's funeral, instead everyone was talking about an email. Frowning I went over to my inbox. Under some junk mail and a forward from David, was the original message…from Marianna.

CHAPTER SEVEN

My first thought was that it was old, or a hack. Some chain message sent via her account after she was dead. One of the ghoulish aspects of technology no one wanted to acknowledge. That after death our profiles and accounts live on, like digital ghosts. But no, the message was from that morning and it didn't look like any spam mail I'd ever seen. It wasn't trying to sell me anything for starters, and it used my name, spelled properly. I chewed the inside of my cheek. What was going on?

The subject line said simply 'My turn'. I could see an attachment underneath. It didn't look like the other rubbish clogging my inbox; nothing about prizes or 'oh my God you won't believe this!' stuff. I checked David's message. He'd forwarded his version of the email to us all, asking if we'd received it as well. That email had his name. From the group chat it looked like everyone had received it, I guessed all of them had been sent with our names. Personalised, not a mass mail out. After a bit of back and forth about the date, the potential for malware, it looked like Ricky had opened the message and attachment. Then everyone else agreed to as well.

I opened the email.

The main body text said only 'Can you work it out in time?'. I opened the attachment. I wasn't sure what I was expecting, some copypasta riddle, a chain letter in a new format, catching me off guard. But it wasn't. The attachment was titled, 'The Second' and it appeared to be part of a story.

2

Night falls again and I have more work to do.

While you sleep I am filled with purpose and energy. This time I do not intend to be merciful. This night ends in fire, or my undoing. There is no in-between. If I succeed it is only through your indifference, your lack of understanding.

I will watch her as she goes about her evening. She is either too arrogant or too naïve, not one to rush and close the blinds when night comes. Perhaps she thinks no one would dare look in? Perhaps she thinks the world a good place, filled with people who wish her no harm? Though her interests surely prove otherwise. Arrogance it must be then. She is too safe, too clever, to be caught out by a night stalker.

I know her habits, I have watched her before. She is curled up on a sofa, a blanket on her lap, tea at her elbow. The laptop lights her face, blueish-white as if she's already dead and waiting to be cut open under the fluorescents.

She may as well be dead, she barely moves. The click of a finger, the twitch of her hand as she shifts for another keystroke. She is absorbed, working towards an ideal only she can visualise. Her headphones contain whatever sounds engage her. She is unaware, even as a cat creeps over and laps at the forgotten teacup.

The backdoor remains unlocked from when she let the creature in only half an hour ago. I open it easily, knowing from observation that it does not squeak. The faint light from the laptop drifts in through the crack in the door to the lounge. It gleams on white tile, knives, the stainless steel of appliances. Everything is clean, sharp, it's like an operating room.

One by one I snap the dials round. A hiss begins, low and expectant. The static sound of weighty silence. The window over the sink is slightly ajar. I close it, then softly shut the door to the lounge as well. The backdoor closes behind me and I am in the dark once more, the biting cold almost stealing my breath.

I wait. Across the road, under an elm by the entrance to the cemetery. The streetlights are far apart here, low energy. I am in shadow, waiting. A family turns on to the street, children dressed as ghouls and witches, swinging plastic buckets of sweets. I watch, motionless as they make their slow way towards me on the other side of the road. They are too busy with the promise of sweeties and the excitement of pumpkin lanterns to notice me.

Any moment now, she will sigh and put the laptop aside. Standing up she will push off the blanket, notice the skin of milk on the cold tea. On her way to the kitchen for another, she will pluck the cigarettes and lighter from her coat on the banister. Her guilty pleasure; the nightly ritual of nicotine. She will already be lighting up as she goes to the backdoor, ready to pay lip service to the no-smoking policy so many landlords set. It is not the pleasure of the cigarette that she adores, but that of having outsmarted the rules. Flouting them with every cloud of smoke. She is clever. Too clever by far, and it makes her foolish. She's so caught up in her work, her cunning, that she doesn't notice the scent of gas.

The explosion lights up the night in vivid orange. Appropriate considering the date. Glass bursts from the kitchen windows and three car alarms are going off before the mother and her children begin to scream.

The flames bite into the house like it's a gleaming toffee apple. Fire licking at wood and wallpaper, turning the windows into the leering face of a giant jack-o-lantern. I turn away. No one is looking at me. My work is done, neatly, as always. Perhaps I have earned a little pleasure of my own?

On my way home I will buy some cigarettes, inhaling the smoke as sirens echo distantly. I will celebrate, because that stupid girl is dead, and I am alive.

I wonder – can you find me before then?

I read over the words again. From the number it appeared to be part of a second chapter. Of what I wasn't sure. Was Marianna writing something, before she died? It was certainly creepy, but it wasn't in the style I usually expected of true crime. Where were the facts, the details, and the hard evidence? It read more like a novel. Or a sort of stream of consciousness poem. Not my thing at all.

I looked at the subject line again, 'My turn'. It was her turn to pick something for us. Perhaps she'd decided to use the group as a sounding board for a crime novel? She hadn't asked, but then, Marianna was a law unto herself with more than just time keeping. It wouldn't surprise me if she just assumed we would be available as her own personal writer's workshop. But how had it been sent after her death?

"What's up? You look all," Adam pulled an exaggerated frown as he brought over an instant hot chocolate.

"I've had an email, from Marianna."

Adam frowned. "You sure it's not an old one? You're not exactly the queen of inbox management."

"No, it's from this morning," I said, pointing to the date.

"Doesn't mean much. Her account's probably been hacked, what is it some kind of scam thing?"

"I thought so, but listen to this." I read him the start of the attached file. "That sounds like something she might have written for us, right?"

"Well, you knew her, not me...but yeah, I suppose it doesn't sound like a scam, if she was into writing and all this crime stuff it makes sense she wrote that. Maybe she was just experimenting with writing, or trying to freak you guys out for a laugh. Oh!" He snapped his fingers, "what if it's like one of those subscription box things you can get? You know, where they send you clues and fake letters and it's like you're a detective being taunted by a serial killer."

"They do those? And how do you know about them?"

He grimaced. "Bang goes your surprise Christmas present. But yeah, maybe she was trying to do something like that with you guys. Roleplay."

The word 'roleplay' conjured up unpleasant visions of David in a plaid miniskirt and Siobhan waving a teachers ruler. I snorted, then tried to steer Adam back to the matter at hand.

"But how did it get sent to us now?"

"I don't know...maybe it's gone weird because your phone was off, you're just getting the notification now."

"But look at the date," I said stubbornly. "Plus everyone else got it at the same time, so it's not just my phone being weird."

Adam shrugged. "No idea then. Is it important?"

"No, I just think it's weird that's all. Spooky."

"So you think it's a ghost or something?" Adam raised his eyebrows. "Is living here starting to get to you?"

I rolled my eyes. "Not a ghost. It's just a mystery that's all. I like solving things."

"I know you do," Adam gestured to the piles of true crime books by the desk. "And I put up with it, mon petit Poirot."

He dunked a biscuit in his chocolate and started playing a game on his phone. I toyed with the dusty marshmallows in my mug and looked through my messages. Checking on the group chat I saw David had popped up again. I closed my eyes in annoyance after reading his message. Of course. Why hadn't I thought of that?

"Delayed delivery," I said.

"Mmm?" Adam said, through a mouthful of biscuit.

"She must have sent the email delayed delivery, so she wouldn't forget to send it after the meeting. She was always late with her picks. But you can send an email and mark it to be delivered on a specific date, or after a chosen time." It seemed so obvious once David had pointed it out. He was going to be oh so very pleased with himself now.

"Mystery of the century solved then," Adam said. "Thank God, that was going to keep me awake all night."

I threw him a look. "Well, it bothered me."

In the chat I ran off a quick message: 'So, are we discussing this on Monday now – as well as Finn's book? For Marianna?'

Katrine sent a thumbs up.

Finn: 'Sounds good to me'

Ricky sent a gif of Freddy Kruger on fire. I interpreted it as an answer in the positive.

David: 'So it's agreed. See you next meeting – Happy Halloween!'

I checked the date at the top of the screen. Sure enough, our next meeting was the day after Halloween.

CHAPTER EIGHT

Adam was working over the next few nights. I felt slightly guilty that he was doing so many shifts. I tried to keep myself busy, distracting myself and tempering my guilt by working on the house. Without a real job I was taking the responsibility for finding cheap or free items on local pages. The move from London had been hurried and despite owning plenty of clothes, books and a few flat pack bookcases: most everything else had belonged to the landlord. Top of my list to find were a washing machine, oven and a bed. I was sick of using the camp stove and sick of the laundrette.

While Adam slept in preparation for his shift, I scoured the internet for furniture and DIY supplies. After a few hours I had a list of things to collect; surplus kitchen tiles, offcuts of laminate, curtain rails and a decently priced rug. Still no bed. At this rate we were going to have to stump up for a brand new one. Most of Adam's salary for October was earmarked for a shower and unblocking the chimney so we'd have some form of heating before the winter really set in.

With each passing day our list of projects was growing. It only added to my guilt. Not only had I lied to Adam to get him to Bricknell, now I was saddling him with the bill for renovating the house. Adam's optimism only made me feel worse. He was so relentlessly positive about the bungalow's potential. After so long spent in pokey rented flats where we couldn't so much a tack a poster to the wall, the idea of a space just for us was intoxicating to him. No more rent hikes, no more begging the landlord to actually fix our leaking toilet or frantic cleaning before inspections. To him, the house was the start of something great for us. To me it was a sword over my head, just waiting to fall.

Guilt made me desperate to make things better. I'd taken him from London under false pretences after all. I wanted to deliver the fantasy I'd conjured to sweeten the deal. A cosy, comfortable home. And since no one was bashing down the door to hire me, that meant all I could contribute was my time and elbow grease.

I drove across town and parked outside one of the addresses I'd received. It was a nice area, with bay windows and very well landscaped front gardens. I felt very scruffy in my un-ironed, laundrette crumpled t-shirt and jeans. I scraped my grown-out hair into a ponytail and tucked my skull necklace into my collar before heading over to the house.

An older man answered the door in slippers. I immediately noticed that in the hallway behind him was a mattress, propped on the wall. Potentially a lucky break.

"I'm Judith, here for the tiles?"

"Oh yes, four pounds wasn't it? I'll just get them."

Don't ask, don't get. "Thanks...are you getting rid of that mattress as well?"

He turned as if just noticing it. "Someone was meant to collect it yesterday but they never came. That's the trouble with these groups – people let you down all the time. Now it's down here for nothing – it's in good condition, I just got a memory foam one."

"How much were you asking?"

"If you take it now, it's free. I would have taken it to the tip but the car's too small."

I eyed my own car; if I folded down the back seats I could probably fit it in if I tied the boot down. The rope from our move was still in the foot well.

"Would you be able to help me get it in there?" I asked.

He sighed, but nodded. "Let me get some shoes on."

Between the two of us we manoeuvred the mattress out of the house and into the back of the car. Alright so I still had no bedframe but a real mattress would at least be more comfortable. Maybe we could go full crack-house and get some palettes to put it on for the time being? Perhaps rebrand it as 'rustic urban décor'?

He held the boot down while I attempted to secure the rope.

"Just moved, hmm?" he said, noticing the collapsed storage boxes lining the back of the car.

"A few months ago, but we're still trying to get ourselves together."

"Have far to go?" he asked, eying the rope dubiously.

I was still struggling with the knots. "Not really. I'm going back to Julien's Crescent."

I sensed, more than saw his sudden stillness. "...you moved into that house?"

Finally getting the knots tight enough, I stepped back and saw his face. All traces of friendliness had gone. The shutters were down. He was looking at me like I'd let my dog mess his driveway.

"Thank you for the mattress," I said, trying to get things back on a friendly note.

"You're welcome," he said stiffly, already turning and heading back to the front door. Before I'd taken two steps he'd pushed the box of tiles onto the doorstep and closed the door. It wasn't quite a slam but there was a finality to it. Our interaction was at an end.

Trying to act like nothing was wrong I picked up the box and put it in the passenger seat. My face was hot and I was sweating. I felt as if everyone on the street was at their windows, watching me. Shame prickled my neck. I was praying that the old man had just disapproved of our choice of home, but couldn't rule out that he saw my mother in me.

I couldn't get out of there fast enough.

When I turned onto our street and saw number twelve on her front step, talking to number eight, a mum in her thirties, I swore aloud. Both of them turned to watch me as I manoeuvred enough to reverse onto our drive. I was so flustered it took me a few tries to line it up right and my face was burning the whole time. Finally I got the car parked up and jumped out, resolutely not looking over at my neighbours.

The rope had pulled tight under the strain of the mattress and I struggled to get it undone. When I did I almost chinned myself as the boot flew up. I heard a snort of derisive laughter. The end of the mattress sprung out like a tongue.

I should have left it until Adam was awake to help, but I was too stubborn to give up in front of the two bitches watching me. After propping the front door open I hauled on the stitched handles and dragged the mattress free. The ground was fortunately dry, I'd only have the dust the side off once it was inside. Huffing and straining, sweat sticking my pleather jacket to me, I hauled the thing inside and shut the door. Through it all, neither of them offered to help, not that I'd expected them to.

Leaving the mattress in the hallway I crept through to the kitchen and stood by the open window. I knew hearing what they were saying wouldn't make me feel any better, but I still had to know. It was a compulsion, like picking a scab until it bled.

"...how you put up with it," Eight was saying.

"Utterly shameless, you should see how they live. No curtains and she walks about half dressed. I see her at night sometimes you know, just standing at the window in the dark. She's not right in the head."

"I feel sorry for the boyfriend."

"He looks a nice lad, can't think why he puts up with her. Working all the hours god sends and she's always out late, stumbling home, pissed as you like. Got up like an overgrown teenager."

"I'm worried about the kids; some weirdo like that living next door. All that was before my time of course but having someone in there, stirring it up...doesn't bear thinking about. No normal person would live there, I'll tell you that much."

"Oh if you only knew the half of it! I know all about what happened back then, and she's no innocent, I'll tell you that much, her mother-" Her voice dropped and I couldn't hear any more.

I felt cold all over at number twelve's words. So, I'd been right, it wasn't just that we were in his house – she knew who I was. She was around back then. She knew some of it, if not all. My mother and Wayfield. Two black spots on Bricknell's history.

I turned away from the window, anger making my chest feel tight. How dare they? They didn't even know me but apparently my genetics made every little flaw of mine evidence that I was a lunatic. A danger to their kids. As if having a derelict house next door was more desirable than having me in it. Perhaps to number twelve and people like her, it was.

I had the sudden urge to slam back outside and let them have it. The pair of them. Gossips and nosy neighbours had always got to me, even when I'd been a teenager at home. It didn't matter if no one knew who we really were, there was still something about us. Like a smell we couldn't wash off. Something foul. People thought we were strange, somehow unwholesome. I'd been aware of it even then, the twitching curtains and abrupt silences when I entered the corner shop or the laundrette. Our flat went without Christmas carollers, trick-or-treaters; even the God squad never came knocking. It was like there was an invisible sign over our door; Freaks Within. A sign that came with us wherever we went, and had now appeared over my own door for those that cared to look.

The worst part was that I felt it too; the wrongness about me. Their prejudice hurt all the more because I knew it wasn't baseless. I was fucked up, twisted somehow. Wrong. I just wanted to know why. Why my father had done the things he had. Why my Mum had loved him, still, after everything. Had she known he was guilty but just denied it to my face? Or had she honestly not known, not believed it. How had he convinced her of his innocence? What was wrong with him, with her, that had passed on to me?

Adam came in, groggy and wearing a dressing gown. "Hey, where'd that mattress come from?"

"Marketplace. It was free," I muttered, filling the kettle.

"Sweet. We should burn the camp beds in celebration – like those guys who burned their ships when they reached the new world – no going back!"

I managed a smile.

"You OK?"

"Yeah, just tired that's all. I'll be glad when we can get this place fixed up like a proper home, you know?" I said.

"We'll get there, I'm sure," Adam said. "Anything on the job front yet?"

"Not yet," I said, feeling my face get hot with shame.

Despite applying for dozens of jobs I'd not had a single interview. Not even a phone call. Was it just bad luck or had word spread locally that I was the freak living in the Butcher's house? Was that why no one wanted me? I'd even looked into signing up as a casual driver on a taxi app, but the idea of locals turning me away when I showed up at their doors had put a stop to that idea. I wasn't sure I could take that.

"What about haulage?" Adam asked, digging about in a cardboard box, looking for the instant porridge.

"Lorry driving?" I felt a prickle on my neck. Wayfield had driven lorries for a living. Up and down the country, stopping along the way to pick up hitchhiking teenagers and stranded women to assault. A part of me shrunk away from the connection. I was already in his house, I didn't want to emulate him any further and get myself in more trouble with the locals. I'd take a minimum wage shelf-stacking job before tempting fate like that.

"I'll look into it," I said, vaguely.

Adam nodded and went to put the kettle on the stove.

After Adam had left for work I took the diaries from their hiding spot. I took them to the living room and spread them out. A scent rose from them, her perfume, lily of the valley. We'd had them at the funeral. Tiny, tightly closed white bells nestled amongst pink roses. Secretive. Demure. Her name was in glittery, pink letters inside the diary cover; Eleanor Pike. Her real name.

They were hard to read, not just emotionally but practically as well. She'd made copious entries but it was difficult to part reality from fantasy. So much of it felt like the wistful dreaming of a schoolgirl, exactly what she'd been when she started writing them. I opened the first thin book around a quarter way through, where I'd left off before. The rounded bubble writing of a teenager greeted me. A torn bit of cardboard fluttered out, my makeshift bookmark. I ignored it and started to read, skimming the few paragraphs I'd read before.

Saw him again today. He was outside the gates when I left after choir. Elaine said he's weird but she's just jealous. No one waits for her outside school. No one even looks at her. But he's there almost every day for me. I wonder where he goes when he's not there? I want to go up to him but I'm worried if I do I'll say something to put him off. He looked so good today in that denim jacket, not stupid anoraks like the boys in our year. He's so cool. I wish I had a picture.

I heard Laura telling Nicole about how David Critchley took her to this place up the canal. There's an old lockup there where they used to fit out boats and stuff. But she says they went behind it to kiss. They were at the back of the art room and I was in the store cupboard looking for fresh markers. Laura said they do 'French kissing' like it was sophisticated. As if putting 'French' on something is meant to make it sound fancy. Like French fries! Still, I'm dead curious about what it's like.

I wonder if He knows how to kiss like that? Does he know about the lockup? I think about what it would be like going up there with him, at night. I could sneak out over the garage roof. I'd wear my new dress. It's black and makes me look older, but it would help me hide in the shadows too. I need nicer knickers. Mum buys mine like I'm a baby who still needs to wear full, white cotton pants. If he saw them he might laugh and I'd just die if he did that.

Her writing was smaller on those paragraphs, like she was embarrassed. She must have been hiding the diary even then but still ashamed of what she was writing. What she was feeling. I touched the pink letters. She had been sixteen then, desperately trying to grow up, be an adult. Desperate for excitement and love. But she sounded younger in her diary, where there was no one to impress. Still a kid.

Had there been even a small part of her that feared him? Was there no prickle to the back of her neck, no weight in the pit of her stomach that told her he was suspect? I wanted to believe she was just innocent, too young to have a sense of the real world. But I'd had those feelings myself. The slight shiver of a wrongness to someone, a gut feeling. Surely anyone could feel those cold currents lurking under the surface, promising to suck you down to the depths? But then, that was with hindsight, wasn't it? I felt those things because I'd seen what happened to victims, in full colour photographs, written up in books. Mum hadn't had that, just a sheltered, small town childhood. Yet, when she'd seen the evidence, later, she hadn't believed it either.

With my hindsight I knew that the man she craved was evil. The man who would, in a few short months, become the Butcher of Bricknell.

CHAPTER NINE

By the time our next meeting rolled around I'd almost forgotten about Marianna's email. Aside from an update from David, letting us know that she was being cremated and sent home to Lithuania for the actual funeral, I hadn't thought of Marianna much at all. I felt bad about it when I realised how quickly I'd put her aside in my mind. Things with the bungalow and encounters with horrible locals had been my top concern.

It wasn't that I didn't care about Marianna, but of everyone in the book club she was the one who showed up latest and said the least. I hadn't known her as long as the others had and, even when she'd turned up we hadn't spoken much one-to-one. I had more of a rapport with David and Ricky. Still, arriving at the Highwayman and finding everyone in subdued silence, it brought home that I would never see her again.

"Hey," I said, putting my pint down and taking a seat. "Siobhan on her way? She say why we had to meet here?"

"Just that her place was too busy. She sent a text out, she's going to be late – her babysitter was delayed," David said, briefly glancing up from his book.

Silence filled the small room. It seemed like none of us knew exactly what to say. There was tension in Marianna's absence. An unspoken awkwardness. Just like at David's I felt that gulf between myself and the rest of them. I was the newest member, the comparative stranger. Besides which, I was keeping a very big secret from them. All of that created distance.

It felt like hours before Siobhan came puffing up the narrow stairs. She had on one of her large collection of hoodies. This one had a black rose and a bunch of convention dates for the vampire TV show she was obsessed with on it. She dropped into a chair.

"Sorry guys, had to wait for Stella to get her act together. If she weren't my niece I'd drop her, honestly, she's so bloody unreliable. And sorry again for not being able to do this at mine. The whole of Tom's darts team came over, very last minute and very inconsiderate."

"Not a problem," David said, cutting off what was surely going to be a long rant about her husband. We got a lot of those.

Siobhan's entrance and chatter seemed to snap everyone out of their stilted silence, myself included. Everyone dug out their copies of the book. I'd made notes, having listened to it rather than read it. Not my preference but the only way I'd managed to juggle reading it with all the work on the garden.

"Louisa Masset then," Finn began. "What did you think of the evidence presented against her?"

"Rather clear cut, I thought," David said. "The brick from her garden, her shawl by the body. Not to mention she was seen at the station and then concocted that letter to the child's minder saying they'd both made the crossing to France."

"Mrs Gentle," Finn supplied. "It's interesting how Masset was essentially convicted on account of her own poor attempts at deception. That she lied about her son going to live with his father, lied that he was accompanying her to France...the only physical evidence they had was her shawl at the station, the brick and the fact she abandoned his parcel of clothes there as well. She might have easily explained away most of the real evidence if she'd had her wits about her."

"I think if she'd been smarter they'd still have got her anyway. After all, she was seen," Siobhan put in. "I mean, you can remember to get rid of evidence and tell better lies but, if you get seen you've had it. Especially back then. If no one saw you, you were home free."

"And who else was it gonna be?" Ricky said. "Her kid, in her care, only her word to say otherwise. Not many other people you could finger for it," he said, with a leer. Mature as ever.

"She said her lover did it though, right?" Katrine said. "This bloke of hers she was going to meet after bumping her kid off."

It was very Katrine to say 'lover'. I'd have said 'boytoy'. Ricky would have said fuck buddy. Katrine had poetry in her of the intense, gothic sort. Lovers, blood oaths and sacrifice were her cup of tea.

"Eudore, the Frenchman," Finn said. "I think there's room for the idea he was behind the idea of the killing, even if he didn't do it himself. He might have given her the nudge to do it. After all if they were going to carry on their affair he wouldn't want her bastard son around."

"So you reckon a girl's only got the balls to kill if there's a man telling her what to do?" Ricky said dramatically, covering his mouth with one hand. "I dunno mate, not sure that's going to go down well in this room."

I snorted, but Siobhan actually looked annoyed by Finn's suggestion.

"Is that what you're saying?" she demanded.

"No!" Finn said, too quickly. "I'm just saying, it's clear from the amount of evidence that she left behind that she wasn't that bright. To have come up with such a convoluted plan, it would take someone else, more intelligent."

"Like a man?" Siobhan said, triumphant. She had him in a corner and he wriggled like a mouse under a cat's paw.

"In this case a man. But it doesn't have to be a man, if that's what you're implying."

A brave attempt to muddy the waters, but Siobhan had already scented blood.

"Not such a clever plan, considering she got caught."

"Perhaps that was his intention," David said, attempting to end the battle of the sexes. "He may have tired of her as a paramour and deliberately set out to have her removed from his life by the police."

"At the cost of her son?" I said, while Katrine scribbled 'paramour' into her notebook and drew a purple heart around it.

David shrugged. "Anyone cruel enough to see a woman hanged just to be rid of her, would be cruel enough to kill a child they had no interest in."

"Perhaps he was a narcissist," Finn put in. "Couldn't see the point in a child that wasn't his, or a woman he didn't want anymore."

I wondered, as they continued to discuss it, which was better. A callous murderer that saw your life as so worthless it could be snuffed out at will. Or a killer who valued you more than anything else in the world, keeping you close. So close you could hardly breathe.

I felt a little bit sorry for Louisa. As an unwed mother life must have been tough back then. She'd fled France due to the scandal and must have been hard up, especially given the extortionate cost of having her son taken care of by Mrs. Gentle. She must have been overjoyed when her boyfriend took an interest. Someone at last, cared about her, perhaps enough to get married. That's what she must have thought. Judging from the wide trail of evidence she left behind, she wasn't the brightest spark. Or perhaps she'd been too blinded by love to indulge the idea that she might be caught. Perhaps to her it had been some romantic gesture, or a test; what a woman would do for love.

"I can't imagine it," Siobhan was saying. "Beating your child with a brick and then smothering him. Pretending like everything's normal and going off for a dirty weekend." She shuddered but her cheeks were pink with excitement. Maybe, like Louisa, she also found the idea of murder in the name of love romantic.

"She sounds like a stupid slag to me," Ricky said, with his usual talent for blurting out the most offensive thing he could at any given time. Though, I thought guiltily, I'd been thinking the same, hadn't I? Love and sex as motive for murder. What was the first blush of love, but lust? Was one more justifiable than the other? Someone was still dead all the same, romantic sentiment or not.

"It's worth noting that she would have been reviled as a loose woman just for having the child," Finn said. "Not to mention the boyfriend. In fact I think it's possible that she may have been condemned on public opinion, rather than the strength of the evidence. Obviously it was a terrible crime, but to have her hanged, with no reprieve, speaks to extreme disgust."

Finn continued to talk for a while on the possibility that Eudore had committed the crime himself and framed Louisa to be rid of her. When he started going into how he'd attempt to prove this with forensics if the evidence were available, I glazed over. Motive and means interested me, the mind of the killer and of their victims. What led them to come into contact with one another. The root of all of it. Not skin cells and DNA testing. That was just so much dust left behind, after the fact.

Finally we took a short break to get more drinks in. We needed it. Ricky had been getting restless and Katrine was as checked out as I was, only with misty eyes, lost in a haze of Victorian romance.

When we reconvened David cleared his throat and produced a printed piece of paper. I almost smiled. David, of course, had no smart phone. Though he could text he did so from an ancient Nokia in a hefty neoprene cover. Ricky called it 'David's walkie-talkie'.

"Shall we...?" he gestured to the paper as if unsure what to say.

"If we have to," Ricky muttered.

After bringing the email up on our phones there was some shifting and sideways glances. No one wanted to be the first to speak. I'd not read the piece since showing Adam and looked over it trying to think of something to say.

"It's a bit weird, I think," Ricky said at last, sparing us from the ongoing silence. "A bit...well, I've never read a book-"

"That we know of," muttered Finn, prompting Katrine to snort indelicately.

Ricky rolled his eyes but turned pink nonetheless. "I meant, I've never read a book that talks like that, all the 'She's' and 'You's', it's like it's talking to you when you read it. Like it's not a story, it's a letter or something."

It was so insightful a comment by his standards that I was lost for words. Ricky was now blushing furiously under his sweatshirt hood, freckles standing out like angry welts. He stuffed his hands in his pockets and shrugged as if trying to look nonchalant.

"I agree," David said, after a few bemused moments. "It's very effective, makes you feel like something's building, then the end, the...explosion, really made me feel a little...aghast."

"I thought it was sad," Katrine said softly. "What with the gas leak in the story and then, you know...with Marianna."

The thought had not occurred to me, or it seemed, to anyone else. An ache made itself known in my chest. Perhaps I felt more about Marianna's death than I'd been aware of. It was certainly a terrible coincidence; two deaths by gas leak, one fictional, one horribly real.

"I wonder why she never sent chapter one," I said.

"What do you mean?" Ricky asked.

"Well, this is chapter two, right? It says 'two' at the top. And the narrator, whoever it is, says that this time they aren't going to be merciful, that they have more work to do. So, that implies they've done something like this before which we should be aware of already. Something less extreme than burning down a house."

"She must have decided not to send it. Maybe she was still working on it," Finn said. "Or she cut it entirely and then forgot to change the number at the top."

"It's a shame, it was really good." Katrine's voice was small and her eyes shone with eyeliner tinted tears. "I wish she'd got to finish it."

The meeting ended in a morose fashion. Being at our normal meeting made Marianna's death more real, somehow. Like we were the only people who knew she was gone from the world. It was ridiculous of course, she had a sister and I was sure she missed her more than we did. Still, as I left the pub and went on my way home through the foggy streets, I felt a heaviness in my chest that hadn't been there earlier in the day.

Normally after a meeting I was tipsy, buzzed and able to relax. Filled with my quota of social contact and ready for a rest. That night however I'd only had two ciders and didn't feel the slightest bit tired. It was already rather late but I knew I wouldn't sleep properly if I went straight home. Instead I took a circuitous route around by the canal and through the housing estate.

The night before had been Halloween and decorations were still up all over the estate. Abandoned pumpkins leered from the porches and fake spider webs drooped from the afternoon rain. Cut-out ghosts and gravestones littered front gardens and sweet wrappers rolled in the night breeze. Someone had left a skeleton hanging from a noose over their porch. The batteries were still working, its eyes glowing red as coals.

There was no one else out at that time. They were either indoors watching the televisions that glowed behind the curtains, or already asleep. The fog and the quiet, coupled with the decorations, made me uneasy. My footsteps sounded too loud on the pavement. Like those of a hapless flower seller in one of the awful Ripper films we'd read about. They echoed and I thought I heard someone walking behind me several times. Though when I stopped and turned, there was no one. Obviously. Stupid as it was, I cut my walk short and stopped in at the 24-hour store for a few cans of cider to keep me company at home.

Inside the shop I was dazzled by the fluorescents and white tiled floors. So different to the crawling shadows of the deserted estate. I felt instantly very silly for being afraid. I'd walked home from clubs and pubs through the dark streets of London for god's sake. The capital, with crime stats many times worse than this sleepy town. I knew the tips and tricks to keeping safe; keys between fingers, can of deodorant as makeshift pepper spray. I didn't have my mother's innocence, even when I was younger. When you grow up knowing your father's a murderer, you can't remain ignorant of danger. You don't get to be innocent.

The floor was wet and I almost slipped, catching myself on a display of papers. The teenage son of the shop owner glared at me for jostling him. He was bent down, sorting papers from a stack. Tomorrow's edition. Time had really gotten away from me on my walk. It was after midnight.

"Sorry," I muttered, turning away, then stopping.

One hand was still on the display, steadying me. I tuned out the late night radio from the front of the shop and stared down at the papers. They were local papers, usually only good for planning application news and school events. Today however the front page had a headline far more exciting than the usual charity drives and record breaking vegetables. In large black letters it proclaimed; 'Gas Leak Causes Fatal Explosion'.

CHAPTER TEN

I arrived home to a house in complete darkness. Adam was at work and inside the bungalow it was freezing cold. I hurriedly locked the door behind me and went to check the back was shut tight as well. There was a prickle on my neck that had nothing to do with the night's chill. I had a copy of the paper clutched tightly in my numb hand.

All the way home I'd told myself there was nothing to be so freaked out about. A gas leak on Halloween wasn't some hugely unlikely event. It was that time of year; heating was going on, boilers working overtime for hot water. Accidents happened. Still, as I sat down and went over the story, my hands refused to stop shaking.

Little was given away by the paper. A woman had died in a gas explosion and resulting fire. According to the 'onsite fire investigation team' it was believed to be accidental. There was a picture of the little house, its ground floor windows blown out, police tape festooning the privet hedge outside like streamers. The picture was in daylight, presumably taken the next morning. No name was given.

I recognised the location, not the house itself but the one next door. They had painted ivy on their door and a terracotta dragon mounted on their roof. It was almost out of the picture, but I had walked past it enough on my way to the high-street to recognise it. That house was opposite the cemetery.

With the paper on my lap I opened the email on my phone. Flicking through, I got to the right section, hoping that I'd misremembered. But no, there it was, in black and white pixels. *I wait. Across the road, under an elm by the entrance to the cemetery. The streetlights are far apart here, low energy. I am in shadow, waiting.*

The story was too similar to be just coincidence. The timing, the victim being a lone woman, the location of the house...that story had predicted her death. I stared at the screen, looking desperately for any conflicting information. There wasn't any. Two weeks ago, I had read a story about this woman's death, and last night it had happened, just as it was written.

My eyes strayed to the email itself, 'Can you work it out in time?'

If I succeed it is only through your indifference, your lack of understanding.

I wonder – can you find me before then?

Someone had planned a murder and then told us when and where it was going to happen. There was no other explanation. To have those details already fixed, to know when and where, they would have to be behind the explosion. I wanted to find it all a big coincidence, but there was something about it that defied disbelief. Maybe because it was the small hours and I was all alone.

A bang made me jump, dropping my phone.

I leapt up, the newspaper slithered to the floor. My heart pounded against my ribs, blood thundering in my ears so hard I could hardly hear anything else. I strained to trace the sound. It seemed to have come from the front of the house. Then the banging came again, from the back door this time.

I was pulled by conflicting impulses; to run, to hide, to confront. Until I was unable to do anything but stand there.

Then someone hammered on the front door. Fist pounding the wood. Not the kind of knock you'd ever want to answer.

I whirled around, taking a few steps away from the front of the house. What was going on? My breathing was shallow, panicked. I swallowed, trying to get myself under control. My eyes darted about for a weapon and I saw a pan on the camp stove. I grabbed it up. My fingers white on the handle. I felt a little better with a weapon of any kind in my hands. Though I wished it was a knife. Too late to go looking for one in the boxes though. There was bagging on the kitchen window now. I didn't dare go back there.

The banging at the back door began again. Now less like banging and more like…shaking. I ran to the kitchen doorway, then stopped, too scared to go any closer. The door was rattling in its frame, the handle cranking up and down as someone shook it, trying to get the latch loose. Cold sweat was sticking my t-shirt to me. My legs were shaking. What if they got in?

A crash broke the spell that held me there and sent me racing back through the living room and into the hall. I saw the smashed window in the front door, tried to stop myself but couldn't. I ran straight onto the broken glass and yelped as a large piece pierced the sole of my foot.

From outside I heard laughter. More than one voice. More than one person. Logic reasserted itself. I needed my phone. I needed the police. Stumbling back to the living room I hunted for it in the dark. My sock squishing with blood. Both doors rattled, beaten by many hands. Voices yelled but I couldn't understand what they were saying. There were too many of them, saying too many things. Only the odd word found its way into my panicked brain.

Bitch.

Whore.

Scum.

Murderer.

On the floor I dialled 999 and felt my injured foot, pulling the glass free. I listened to the mechanically burring of the phone as terrified tears ran down my face.

"Hello?" I yelped as soon as the operator began to speak. "I need the police, there's people outside trying to get into my house. They've broken a window, please I need help." My voice came out too high. I hiccoughed, unable to catch my breath.

The voice on the phone was clipped and calm, almost robotic. "What is your address?"

I gave it and she told me to stay put, someone was on their way. I couldn't have moved if I wanted to. Now that I was huddled on the floor some instinct kept me frozen there. Curled up like an animal awaiting attack.

Another crash made me jump. The sound of breaking glass unmistakeable. I heard the strangers outside whooping as the glass from the kitchen window rained down over the floor. The woman on the phone spoke to me but I couldn't understand her. I just held the mobile to my ear and sobbed until the police came.

Once two constables had arrived and managed to talk me into opening the door, I'd cried myself out. Feeling a little calmer I waited while they called Adam for me. I couldn't tell them when the banging stopped, but it must have been while I was crying on the phone. The pair of police officers split up and he took a walk around the outside of the bungalow while she wrote down a statement from me. As if I was a hysterical woman who needed another woman to comfort her. That's exactly what I was of course. I felt humiliated. I wanted Adam. They called an ambulance to come and look at my foot. Which was even more embarrassing. Had it really only been an hour or so ago that I'd convinced myself London had hardened me? I felt like a complete idiot. The worst kind of fluffy headed fool.

The officer from outside returned, his phone out as if he'd been taking pictures.

"There's tire tracks all over the front garden. Looks like kids on bikes," he said to his partner. Turning to me he adopted a sympathetic frown. "There's some graffiti and it looks like they've thrown stuff at the windows; dog shit and some stones. Little fuckers."

"Pete," said the woman, reprovingly.

"Sorry...dog *mess*."

I let out a shaky laugh. She rolled her eyes in mock irritation. They were trying to make me feel better, at ease, but I couldn't stop shaking. Fear and humiliation turned me hot and cold by turns. From what they'd said it was just kids running wild, some post-Halloween prank gone too far. But that email and the things it had said...I'd genuinely thought someone was coming to kill me. Sitting there while the two of them tried to placate me, I felt ridiculous. Their kindness embarrassed me. The state of the house embarrassed me too, having them see the camping stove and the floor mattress in our squalid living room.

When Adam arrived I felt even worse. He looked so panicked, so tired. I wished they hadn't called him. By then I'd had my foot seen to, it was all bandaged up and the ambulance had gone on to another call. Someone who actually needed help. The policeman had even swept the broken glass in the hallway to one side, so no one else stepped on it. I hadn't so much as offered them tea.

Adam flew to me and knelt down, hands on my shoulders.

"What happened?"

"Kids," I muttered, too humiliated to meet his eyes. "It was just kids…I…I overreacted."

"It looks like a bit of leftover Halloween hooliganism," the policeman said. "Obviously no laughing matter, considering the injuries to Miss Broch and the damage to the property. We'll be checking to see if any of your neighbours saw anything or if they have CCTV."

"What about fingerprints, or DNA?" Adam asked, finally taking in the state of the kitchen window.

The constables exchanged glances. "We've collected the stones that came through the window but…I'll be honest with you Mr…"

"Powell."

"Mr Powell, in cases like this we have more chance of finding the culprit through video or witness statements."

What she wasn't saying, but what I knew from Finn's obsession, was that any evidence they gathered would be low priority. Probably not processed for an age. And unless they found someone to compare the prints to they were fairly useless. They weren't going to waste time and money on it unless the bastards had been caught on camera.

"We'll be in touch with an incident number. You'll need it for your insurer. For now I'll leave you with the number for an emergency glazier. You should get the windows boarded up." The policewoman smiled at me reassuringly. "The important thing is, you're safe and we'll have a report on file in the unlikely event something like this happens again."

I thanked them and Adam walked them out, spilling gratitude and apologies as he went. When he came back he slumped down next to me. He was still in his work uniform, his steel capped boots thumping on the floor. Realising he'd probably left everyone else in the lurch to unload all the incoming deliveries, I felt even worse.

"Are you alright?" he asked.

I nodded. "I got freaked out but...they're right it's probably just kids."

"When I got here you looked like you'd been attacked, like, for real – your eyes were everywhere, like you thought someone was coming after you."

I swallowed. When the police arrived I'd been so relieved and felt so stupid I hadn't mentioned the email, the story or the fire. With other people around it seemed so ridiculous. What was I meant to say? 'Sorry for freaking out, but I thought a serial killer was targeting me and that it was him outside, rattling my doors and throwing dog shit'?

"I was a bit spooked, that's all. That story from Marianna's email? Turns out a fire just like it happened on Halloween."

Adam looked at me a moment with an unreadable expression on his face. Then he sighed. "Jude, come on."

"What?"

"I mean...it's not real. That was just a story. You read too much of that stuff and you'll be afraid to leave the house."

"The stuff I read is about real crimes," I pointed out, irritated. "Those things actually happened."

"Yeah...but like, hundreds of years ago, or in the 60s when everyone was joining cults and taking LSD. They catch people now, Jude. They'd have Bundy's phone tapped before he could plan his first murder. And anyway that story wasn't real. It was just Marianna trying to write a creepy book. Don't let it get to you."

"But the fire happened, just like in the story. A gas leak, the same night, opposite a cemetery – that's not a coincidence!" I realised I was nearly shouting and snapped my mouth shut, alarmed.

Adam raised his eyebrows. "The cemetery here, in town?"

I nodded. Finally, he was getting it.

But instead he rolled his eyes. "Jude, that place is in the middle of three estates. There's got to be like...a hundred houses on streets opposite it. And people go out and get plastered on Halloween, let off fireworks, have spooky candles out. Accident waiting to happen. I mean, come on – just because someone stumbled home for some beans on toast and left the gas on doesn't mean there's a murderer in Bricknell."

It made sense. That was the annoying thing. I felt so stupid. On my own, late at night with the paper and the creepy story still running through my head I'd been so sure. Now, with Adam there, it just seemed ridiculous. Hadn't the paper said the police were certain it was an accident?

Adam got up and rubbed a hand over his hair. "Listen, I've got to get back. Are you going to be OK?"

"Back?" I was incredulous. "The windows are smashed in and you want to leave me here, alone?"

"It's just the door and the kitchen fanlight. No one can get in through there. Even if they could reach in, they wouldn't even be able to unlock the front door without the key," Adam said, ever logical. "The police probably scared them off home to their parents."

"Can you not just stay, there's only a few hours left on your shift." I hated how whiny I sounded. I was not a whiner. I wasn't a victim.

"It's like five hours and we really need the money. Besides I can't leave everyone else to manage." As he turned away I heard him mutter, "They hate me enough as it is."

I wanted to ask him what he meant, but he was already picking up his phone and keys. I glanced at my own phone. The screen was cracked from where I'd dropped it, making the display nearly impossible to read under its spider webs. Great. Another expense. Adam was right, we needed the money. I needed to be strong. I was strong.

"Leave the rest of the glass. I'll clear it up tomorrow," he said, on his way out the door. "Just get some sleep. We'll talk later."

What about, he didn't say.

CHAPTER ELEVEN

Before going to bed I cleaned up the broken glass. I was feeling more in control and didn't want to leave it for Adam after his shift. There was blood on the floor as well from my foot and I wiped it up with a cloth. It didn't take long before everything looked normal again, aside from the broken windows. But hey, we already had the glazier's number saved. Adam had been right, they weren't big enough for anyone to get in. All the same, I took a kitchen knife and went to hide it under the mattress.

On my way I stopped and looked at the blade in my hands. Could I use it, if I had to? Even the Butcher, despite his name, had never stabbed someone. That I knew of a least. Could I push a knife into someone? Feel it pierce skin, fat and muscle, blood spilling onto my hand? It made me feel shaky just to imagine it.

In my early teens I'd gone through an emo phase. It was then that I started to dye my hair black and wear eyeliner and dark clothes. It made me look less like my mother, which was all I cared about. But at the time I convinced myself I was deeply into death, despair and poetic depression. That had ended when I'd tried my hand at self-harm. I couldn't make myself cut into my skin. Not even a scratch with the razor blade I'd stolen from the chemist. If I couldn't even scratch myself, how could I hope to stab someone when my life depended on it?

I put the knife under the mattress anyway, defiantly. But I remained afraid, because I knew I couldn't use it. Wouldn't use it. Like my mother, it seemed I hadn't a single drop of self-preservation in my body.

Sleep didn't come easily. Despite Adam's reassurances. I felt like I was back in my student days, pounding energy drinks until my heart was in my throat. Even with my eyes burning for sleep my legs kept twitching and I rolled over and over, unable to relax. I wanted a cigarette but like hell was I going to the shop right now. Instead I decided to see if anyone in the group chat was up to keep me company. On my cracked phone I brought up the local paper's website and sent the book club a link to the explosion story.

Jude: Anyone seen this? Looks like that story of Marianna's??

No one messaged back. It was two in the morning and clearly everyone else was asleep. I put on a podcast, 'Late Night Investigations'. It was one I'd stumbled on when we'd first moved to Bricknell. Podcasts weren't really my thing, but this one had an episode on the Bricknell Butcher. The presenter was a woman, British, with a low voice. I hoped it would help me sleep. Perversely, it usually did.

Tonight we dive into the life of Raymond Wayfield, better known as the Butcher of Bricknell. In 1991, while working across the UK and Northern Island as a lorry driver, Wayfield became a suspect in a string of sexual assaults. Many unsolved attacks have been linked to Wayfield over the years, though he was never charged until something, perhaps a growing thirst for violence, prompted him to turn his hand to murder…

Lulled to sleep by the familiar facts I didn't wake up until Adam came home just after six. I blinked awake just as he was kicking off his boots in the hallway. He looked done in. While he got undressed I pretended to sleep. Whatever he wanted to talk about could wait until he'd had some rest. I didn't get up until he was snoring.

After getting dressed and easing my boots on over the foot bandage, I went to check the damage outside. In the stark light of a clear November morning, it was hard to believe I'd been so frightened. The graffiti was predictably childish; swear words in unpractised spray paint, some misspelled. It might have shocked someone else but I'd seen my share of scrawled obscenities in London. The dog shit made me wrinkle my nose but again, it wasn't upsetting, just gross and annoying. Without the silent darkness of midnight and the idea that there was an email from a killer sitting in my inbox, it wasn't frightening.

With the aim of letting Adam sleep I drove to the nearest petrol station and got a coffee and a stale muffin, then parked on the heath to make some phone calls. Outside, early morning golfers trooped about in thick coats. Gulls wheeled overhead and traffic rushed past on the main road. Everything felt gratifyingly normal. I arranged for the glazier to come and board the windows over. Then I checked in on the group chat.

My message hadn't caused the stir I'd been imagining. I wasn't sure what I'd been hoping for, maybe just some interest or acknowledgement that it was a weird coincidence. Siobhan and Katrine had dropped generic 'that's so weird' messages. Ricky had added a gif of some conspiracy theorist guy with a board covered in red string. Finn was as coolly logical as Adam had been, even pointing out that Marianna's story hadn't even specified Bricknell as the location. For all we knew she'd been writing about some other town. It made the coincidence all the more banal.

Only David, ever cautious, had asked if we ought to tell the police. The idea of doing so after my embarrassment the previous evening made me flush all over. No, I did not need to involve the police again. I'd look even more hysterical than they already thought I was.

David had also asked if anyone else was free to meet Marianna's sister that morning. She was heading home but had some things of Marianna's she wanted to hand over to us. Knowing Adam would be asleep for a good few hours yet I told David I was able to meet. Ricky and Siobhan were also going. Finn was at work already and Katrine was at a seminar.

We met in a little café just down the street from The Highwayman. It was run by a chain and had the same quirky décor as all the others; fringed lampshades, weird paintings and uncomfortably modern chairs. David was already there when I came in, seated at a scrubbed wooden table, alone.

"Hey," I said, dropping on to a seat that had looked much softer from a distance. "So…do you really think there's something to the story then? It's not just me being dramatic?"

"It's certainly a strange coincidence," he said. "Though I think I agree with everyone else that it's not a matter for the police."

"You think that's all it is then? A coincidence?" I said, feeling some disappointment along with my relief. What had I been hoping for, that we really were being contacted by a murderer? I needed to get a grip.

"Finn made some good points. It seems very unlikely that someone would plan something like that ahead and then tell us, of all people."

"Mmmm," I said. "Marianna would have found it funny, I bet. That we believed it, or at least, I did."

He smiled slightly. "I imagine so, yes. Though she'd probably be more flattered than anything. You know, that message was rather good, wasn't it? Product of a talented mind. Such a shame," he looked down at the table, lost in thought.

"Did her sister say what she was bringing?" I asked, trying to change the subject. David looked up and frowned.

"Diana? No, she didn't. I expect it's not much. I suppose as she's going home she wants to sort everything out now. So much domestic clutter when people die. You wouldn't believe how long it takes to sort out, I remember when my mother passed away, it took weeks. And a skip." He winced, guiltily. "Of course not everything was thrown away."

I nodded, understanding better than anyone the kind of mess a death in the family left you with. "Where's she from? Diana – I mean, I know their family is Lithuanian but she lives in the UK, right?"

"Yes, but I'm not sure where. It was all such a muddle when we spoke, I'm not sure I remember…she was quite upset, understandably. I got the impression it was a way away though. The police called her when Marianna was found and she said she'd been on the road a few hours to get here."

"I can't imagine getting a call like that," I said, because I felt like I should say something. In reality I had of course experienced it firsthand.

A perky student came over to take tea and coffee orders. I winced at the price of a single latte, easily twice what I'd paid for my petrol station breakfast. As she was leaving Ricky and Siobhan appeared. He with a backpack, her with a pushchair containing twins. I groaned inwardly. I had no patience with children at the best of times and Siobhan's were some of the worst. Loud, demanding and usually completely ignored by their mother. One was already squealing, the other had a face plastered in dried snot.

"Alright?" Ricky said, sitting down and knocking the hood of his sweatshirt back. A waft of zealously applied Lynx washed over me. I nodded and he looked around before snagging a menu.

Siobhan tightened her already vicious looking ponytail, unaware of the snot trail on her *Game of Thrones* hoodie. One of the two kids (what were their names? Galadriel and...Caspian? Poor bastards) started to bang a plastic toy against the table leg. She ignored it. I noticed David wince as the noise grew louder.

Finally am woman I took to be Diana arrived. She stood in the doorway, glancing around until she saw us. She had an archive box in her hands. That was how I recognised her. I thought, somewhat guiltily, that Marianna had inherited the looks in the family. Diana had the same long dark hair and brown eyes, but her skin was leathery from the sun and pockmarked in places with old acne scars. Her lips were thinner, less generous, and her jaw was heavier. She had on a mid-length black coat, over a funereal suit and white shirt. Everything looked a bit big on her as if she'd just lost weight. She arrived as our drinks did and declined to order for herself.

"I'm double parked," was all she said by way of greeting. She'd already put the box on the table. "I've had most of her things moved to storage, but I thought, based on what she told me about you, that you might like these."

She lifted the lid of the box. Inside were books, DVDs and some magazines. All of it was true crime stuff. Some of the books I owned myself, though I wasn't that into conspiracies and assassinations. They were titles we'd discussed for the club. The DVDs were documentaries and biopics.

"I did want to stay and sort things out from here but, I really can't miss any more work," Diana was saying. "So it'll probably all go to charity. But I know you were her friends and this is a...thing you did together." Clearly not a thing she approved of.

"What is it you do?" Asked David.

She put the lid back on the box. "Finance. Bit technical, but very high pressure. They can't do without me. I really do need to go. I'm sorry, about the funeral thing. I would have liked to do something for her friends here, it's just…" she waved a hand to encompass the weight of the situation.

"We understand," David soothed. "And we're very sorry, for your loss."

"Thank you," she said, looking down at her hands, the nails were bitten short, the skin around them gnawed. Stress. She was missing her sister, or just stressed about work. It was hard to tell. Her eyes were swollen, perhaps she'd already been crying.

"You can call, any time, if you need some help on the ground, sorting things out," David said.

"Yeah, we'll help," I said.

Diana nodded, blinking rapidly as if to stall tears. "Thanks. I'll phone if there's anything. Sorry I really have to go." She hurried away and as she passed the café window I saw her press a tissue to her nose and mouth, shoulders quaking. I quickly looked away.

After she'd left Siobhan opened the box again, ignoring her squalling twins who were now flailing at each other.

"How do we divide this up then?"

"Dibs the DVDs," Ricky said.

Siobhan picked up a thick book on Bundy. "This looks new – it's still on my wish list."

"We should ask Katrine and Finn what they would like, to remember her by," David said.

"Maybe we could divide them at the next meeting?" I suggested.

"Sounds like a good idea," he said. "I would take it back with me but I'm on the bike today. Would you be able to take them home and bring them along next time we're all together?"

I nodded and stashed the box by my chair. Over the rest of our drinks we talked a bit about how we were finding our latest book and some new drama Siobhan had just started watching.

As we paid and were on our way out, David touched my elbow to get my attention.

"Judith, I meant to say, what you said about the cemetery reminded me. You're still researching the Butcher, constructing a timeline, yes?"

I nodded. I'd been working on it since we'd moved to Bricknell. A timeline of confirmed or possible Butcher victims. Slow going without many sources to go on, it was based mostly on what the others at the book club could tell me. Most of the assaults were all over the country, hard to match up with what few jobs I knew for certain he'd taken.

"Well, you should look into Evelyn Scott, if you haven't already. As a potential victim."

"Oh, right…who was she, one of the roadside assaults?"

"An assault, but not on the road. Local girl. It occurred to me the other day that it might be connected. Or at least, it could have inspired his sudden spree of murders. Never actually confirmed as one of his, bit of an outside chance but it might prove interesting. Let me know how you get on with it."

I hefted the box onto my hip. "I will. Though it's not likely to be one of his, an assault on his own patch. What reminded you of her?"

"The newspaper article about the fire. That's where she was assaulted. In the cemetery."

CHAPTER TWELVE

A dam was still asleep when I got in. I felt guilty for being so relieved. Last night had been awful and I wasn't in the mood to rehash it. I left the box of books in the hallway and went to the bathroom. It was only then that I realised my phone wasn't in the pocket of my jeans.

I panicked. Where had it got to? I couldn't afford a new screen, let alone a new phone. I thought back. I'd been using it in the car, on the heath. I went out and had a look around the driver's seat. Nothing. Had I taken it into the café? Maybe. That meant it could still be there, if someone hadn't run off with it. The thought of walking all the way back into town made me want to groan aloud. Paying for another parking spot was just as off putting.

In the interest of not wasting my time, I went to get Adam's phone. We had each other saved on 'locate my device'. At least then I'd know if it was at the café or out of sight in the car somewhere. I tapped the screen, but instead of showing our smiling faces on the background, there was a lock screen. I blinked at it. Since when had Adam started locking his phone?

I glanced at his sleeping form. He'd been acting a bit off recently. First the shift he'd lied to me about, apparently so he could surprise me with a night at a hotel. But then he'd acted kind of weird about me borrowing his phone. Now it was locked? Why was he suddenly being so cagey about his mobile? Again, the worry that he was cheating popped into my head. It wasn't that I thought he'd lie to me, or hurt me, it was that I knew he deserved better than me. What if he'd finally found it and was pulling away?

The sound of my mobile chiming with an email made me jump. I quickly put Adam's phone back on the desk. He was already stirring, alerted by the noise. I hurried into the hall and dug my phone out of the box. I must have swept it up with the books Siobhan had removed and not realised.

"Jude?" Adam called sleepily. "That you?"

"Who else would it be?" I called back, trying to sound light and casual.

"The midnight killer of old Bricknell town?" he muttered.

I went into the lounge and found him pulling on a jumper over his pyjama bottoms. He went over to his phone and tapped away for a moment. Then he turned and waved it happily.

"Just been paid. 'Bout time too, this place is freezing." He crossed his arms and made a dash back to the duvet. "We can get the chimney done and have a proper fire."

"Just before winter too," I said, trying to sound optimistic. "I'll make some tea. By the way, I called the window people, they had a cancellation so they're coming in an hour or so to board us up."

Adam sighed. "One step forward, two steps back. Those little shits."

"At least there wasn't too much damage...I'm sorry about freaking out on you."

"No, I'm sorry," Adam waved a hand. "I was in a shitty mood and I shouldn't have made you feel bad about being scared. It was the middle of the night and you had every right to be."

His apology only made me feel worse. I busied myself putting the kettle on and cranked the gas up. The hiss of it made me shiver, thinking of Marianna, of the explosion in the paper. Adam didn't seem to notice. He was jotting something down on the back of an envelope. Frowning. By the time I'd made the tea he had a whole list of figures written down.

"I think we can just about run to the shower and the chimney sweep. It's not going to be top of the line, but it'll be cheaper than filling that swimming pool of a bath up and more comfortable than that hose attachment."

"So the bath is staying?" I said, not sure if I was happy or not. Since that night Adam had mentioned his suspicions I couldn't shake the image of limbs piled up in it like pale sausages.

"We can't really afford the whole shebang – shower over bath is the cheapest option." He didn't sound too thrilled. "That or we rough it for a few more months until we can afford to get it all ripped out."

Not an appealing thought. "No...it's more sensible to get the shower fitted over the bath."

Adam nodded, then sighed and put the envelope aside. "So...last night was a shit show."

Apparently we weren't finished talking about this. My heart sank.

"I saw the graffiti outside," I said, face already burning with shame. "When I went to meet up with David and the others. Shouldn't be too hard to remove, right? I'm sure I saw an old broom in the garden the other day so, I'm going to give the walls a scrub later, see if I can at least get the shit off."

"I think we should move."

I sat down heavier than I'd intended and the beanbag nearly fell over. "What?"

"Not right away but...as soon as we've done enough work on this place to flip it, we should sell it and move." Adam's face was closed off and he wouldn't quite meet my eye. But he sounded completely convinced.

"But...we've put up with so much trying to get it all fixed up. You don't want to enjoy it once it's all done? Or at least wait for a while and then get the best deal on it?" I said.

"I don't see that there's much to enjoy about being here," Adam said, looking into the depths of his tea. "I mean, you've seen the way people act towards us; the neighbours, now these kids. Why should we stay and put up with this crap?"

"So some kids chuck shit at the house and you're willing to move away?" I said, harsher than I intended. Anxiety was zipping through me. I couldn't leave now, not when I was starting to make progress. Getting closer to finding out what my mother had refused to share with me. Refused to even believe. Little by little I was gathering all the knowledge I could. When I finally faced Wayfield, I'd be the one in control – he'd have nothing to bait me with. No secrets with which to tempt me.

But, a little voice chirped in the back of my head, if I did just sell the place and leave, Wayfield would never be able to write to me again. Wasn't that what I wanted?

Did I want him to leave me alone, of course. But I wasn't going to run from him, like I'd been doing for years. Hiding from his letters, his notoriety. This was about more than facing up to him. It was about getting control of my life. Control of the facts.

"It's not just the kids though, is it?" Adam said, cutting through my thoughts. He was more agitated now, clearly upset. "I've been working at this new warehouse for six months and they still treat me like crap. They act like I'm not there until they have to interact with me and then it's like they don't want me there. Like I'm...intruding."

"I didn't know that," I said quietly in the silence that followed. Adam hadn't really told me much about his work, I realised. Back in London he'd always been full of stories or plans to go out for drinks on a Friday night. I'd thought he'd been saving money by not going out, stupid of me.

"Yeah, well...I didn't want to say anything. But I think it's getting worse. My stuff keeps going missing, they've been messing with my phone, my bag. I'm getting every shit job they can throw at me. It's like they're trying to force me to quit. Or trying to get a rise out of me so they can get me fired."

It was all coming out in a rush now and Adam couldn't even look at me. How had he kept this from me for so long? I felt a stab of guilt at the thought. Hadn't I been keeping things from him since we'd met? Far more important things at that. About me, my life before him. My real name. If he'd tried to tell me, would I have listened, or would I have been too caught up in Wayfield to pay attention?

"I thought it was just about me being new. That maybe they were suspicious because I've come in from London and I asked about a few things they do here. Maybe they thought I was going to cause trouble, be a jobsworth. Then I thought it might be the house, after you told me about the history – but it feels like more than that. It feels like they hate *me*," Adam said at last, dropping his head into his hands. "I didn't want to believe it at first but...well, I know people say small towns are more conservative, more prejudiced but this...I didn't expect this."

It was a good thing he wasn't looking at me, because for a second I couldn't speak. My mouth moved but I couldn't make any words come out. I felt so awful. I'd not considered how it must look to Adam; the stares and the aggression, the whispering and pointed avoidance. To him, the only black person on our street, it was probably at the forefront of his mind that his appearance was the reason for our frosty reception. As opposed to mine.

"Adam...I'm sure it's not that. Maybe some of the old bastards around here but...we're just new." I said, desperately wanting to reassure him, to wipe the hurt from his face. "Places like this, they don't adapt or adjust quickly. There's probably people that've lived here for ten years that aren't considered 'proper locals' and yeah, maybe being in this house in particular is making us less than popular but...I'm sure it's not as widespread as you think. We just need to give it time." I said, feeling lower than shit as I said it, because no amount of time was going to fix what was really wrong. It wouldn't end until I left.

"You don't know how it feels," he says, looking at me for the first time. "I do. This is not the first time I'm dealing with this shit but before..."

Before he had his friends, his family. I loved his parents, Adom and Sabrina, their flat was always full of his brothers and sisters. The kind of family I'd always wanted. Close and supportive. Without them it was obvious Adam would be lonely. So why hadn't I seen it? I felt terrible. I'd been too caught up in myself and my obsession to see that he was struggling.

"You're right. I don't know how it feels," I said, truthfully. I had no idea what it was like for him. The hatred aimed at me was earned. "But I do know that we have every right to be here and they can all get fucked. And...when this place is done up, if it's still not working for us here. We'll move. I promise. I don't want you to feel like this."

I could have cried, the guilt was so thick in my throat. I wanted to say we could just leave tomorrow. Sell the house, like I should have done months ago when I first received that fucking solicitor's letter. I never should have accepted it. Never should have lied. Only we'd been so desperate for a place of our own, a way out of the vicious cycle of renting that never left us anything to save. To be given the keys to a place that was, if decrepit, at least bought and paid for, had been a kind of miracle. But Adam deserved better than the lies I'd fed him. Better than me.

"You're sure?" Adam asked, snapping me out of my panicked thoughts. "This place seems like it means a lot to you. I don't really know all about how it came to your Mum, but if it's important to you..."

"It's just a house," I said, even though nothing was 'just' anything where Wayfield was concerned. Not to me. "We get what we need from it and then we go – nothing is worth you feeling like this. Nothing."

That at least, was the truth.

*

After our talk Adam seemed in a better mood. He got dressed and went to the nearest DIY superstore to see about a shower and some other bits we were in need of. Watching him go, so determined to get the bungalow fixed up, I felt like the worst kind of traitor. He had been so good to me and I'd been so dishonest I was starting to think he was the one hiding things from me. I needed to get a grip.

I dumped a bottle of floor cleaner into a bucket of water and went to scrub the brickwork. As clumps of dog shit fell and red-tinted water splashed on me, I accepted it as my penance. I would get things fixed up, I would find my answers and then I would keep my promise to Adam. We would leave.

As for what I'd do if my answers weren't forthcoming, I didn't want to think about that. I didn't want to have to make that choice.

As I scrubbed I became aware of eyes on me. Glancing around I saw the old hag from next door peeping from her window. I felt anger burning up my spine. How old would she have been when Wayfield was arrested? Forty? Had she lived there then, right next door to him? Had she spoken to him, exchanged greetings while walking some other ratty little dog? Had she suspected that there was anything untoward about him, I wondered. Probably not. Yet she judged me, when I had less to do with the whole sordid affair than she did.

It was Wayfield's other neighbour who'd discovered the bodies. An elderly man long since placed in a home, his house sold to the young couple there now. While Wayfield was away on a long drive north a storm had come in. The shed at the end of his garden was blown over and the neighbour, being a friendly sort, went to right it.

It was safe to say he had not been expecting the bodies. Hidden under a large cut out portion of the shed floor was a pit. Inside, the disarticulated bodies of three women, all buried in quicklime. There was a chair in the shed. Neighbours had seen light through chinks in the wooden walls often, assumed that Wayfield had some hobby or other to keep him in there for hours of a night. He had liked to spend time with the girls. His possessions.

She'd lived next door to that, and never suspected. I scrubbed with renewed viciousness. The unfairness of it all making my vision blur.

"You alright Luv?"

I turned and found myself face to face with a man touting a toolbox. Behind him a van was parked at the curb, an assistant already unloading sheets of plywood. The glazier.

"Sorry, miles away," I said.

"Little shits, eh?" he said, nodding to the broken windows. "Ought to be made to pay for it."

"Agreed," I said, mustering a smile. "Let me get the door."

After letting them in I picked up the bucket of water to dump down the outside drain. I'd been cleaning in a daze and the graffiti was now mostly gone, leaving several red patches behind. Between that and the boarded up windows, it was going to look like a budget haunted house.

When Adam returned with the shower unit he seemed more himself and was happy to chat to the workmen, neither of whom was local. They admired some of the bargains he'd picked up and exchanged tool talk and complaints over the weather, football and the state of the local roads. I left them chatting about their gaming setups and went to look up a quote for plastering the bedroom.

It was only then that I looked at the email that had pinged my phone hours previously, waking Adam from his sleep.

It was from Marianna.

CHAPTER THIRTEEN

This time there was no mistaking the feeling that went through me when I saw the email. I was not confused or surprised that my dead friend appeared to be messaging me. I was afraid. In that moment every reasonable counter argument Adam and the others had provided fell away. I was left only with the certainty I'd felt on seeing that newspaper. This was real, and it was happening again.

I clicked the attachment and as soon as it opened, my heart was in my throat.

3

Oh dear.

It looks like this round goes to me. I'm quite surprised actually. You'd think, given the stakes, that you'd try just a little harder to outwit me. I gave you the day, as good as told you the location – yet still you failed to find her in time. Now Lara Preston is dead, because of you.

It's almost embarrassing, given your obsession with murder. You convince yourselves that you're smarter than the police, the FBI, the very killers who remained unidentified for centuries. Who died free men, their guilt going with them to the grave. You think that you are the authority on these things, that a handful of books and salacious podcasts give you some insight. But you have no insight. You are not detectives.

You are ghouls.

The screaming masses fighting for a piece of the hanging rope.

Numbed by your own unique fetish, looking all the time for more depraved acts to satisfy your curiosity.

I will not disappoint you.

I have already chosen my next target. He is a very boring man, more so even than Miss Preston, who at least varied her routine from day to day. This man is almost a ghost, tied to repeat each day just as the last, as if cursed. I watch him from the bushes outside his maisonette. Almost dozing in boredom myself as he wakes up, eats the same cereal and watches the same news every morning. Then he leaves home just in time to reach the betting shop as it opens.

It is safe to leave him there for a few hours before he ventures to a pub to drown his sorrows. He is not a winner after all, almost a born loser in fact. Even the small amounts he makes at his favourite pastime are inconsequential beside his losses.

Then home, not drunk exactly but unsteady. Weakened. He will spend the afternoon online, typing earnestly away. He thinks of himself as an academic, a man struggling to bring enlightenment through his work. Sharing his small store of knowledge with anyone he comes across, while they cast their eyes around for any excuse to escape his rambling. He refuses to consider that he may be wrong on nearly all counts, that he will never be accepted by those he idolises. Will never achieve his long held dreams. He is, in short, a joke.

When he feels his work is done he will retire to the velour armchair, pour himself a whisky and watch the history channel. He fills his dreams with Roundheads and Vikings, WW2 soldiers and Tudor kings.

Sometimes he narrates to himself as he fetches another drink, imagining he is the one being filmed in his tweed jacket outside Hampton Court.

I watch and wait for him to drink himself to sleep in front of the television. That is when I will make my move. Fire and air have been kind to my efforts, but now it is time for water to be tested. The bath, I think. As much as I do not want to see his gnarled body without its worn and musty clothing. It is a sacrifice I am willing to make.

Even in death he will be but a footnote in history. His name forgotten, lost under a new title; Victim.

Try harder. His life depends on it.

I went to the group chat immediately. Apparently I was the first one to have read the email. Most everyone else was at work or college. Siobhan was likely busy with her kids and god only knew what Ricky got up to during the day, before the pizza shop opened. I was surprised that David hadn't yet seen it. He seemed one to be fastidious in checking his messages. He was also, as far as I knew, home all day. Always around in the chat or on forums of one kind or another.

I typed out a message asking everyone to check their email. Then I waited, rereading the email until it was embedded in my memory.

One email from a dead woman could be explained away as a quirk of technology, an ironic attempt at organisation. Two was no coincidence. Someone was using her account to mess with us, and I could not for one more moment believe that their intentions were benign. A quick google revealed the name of the woman killed in the gas explosion; Lara Preston. This new chapter, or letter, whatever it was, claimed responsibility for the fire on Halloween. Named the woman killed. Her death had been predicted.

Why did her name sound so familiar? Why had she been chosen, and why were we being singled out to participate in this game? What connection did she have to the rest of us, if there even was one? I had no answers, only a pit of dread in my stomach. If we didn't find the person in chapter three, they were going to die. The writer, or 'the killer' as I couldn't help thinking of them, had said as much. His life was in our hands.

A message appeared in the chat.

David: Should we go to the police now?

Me: If this is real, we have to, don't we?

Ricky: Fucking hell you guys what the fuck is going on? Jude, is this you? Because it's not fucking funny.

Me: It's not. Why would I do this?

Ricky: Idk, as a joke? Try to prove you're cleverer than us?

Me: Jesus Ricky. No. I wouldn't do that. And that Lara woman? She's actually dead. She's the one who died in the fire on Halloween.

Ricky: Fuck me.

Siobhan: This isn't real. Why would anyone do this? It's just someone messing with us.

Ricky: HE KNEW HER NAME. HE KNEW HOW SHE WAS GOING TO DIE

Finn: He's playing us. It's all just the power of suggestion.

Ricky: Like fuck it is!

Katrine: I'm freaking out.

The messages cascaded, one after the other. Ricky and Katrine were panicking. Siobhan seemed to be in denial, unable to believe what was going on. Finn, who really should have been busy at work, was being condescending and David was trying to keep the peace. I closed my eyes for a moment to calm myself down. There was little doubt in my mind that this was real. Someone was out there, killing people and playing a weird game with us. What had we ever done to anyone? Read some books, discussed some history? Not the kind of thing vendettas were built on. Maybe we'd been chosen at random? Someone had happened on a forum post one of us had made and decided to play a twisted game with us? The only comfort in thinking of it that way, as a game, was that games had rules. Games could be won. Only we didn't know the rules. How could we? We'd never been told.

The thought of going to the police frightened me. No one was going to believe us. I'd already embarrassed myself in front of them once. What scared me was the thought that Adam might insist we move if I freaked out again. He already thought I had murder on the brain, an obsession that was sending me into hysterical fits of terror at the slightest bit of hooliganism. If I told him I thought a murderer was after me he'd insist we go back to London. For my mental health if nothing else. I couldn't do that. I had to stay in Bricknell. I had to get my answers.

When I glanced at the chat and saw that Katrine was suggesting we report the information anonymously, I could have cried with relief. After some back and forth about handwriting identification and fingerprinting, it was agreed that Katrine would send an email. There was a computer at the college left logged in to a spare account so students could use some kind of design software via a subscription. She would send the email from that account. It could be accessed by anyone who walked into the studio, which was anyone passing by. Among several thousand students, staff and visitors, it was unlikely to be traced back to her. We'd be safe from scrutiny, and embarrassment, if this turned out to be nothing.

It would turn out to be nothing, I told myself. After all, my life had already been torn up by one serial killer. A second would be more than just bad luck, it was about as likely as being hit by lightning, twice.

I agreed to the plan, then added: Will they find him you reckon? This guy in the story?

David: I'm sure they will. Or they'll put out a news bulletin to let people know to be careful. Someone's bound to recognise the details of the man's routine.

Finn: Not much to go on though is it? Should we not have a go?

David: We shouldn't attempt to engage with this person. There's no threat to us, so as long as we've informed the police of the issue, we'll be fine.

Me: What about Marianna?

David: That was an accident. There's no evidence to suggest otherwise.

Me: Bit of a coincidence though, isn't it? Her dying.

David: We have no evidence that it wasn't an accident.

Finn: idk he seems pissed that we didn't find Lara. What if he gets more angry that we aren't trying to solve this one?

David: In all likelihood this is still just someone trying to frighten us. They could have easily searched a similar fire to the one they described and then used Lara's name to make themselves seem legitimate. If we report it, we've done our duty, but I don't think we need to be afraid.

It hadn't occurred to me on reading the email, but David was right. Whoever was writing these messages hadn't revealed Lara's name until after she was dead. He could have found it just as I had. There were still too many supposed coincidences for me to be comfortable. A gas explosion on that night, in that location, with a woman as the only victim; just as the email had predicted? I wasn't as keen as David to write the whole thing off as a sinister prank.

Still, he had a point. The police would get the tip and they'd have to take responsibility for finding this person, if they really were in danger. We had nothing to go on other than his habit of going to the bookies and getting drunk alone of an afternoon. Not exactly a huge amount of information with which to find someone. It could have been any bloke past retirement age.

Me: 'David's right. We've done all we can, now it's up to the police. But everyone should take care. Even if they're not really a murderer, just pretending to wind us up, someone IS still messing with us, and we don't know why.

Katrine: He said about us being ghouls. He thinks we like murders and torture and stuff, for fun.

Ricky: So the sad fuck just wants to scare us because we like true crime? Us and millions of other people. That's like gunning people down cos they like action movies.

He had a point. I couldn't imagine someone setting out to snipe Adam just for his taste in online games. Ours was not an unusual interest. There were thousands of books and documentaries about serial killers and murderers coming out every year. Most streaming services had a whole category for this stuff. It was like nature documentaries or Second World War biopics. It was just an academic interest. So why was this guy so bothered with us?

Whatever the reason, I hoped he'd get bored once he realised we weren't playing his little game. I had more important things to worry about than some keyboard warrior's idea of poetic justice.

CHAPTER FOURTEEN

Having decided that we were being targeted by a prankster, rather than a killer, I put the issue out of my mind. With Adam determined to move as soon as the house was in a sellable state I had to spend some time with Mum's diaries. Reading them for the first time in her home town was like stepping into the memories she had never shared with me. The secrets she'd held behind every protestation of Wayfield's innocence. I was seeing him through her eyes, learning about him as she did.

While Adam was working I got the diaries from their hiding spot. Soon after Mum wrote of her crush on Wayfield, she'd started writing in 'code'; though not one that anyone would have had a hard time cracking. It was numbers zero to twenty six. Zero being 'A', one being 'B' and so on. A child's idea of subterfuge, probably just a way to keep her mother out of her business. Still, I had to translate it as I read, scribbling between the lines in pencil.

Before I started doing it I thought sneaking out would be hard. I was worried Mum or Dad would come running down the street after me or phone the police. It was like I'd been taught to believe that leaving the house after they'd gone to bed was impossible. It wasn't! I've been letting myself out on the weekends when He's not working. I didn't even need to climb down over the garage. I just let myself out the front door.

They lie to you, make you think it's impossible to keep things from them. But it's all rubbish. Bullshit, as He says. They don't know anything. Can't see what's right in front of them because they're too safe and secure in the idea that a locked door is enough to keep the world out, and their daughter in. More fool them.

Tonight we met up in the graveyard. It's so much more creepy than the canal but it's also much more private. There's this little shed where the lawnmower and watering cans are so it's the best place to go when it's raining, or if we don't want to be interrupted by other people looking for a place to snog. I asked if we could go to his place once but he lives with his Mum and she's not very well. I get it. I wouldn't want him in my room if Mum was home – even she wouldn't be able to ignore THAT! It might almost be worth it to see the look on her face!

He's gone a lot for his job. Driving all over. He says he misses me when he's away. They make him stay in awful hotels or even just in the lorry. He says if there were better places he'd take me with him. He brought me a present back from his last work trip. It's a teddy with a red velvet heart on its lap. I'm going to keep it at the back of my wardrobe because if Mum sees it she'll ask where it came from. She's always nosing about it my room. He also brought vodka! We were drinking it in the shed and it tasted horrible, but it did warm me up and made me feel more relaxed. Usually I'm worried about someone maybe hearing us or coming in.

Tonight he kept putting his hands up my skirt and I had my top AND bra off. He makes me feel so good, I had no idea how amazing love would feel. But I'm still not ready to do IT yet. Joanna at school told Elaine that she did IT and it really hurt, plus she got blood on his parent's bed. Which is disgusting. He would never ask me to get in his Mum's bed. He's already said that when I'm ready we'll got to a hotel – a proper grown up one with champagne and chocolate in the rooms. Because he loves me.

I'm a bit scared though, because Joanna got dumped after the bloody bed incident. What if He gets bored of me or I'm not good enough and he goes after another girl? I've been sneaking out of the children's part of the library and looking at the women's magazines. There's all kinds of stuff in there and I'm already saving up for a razor and some shaving cream. Maybe some perfume as well. Mum doesn't bother with all that and if I ask her for it she'll tell me I'm too young.

I realised I'd chewed my lip raw while reading. There was no graveyard in town. A graveyard was attached to a church. Mum must have meant the cemetery; a burial ground without a church nearby. They'd met there and kissed, fooling around like a pair of teenagers. At that point she'd been sixteen, he was twenty-two. Hiding her away from his mother or anyone else who might get the police involved.

He'd been telling the truth about his mum being sick. I'd done some digging and found a picture of her. My paternal grandmother, in a wheelchair at a local fundraiser for research into Multiple sclerosis. Something she'd been diagnosed with leading up to her death. She looked very small in the picture, bird boned and sharp-faced. He wasn't with her, but she had a walking stick across her lap, knuckles tight on it like she was ready to swing it. Had he been scared of her I wondered? Was she the reason he'd hurt so many women? I wondered what she'd have made of my mother. Judging from the diaries they'd never met. Probably she'd have thought her a stupid little girl. But would she have wanted to meet me, to know me, as her only grandchild? I'd never know. She died before I was born.

Reading the diaries it was clear my Mum was basically still a kid. I'd always imagined that she was more aware of what was going on, but at this stage at least, she was totally ignorant. Her parents though. My grandparents. They should have done something, noticed something. It wasn't all her fault. Still, I found myself getting angry as I read her rapturous accounts of the time spent with Wayfield. How had she not known what he was? How could she have been so ignorant of the warning signs?

The simple answer was, obviously; because she was in love. Because she was young and didn't know any better. Because it was another time and she was on guard for creepy older men, not handsome ones. Which wasn't her failure, it was theirs. Her parents. Though, I doubted anything could have kept her from him once she was captivated. Stubborn as hell, that's what she was. A trait I had inherited.

What else had made its way into my makeup?

Judging from the date I knew Wayfield's mother was only a month from dying. Flipping ahead in the diary I read that Wayfield was 'depressed' afterwards. At least my Mum thought so. He said his mother had some kind of spasm and fell, hitting her head on the coffee table. I had my doubts. If he wanted her out of the way and ownership of the house, he could have killed her.

Finn had copies of her death certificate and theorised that Wayfield might have withheld her medication, causing her symptoms to worsen. Perhaps she hadn't fallen at all, he could have pushed her. It was a divisive topic when discussing the Butcher. I thought it was probably a spur of the moment thing, cascading anger and frustration.

He was too under her thumb to plot against her, hide things from her or confiscate her medication. Even with his mother's declining health he'd been too afraid of her to bring his teenage girlfriend home. She had some kind of power over him; a single mother ruling with authority and a hefty leather belt. A belt Wayfield had shown my Mum, once the house was his, for sympathy. For her to cry over. Poor Ray. The idea made me sick.

The first entry after Miss Wayfield's death was all about him and how sad he was. My Mum's attempts to talk to him about it were shrugged off and she was scared he was going to break up with her. If he had she'd have had a lucky escape. Instead the next entry was a looping treatise of ecstasy.

Tonight was the night! We didn't need to go to a hotel after all, which was a shame because I was kind of looking forward to it. But he bought champagne and even though it wasn't as nice as the vodka it was still pretty great. He bought me a rose and I'm going to dry it and stick it in here to keep forever.

I think Joanna was being a baby because it didn't hurt THAT much. Maybe she wasn't ready. I was. I know now that we're going to be together always. He told me so. When I've finished school he said we can get married and I can move in with him. Then the house will belong to both of us.

Elaine is talking about going to college and getting work in an office. She wants us to get jobs in London and to take the train there every day. Go to nightclubs after work and go shopping on Oxford Street on our days off. It sounds quite glam actually. But the idea of working all those long hours puts me off. He says I don't need to. He has enough for both of us.

I don't think he likes Elaine very much. I said something about her once, I can't really remember what, and he said she was immature and that she was never going to find someone to marry her, because she's so plain. When I mentioned the office thing he said she'd probably still be there at sixty, bored out of her mind. That or she'd get knocked up by someone she met in a club. He said she'd either be boring and alone, or ruined. No one was going to marry her either way. I've gone off her now. I'm too busy with Him most nights to do anything with her. I don't even really want to tell her about having lost my virginity. She'd only get all scrunched up and tell me off. She looks a lot like her Mum when she does that.

I wonder what she'll say when I show her the ring he's going to buy me????

The opposite page had a brown stain on it and some dried glue remnants. If something had been stuck there it was long gone. The smell of sweet, floral decay wafted up from the page. I wrinkled my nose. It reminded me of funerals.

Putting the diary aside I got up and went into the hall. The bungalow had two bedrooms; the larger one at the front of the house and a smaller one on the other side of the bathroom, at the rear. That was going to be the 'office' or so we'd decided when it looked like we were staying for a while.

Standing in the middle of the damp smelling space I wondered if this was where my Mum had slept with him. My Mum had walked these floors and seen these same walls, maybe looked through the same pieces of stained glass. I might even have been conceived in the back bedroom. A thought that turned my stomach.

I'd visited her old house of course. It was a nice little semi-detached property on the older side of town, far from the estate. I hadn't felt a connection to her there though. It was occupied and changed; an extension, a modern skylight and large windows looking in on a minimalist living room. The garage she wrote about had been knocked down and replaced by gravel and succulents. This place though, was like a time capsule.

I returned to the diaries and read a few uncoded entries about school, friends, some party she'd been invited to and turned down to see Wayfield instead. Then a new entry. This one was not only coded into numbers, but written underneath an old birthday card, which had been stuck over the top and had to be gradually peeled away. I'd only seen it because one corner had curled up with age. I didn't have to read it to know what it would say, the dates told me enough. Still, it beckoned to me. I wanted to know how she'd felt in the moment. I already knew what had come after; the blame and resentment. But maybe, in those first moments, there might have been something like...joy. After all, she loved him, why not me?

I was kidding myself.

I don't know what to do. My period is two weeks late and I'm not sure if I should be worried or if this is normal. I've just started doing it, maybe that's made me skip one or changed something down there? There's nothing in any of the magazines about that happening. But maybe that's the case? I want to ask Elaine but I doubt she'd really know. She likes to think she knows all this stuff because she reads things from the adult library but really she's clueless about a lot of it.

I could ask Ray but I don't want to worry him. What if he panics and stops wanting to see me? I can't be pregnant. I'm too young.

A short gap followed. I assumed that she'd not been able to confront her worries as the time stretched on. The entry was covered over, she hadn't wanted to even look at it. Perhaps she'd hoped that, unacknowledged, I might cease to exist. It was not the last time she would apply this tactic.

Then came a long entry, etched into the paper with such force that it had torn in places. The pen puncturing through to the next page and leaving smears of ink. The words were blurred in places as if by tears, or perhaps she'd spat on the page. There was enough hate and despair in the writing to justify either.

I am never going to speak to those people again. They don't exist anymore. I am an orphan.

Mum and Dad were waiting when I got home from seeing Him. One of them must have woken up and realised I was gone. They were in their pyjamas, sitting in the lounge like someone had died. It was pathetic. They looked so old, the pair of them. Like bloody pensioners.

Dad shouted a lot and when I wouldn't tell him where I'd been or who with he shouted more. Mum was crying and she only stopped to shake me and demand I tell them what I'd been doing. I wouldn't. They sent me to bed. I could hear them talking downstairs for ages before I fell asleep.

Today was Monday. I was meant to be going to school but when I woke up it was after ten and no one had woken me up. When I went downstairs they were already there and Mum asked me flat out if I was pregnant. I couldn't think of anything to say. I couldn't believe she knew – how??

She just started shouting about 'how could I be so stupid' and that she knew something was wrong. Turns out she's been keeping track of the pads in the bathroom and knows I haven't been using them. She kept crying and calling me names and then begging me to tell her who I'd been with. It made me cry but even then I wouldn't tell her.

Then Dad told her to go upstairs and do 'what they talked about'. And she went but he wouldn't tell me what was going on and then he HIT ME. Right across the face and called me a stupid little bitch – he actually said bitch! - and said he was ashamed of me. So I said I hated him and he got hold of my shoulders and said, right in my face, that he and Mum had loved me more than anything and that I'd disappointed him so much that he didn't want to look at me. I started to cry more but he didn't care.

After a bit Mum came back and just nodded at him. He told me to put my coat on because we were going for a drive. I asked where but he wouldn't say. So I thought he was taking me to the doctor and I told him I wasn't going anywhere. But he got my arm and made me get into the car. I wanted to scream, embarrass them, but it was all so fast and then I was locked in the back of the car. Then him and Mum put some bags in the boot and I realised she'd been packing my stuff.

I screamed and I BEGGED but they wouldn't let me go and the child locks stopped me jumping out at the traffic lights. I tried grabbing at Dad to make him stop driving but Mum grabbed my hands and hurt my wrist. They wouldn't tell me where we were going. Wouldn't talk AT ALL. I looked out the window when we passed the Crescent but Ray wasn't there – he was back working. I don't know where he is. Then we were on the motorway and it didn't matter anymore. I just cried until we stopped driving.

I'm at Aunt Jill's now. She lives in a pokey little flat in Liverpool and now I live here too. Mum and Dad arranged it last night while I was sleeping. The bastards. They dumped me off with her and said I'd be staying there until the baby came, then I could come home IF I told them who the Dad was. I told them I would rather die than go back to Bricknell with them.

They left. Mum was still crying. I think Dad was too.

Aunt Jill is a bitch. She's Dad's sister and her husband died ages ago. Probably to get away from her. Her flat smells like chips and cat pee. There's a big picture of Jesus in my room and she has the key to the front door on her all the time. I can only go out on the balcony and it's like twelve floors down. I can't get away but she's going to have to take me out at some time – even if it's only to the doctors.

Tomorrow I'm writing to Ray and as soon as he finds out where I am he can come and get me. We can go live somewhere else and never see those people again.

She seemed so certain. I could tell from the way she wrote his name, the loving curve of the numbers that represented it in her code, how they were larger than those around them, that she adored him. He was the most important thing to her. I didn't have to imagine it; she'd told me as much. All through my childhood, 'If he didn't want you, you'd be out of here, so be grateful'. It was strange to think that as she'd written the words I was reading, I'd been developing inside of her.

I felt numb when I finished reading that section. I'd moved to Bricknell to go where she had gone, see what she had seen. To try and understand her. But, I realised, holding that diary, that there was more to it. I hadn't wanted to admit it even to myself but I was also there to find out if, even for only a moment before my birth, she had actually loved me. Amongst all the anger, longing and fear, I couldn't see one word that spoke to anything but a desperation to be rid of me. All her care was for him; the Bricknell Butcher. My father. All her hopes were pinned on him.

And he was never going to come through.

CHAPTER FIFTEEN

I binged the next diary like a bag of sweets or a litre of vodka. It made me feel sick and jittery but I couldn't stop. The sheer, unbridled hatred that leapt off the page was like a drug. It coursed through my veins, burning all other emotions away like acid. After a lifetime of her cold indifference and barely concealed resentment I was finally seeing into my mother's heart. Inside there was only room for one person; Raymond Wayfield. Around that burning core there was only fury and hate. For her parents and also, for me.

From the point she was foisted off on her aunt my Mum stopped keeping a regular diary. There were no dates and very few references to real events. I guessed that this was during her confinement in the flat. There was no school or anything else to occupy her. Her parents had opted to lie that she was going to a private school. In reality she was enrolled nowhere. All her 'learning' came from workbooks her parents sent to her, which she ignored. She didn't care about school. She only wanted one thing; Raymond Wayfield. Nothing else mattered. He was her horizon. She couldn't see beyond him. There were no dreams in her diary that didn't involve him. No aspirations other than to see him again.

Even her aunt seemed to barely interact with her. I got the impression that she was being paid to keep my mother with her. At no point did the diary mention her going to work and conditions seemed to hover just about the poverty line. Mum made one mention of her parents 'writing more cheques than letters'. I guessed it was those cheques that made the aunt put up with her. It couldn't have been love. Even taking into account Mum's bias against her family, it seemed there was no kindness in that flat.

Instead of documenting her life, my mother ranted. Each page was dense with text detailing how much she hated 'those people' her 'former parents'. How she never wanted to see them again. How she wished her aunt would fall down the stairs and die while taking the rubbish out. She longed for escape and, more than anything, to be reunited with Ray.

I managed to send him another letter today, while we were at the doctors. Jill has books of stamps leftover from Christmas cards and I've been taking one stamp from each ever since I found where she keeps them. I keep them hidden in my diary. I think she's been searching my room but she's never going to find my hiding spot. I suppose I should be glad this shitty flat has ceiling tiles. Though there's probably rats up in that ceiling. This place is the absolute pits. A rat infested dungeon.

I think the receptionist at the surgery hates me. She looks at me like I'm something someone's trod in and scraped off on the carpet. But her assistant is young and I think she feels sorry for me. I told her the letter was for my Dad and she said she'd post it for me. The first one I got in a box myself on the way to the surgery for my first visit. SHE was busy nattering to some other old biddy. I just wandered over and did it. He can't write back though. I don't even know the address of where I am, just the flat number. I tried looking for a street sign but it's been knocked over and taken away. There's just an empty post. Even the building name has been vandalised so badly it's just random letters. I could probably find it from the streets around us, but Jill doesn't have a map. Or the internet. I'm going to get my hands on a letter to Jill and then tell him where I am.

I did tell him, about the baby. His baby. I thought maybe it would make him try harder to find me, that he'd be worried about it. About me. He said he wanted us to get married. Maybe he'd be happy about the baby?

Sometimes I think I feel it move, even though it's too early for that yet, according to the doctor. I put my hands on my stomach and try to feel something, but there's nothing there. It scares me a bit. I always thought Mum had loved me right from when she knew she was going to have me. But I don't feel anything like love. I wish it had never been made. If it hadn't been I'd still be with him.

Most of me doesn't care that everyone expects me to give it up. I wish I could hand it over now and just go back home to Ray. But I'm also worried because he might hate me if I do give it up. It is his, after all.

After reading that section I helped myself to a bottle of red wine. Downing glass after glass didn't help me forget that my only value to my mother was my relation to a serial killer, but it did help numb the parts of me that hurt.

She'd arrived at her aunt's on the sixth of January, that was in the diary. Two days after that was the assault on Evelyn Scott that David had told me about. It happened in the cemetery where Mum and Raymond had met in secret. Other than that, there was no real connection or evidence that Evelyn was a victim of the Butcher. Of course no one else knew about that connection. It was just the fact that it happened in Bricknell that had turned David on to it.

Leaving aside the issue of his mother, Wayfield had supposedly never attacked on his home turf before the canal murder. His previous sexual assaults, although violent, had not been as brutal as that on Evelyn. Was she the bridge between his sexual assaults and the murders? A girl he'd beaten almost to death, then realised he had a taste for killing?

To me, it made sense in the timeline. Two days after his girlfriend was whisked away Wayfield was likely angry, powerless to get at my mother, feeling impotent. Just like when his mother had control over him. If he had killed his Mum to get away from that feeling, it stood to reason he'd want to attack someone else to block it out again. He couldn't wait for work to take him away from town. So he'd attacked a lone girl in the cemetery; a girl around my mother's age. A way to take back what had been stolen from him? Wayfield had broken the girl's jaw, her nose and fractured her skull. Left her unconscious in-between some graves. Left her for dead most likely. She had nearly died – choked on her own blood. Some drunk locals were taking a shortcut when they found her and shoved her into the recovery position. Lucky for her.

She wasn't considered a 'canonical' Butcher victim due to the lack of sexual assault, her location in Bricknell and away from the main road. The Wayfield assaults having all been assaulted while he was working and then left at the side of the road. Unlike his later murders, she was left to die of her injuries, not purposefully strangled. The victim dumped in the canal, only four days later, had not been beaten at all. That night he'd been more controlled, determined.

Clearly, my mother's disappearance had provoked a change in him. That or the news of her pregnancy. Perhaps both. Had he hated me as much as she did? Or was it being deprived of his child and his young girlfriend that drove him to such rage that he murdered four, almost five, women? The idea that he might have killed because of my very existence chilled me, even after the diaries were safely out of sight.

I knew he couldn't hurt me. Not physically at least. I hadn't seen him in a long time. Then he'd given me his house. A bribe to get me to return to him? To make me feel like I owed him some attention, some pity? Did he just want to control me, or torment me? I'd told myself I'd never go back to see him. Every day there was the threat of another letter, a phone call that Adam might pick up instead of me. I would have to see him soon, either to protect my fragile life from destruction, or to satisfy my own need for answers if the diaries left me with unanswered questions.

While I was making progress on the diaries at night, I distracted myself in the day by working on the house. It was like a balm to my guilty thoughts. Doing something for Adam, even while he continued to believe my lies. While he slept in the mornings I watched tutorials online and started retiling the bathroom. He helped fit the shower and then I laid an offcut of lino to cover the old vinyl floor. I also collected a bedframe from the larger town nearby. It had two broken boards in it, but it was free and I replaced those with an offcut of MDF. For the first time since moving in we weren't sleeping on the floor and could shower at home.

It should have made me happy, but I could hardly summon the will to smile at Adam's pride in my efforts. Inside I felt hollowed out. Scraps of my mother's diary entries went round and round inside my head. Even when I tried to sleep I couldn't stop hearing the words her teenage self had written. I could imagine her adult voice all too well and in it I heard all the things that were worse than the insults she'd heaped on me directly. All the things I'd known anyway, intuited from her actions and her silences. Now confirmed by her own diaries. Not just that she only kept me for the sake of being allowed to visit him, but that she wished I'd never been born, wished I'd died inside her. That she only wanted me as a thing to gift to him.

I carried on with the work on the bungalow, half in an effort to distract myself from the diaries and half trying to assuage my guilt towards Adam. Every time he came home from work, beaten looking and quiet, I knew it was my fault. He was being targeted based on our presence in the house and my resemblance to my mother. I knew he wanted to leave just as much as I couldn't bear to.

I made myself promises to get through the days; once the house was finished, once I was able to put the past to rest, I would tell Adam everything. About Mum, about Wayfield. I would come clean about all the things I'd kept from him since we'd met. I'd never meant to lie to him or mislead him. Our relationship had developed so quickly, turning from flirtation to affection to love all too easily. By the time I was ready to trust him I was terrified of losing him. I would change that, I had to.

Still, a traitorous voice in my head told me I would do no such thing. I was a liar, unworthy of Adam. I was an unfeeling monster, just like my mother. I was a craven manipulator...just like my father. As much as I tried to push those thoughts away, they came back stronger. It was as if the house itself was whispering to me, feeding me my own insecurities, magnified a thousand times over. The harder I fought to ignore it, the greater Wayfield's presence seemed to grow. Like a ghost following me from room to room, yelling obscenities that only I could hear.

The diaries overshadowed everything, even my anxiety over our mystery emailer. As far as I was concerned the prankster was nothing compared to confronting my Mum's past. When the two week mark came and went with no news stories appearing about accidents or deaths, I was barely relieved. Internally I had already let go of the idea that we were in any danger. When no new email arrived, I assumed whoever it was had given up their game. Frustrated by our lack of response.

I was nothing if not adept at self-deception.

We had a fairly normal meeting that night. The absence of Marianna didn't cut as deeply anymore. It almost felt like we were back to normal. Ricky's pick was predictably a bloodthirsty and poorly written one about a spree killing. All grisly pictures and shocking acts of cruelty. David kept his comments to a minimum but his pinched up face said it all. He was disgusted. It was almost funny; Ricky's books were basically what the coverage of the Ripper had been at the time. Fiction and gory fact interwoven with scandal and superstition. I thought of the famous 'From Hell' letters that the Ripper had supposedly sent the police. So similar to the emails we'd received. I shivered, it was a sobering thought.

We got onto the subject of the Butcher again. We usually did once talk about the book had run out. Only this week Finn brought up the Butcher's child. One of the great mysteries of the coverage of his trial. To everyone else. Not me. I already know how that mystery ended. It was not something I planned to share. Though, ever since I'd cottoned on to the whispering on our street I'd been worried that the gossip might reach someone from the group.

In my more paranoid moments I suspected that one or more of them might know about me already. Thought I knew if they had found out none of them could have kept it to themselves. I told myself it was unlikely. It wasn't like someone had taken an ad out in the papers. It was just neighbours gossiping, and then, only those who had known my mother enough to remember her face. The few pictures of her that had appeared in newspapers around the time of the trial didn't do her justice. In them she was sun starved, had recently given birth and was bundled into winter clothes. A blurry figure in newsprint that even I had trouble identifying as my mother.

The localised gossip of my neighbours and some people at Adam's work was hardly likely to reach Katrine at college, or Siobhan all the way across town, barely seeing anyone but us and her own kids. Finn and David were loners and I doubted Ricky had any friends that weren't ones he played online shooters with. When it came right down to it, none of the people in my little book club were that sociable. They were the odd ones out just like I was, in their own way. No one was going to tell them anything.

"Where do you think that kid is now?" Ricky asked.

"No idea," David shrugged. "The papers talked about them at the time but, I've not seen anything since. Not even a picture."

"Therapy, hopefully," Finn said. "Debateable who was more cracked; the killer or the woman defending him."

I bit my lip. It was too close to my own thoughts.

"I've tried to trace them. Can't find any record of Eleanor Pike ever appearing on a birth certificate before she vanishes entirely. There might not even be one. So, no record of the birth sex, location or even date of birth of the child. Like looking for a needle in a haystack. My guess is she got knocked up and the family kept it quiet, you know, like the good old days. Pack them off to a convent somewhere and hand the baby off to some childless couple," Finn said.

"That's awful," Siobhan said. "That poor baby."

"Better to be raised by a teenager with a fetish for murderers?" Ricky said. "I think I'd rather not know. Though it might come in handy on the playground. Not so much 'my dad can beat up your dad' as 'my dad could strangle your mum'."

"As I was saying," Finn said, rolling his eyes. "I can't find any mention of the birth in public records. Then Eleanor Pike disappears. It's likely she changed her name, unofficially, since there's no record of that either."

"She'd have to, wouldn't she? After what she did." David said. "Disgusting really."

They all nodded, I did too. Inside I felt dirty. Like my innards were covered in thick, rancid gunge. Rotten to the core.

By this time I'd reached the entries of Mum's diary that led up to my birth. She'd convinced herself that Wayfield was angry with her. That he had mistaken her 'kidnap' for desertion. She wrote reams on this, torturing herself with his perceived heartbreak. In her mind they were Romeo and Juliet, kept apart by an unfeeling universe and the actions of her hated parents.

In reality of course, Wayfield had no idea where to find her. Mum had never managed to work out where in Liverpool she actually was. I expected that her aunt was taking great pains to keep her in the dark about that. Mum's infrequent letters might well have reached him, but without a way to find her or control the situation, he began to spiral. The murders confirmed this. Over the months between Mum's departure and his arrest he killed four women, nearly five if the cemetery assault was in fact his handiwork. All of them local. I had no evidence that he had stopped working, but it made sense that he'd stay close to home. He was waiting for a clue that would lead him to her, to us. Waiting, and growing impatient, lashing out.

Finally, perhaps pushed back into work by his dwindling bank balance, Wayfield set off across country. It was almost poetic that on his first absence from home, a storm would hit and the bodies would be discovered.

Mum didn't find out right away. Her diary continued to be a mixture of rants against her parents and aunt, and dreams about Ray and their reunion. She wrote lengthy pages about the life they would have together. None of these mentioned me. Her fantasies of rescue became wilder and her devotion, if anything, only burned brighter the longer they were apart. It was all she had. What was happening outside of her fierce internal life must have been of only passing interest. I got the impression that she was isolating herself in her room, away from her aunt and consequently, the television and papers. It must have come as a shock when she finally saw the news.

Today at the doctors I saw the most awful thing. The newspaper says Ray has been arrested for MURDER. I can't believe it. RAY?? He's the gentlest person I know. He cared for his Mum so well. There's no way he's guilty of what they said. All those women. It's sick!

I took the paper, hid it in my coat. There wasn't time to read it all. There were pages of it. Pictures. His house, the garden. They had a photo of him. I don't know where it came from, maybe his work? He's wearing a uniform shirt. He looks thinner. I was always reminding him to eat properly before – he'd live on tea and toast otherwise. He needs me.

I've cut the picture out and I'm going to keep it behind the picture of my parents. They sent it up and Jill put it on my bedside table. I've had it face down but she keeps picking it up. Now I'll have him hidden in there and only I'll know.

The paper says they found bodies in Ray's garden while he was away. But anyone could have buried them there! He's away all the time and people sometimes climb over the fence and use his garden. He used to get really annoyed about it because they left beer cans and stuff all over the place.

I don't know what evidence they think they have but it can't be much. He didn't do this. It's so unfair. Now I know why he hasn't found me, he's been locked up – unable to track me down. I had this idea in my head that he'd go round to my house and get it out of them where I was. That or come to Liverpool and look for me. I don't know the address of this place but I've written to him about what I see when we're on our way to the doctor. The other street signs, the swimming pool…if he'd been able to he would have found me. But they've stopped him.

As soon as I can, I need to get back there. I have to tell them they're wrong about him. And this baby, he might not even know about it. I can't give it away until I know what he wants. They can't lock him up if he's going to be a Dad!

Reading that part turned my stomach. According to my estimates on when it was written, she was only weeks from giving birth to me. But I was still 'it'. I was still a thing to her. Worse, I was a bargaining chip, something she thought she could use to guarantee Wayfield's freedom.

In her mind Wayfield was a hero, held back from rescuing her. To me, the idea of him going round to her parents to demand her whereabouts was ridiculous. He was a grown man who attacked girls and his own elderly mother. He wasn't going to square up to a grown man, much less put himself in danger of being revealed as having groomed a teenager. Wayfield might have been losing control but only on those who couldn't fight back. He was keeping himself in check, if barely.

I felt a deep shame reading those entries. A kind of hot, squirming, second-hand embarrassment both for her and for myself. She was so naïve, completely besotted with a murderer. Even after he'd essentially groomed her and ruined her life, even holding a newspaper that called him a murderer, he was still her true love. He was still the man she thought needed looking after, babying. Her actual baby meant nothing. I meant nothing, without him.

And she was about to sacrifice me, my future, for him.

CHAPTER SIXTEEN

While Adam slept off his last night shift for the week, I walked into town. I needed to get out of the house, away from the diaries and away from my own thoughts. I needed fresh air and some anonymous human contact.

From the high-street I took the bus to Newston, the larger town about half an hour away. Or at least, it was half an hour by car. Money was tight since buying the shower and arranging for the new plastering. I wasn't keen on taking the car out for a jaunt and wasting petrol, not to mention the cost of parking. So, bus it was, and it took forty-five minutes of bumpy, jerky travel. The country roads were potholed to hell and back. I felt sick by the end of it.

Still, as soon as I stepped off the bus and into the swarming pre-Christmas crowds, I was glad I'd come. I felt myself relax almost immediately. It was reassuring to be milling around large shops with throngs of other people. Almost like being back home in London.

I went in and out of a few places, looking at the jewellery, touching clothes and sniffing candles. I was just letting the atmosphere wash over me. The beeps and crashing tills, the chattering voices, it ate into the black cloud around me and left me feeling buoyed up. Christmas was spread over every available surface; fake snow, fake trees, fake presents. All reassuringly normal. I was as far away from 1992 and my great-aunt's squalid flat as it was possible to be.

With no money to spend I window-shopped happily. Back in my teenage days the lack of funds wouldn't have stopped me; I'd been a great thief, caught only a handful of times. Although I never had any money I'd come back from town with pockets full of costume jewellery and makeup, layers of clothes under my own, bottles of drink in my bag. Partly because I had no money, partly because it was the only time Mum seemed the least bit pleased with me; when I had something for her.

Despite our bad relationship, Mum hadn't purposefully made me do without. We'd been incredibly hard up and neither of us had money for new things all that often. For all her indifference Mum had ticked the boxes of what a parent should do; fed me, clothed me and told me to do my homework. She never made sure I'd actually done it. But she did tell me. She went to parents' evenings and Christmas plays. But it was all on sufferance. Her role was performed automatically, by rote.

She'd sit in the audience but didn't take pictures or wave to me. She never remembered foods I didn't like or bands that I did. When I told her stories about my day she'd nod but not take them in. When she wasn't actively doing something for me it was like I wasn't even in the flat. She took care of me, but she didn't care to know me. I was a means to an end.

When I'd started shoplifting, bunking off, drinking in the park with other kids, she'd treated it with the same indifference. If I was bringing back something for her, what did it matter what else I got up to? Whether I was star of the Christmas play or coming home reeling on cheap vodka, stinking of weed, it made no difference. She didn't care. Even my stolen gifts were treated as just her due, getting me a slight smile or a nod of acknowledgement. Nothing more.

The only time she actually showed some kind of reaction to me, was when I threw an old teddy of hers mid-tantrum. I was six. I now knew it was the bear with a heart that Wayfield had given her. She screamed at me then, so much that spit came out of her mouth and her cheeks went red, then white with fury. She called me awful names. Bitch was the least of it. Utter filth. Stuff I'd be ashamed to say to anyone, much less a child. She'd nearly dislocated my arm dragging me to my room, then smacked me, hard, with a belt, until I bled.

I didn't touch that bear again, not until after she'd died. Then it went into the bin with the rest of her shit. I stood on the street and tore the little heart form its paws. Fuck you, I thought, as the whole thing dropped into a pool of rancid curry sauce. Fuck. You.

Pushing aside thoughts of my childhood, I did the rounds of the pharmacies. It kept me busy for a while, pasting lipsticks on my hand and testing eyeshadows that looked more like a toddler's finger paints from so much swatching. I stopped only when my feet started to hurt from standing.

I headed to the library. It was the only place I could think of where I could sit down in the warm without paying anything. The next bus wouldn't be through for another hour and a half. Another downside of rural life. But at least the library had crime magazines, those were expensive to get hold of otherwise.

Hidden away between racks of old newspapers and a window, I flipped through the magazines, reading the stories. Most of them weren't detailed enough, but unlike books they had colour pictures. A little window into the crime scenes themselves. I always found these the most interesting. Not the blood, or the police tape or the signs of a struggle, but the mundane elements. The Monopoly box on the side table, what books they had on their bookcase, how they decorated their homes, signs of pets, of children. I wanted to know who they'd been before this terrible thing happened to them. Who they'd pretended to be before showing their violence, their inhumanity.

Flicking through I came to the adverts at the back. Most of these were for self-published books and memorabilia, be it military, historical or film. A few smaller adverts were for private courses and talks on criminology and related subjects. I noticed a tiny black and white advert at the bottom of one page. The words 'Bricknell Butcher' caught my attention. It was one of those books you had to order. Print on demand or eBook. All about the Butcher. I snapped a picture on my phone. It was likely nothing special. Between my research and everyone else in the book club we probably knew more than anyone else. Still, I'd been surprised before.

The cover image was a little blurry, the resolution not up to being printed, but I could make out that it was a black and white line drawing of a shed. The style was simplistic, like a child's drawing or a company logo. Underneath was a ragged section of black, clearly meant to represent the pit. The blood was the only colour, a vivid poster paint red leaching into the ground and spreading out like the tentacles of some monster. An above average attempt, better than some of the books the others had picked for us to read. By Howard Stepp. I'd never heard of him.

Sitting back on the square, foam seat, I asked myself what it was I hoped to achieve by staying in Bricknell. More and more the idea of leaving was on my mind. For Adam's sake and for my own. Whatever I had hoped to find in Bricknell was not coming to me with ease. The more I poked about behind my mother's stone walls, the less I found of her, and the more I saw of Wayfield. He was like a cancer, taking up all the love and all the space inside her, until there was nothing left. Nothing even for herself. I'd been kidding myself to believe that she'd admit the truth of what he was in her private diaries. Even inside her own head she was lost to him.

I was looking out of the slightly fogged up window sightlessly, when I saw Adam. I blinked in surprise. What was he doing in town? My first instinct was to rush out and join him, maybe sneak up to surprise him. But then I saw who he was with and I froze, confused. It was Diana, Marianna's sister.

For a second I just stared. The two of them were across the road, standing together at the entrance to an alley between shops. Adam was saying something, he looked surprised, angry. Diana was holding his sleeve but he shook her off, backing away. She looked like she was shouting, I could sort of hear their voices but the distance and the glass made the words intelligible. People around them were looking but not stopping or trying to intervene. What was going on?

I watched as Adam took another step back. Diana was turned more towards me now as he circled round her to get away. Her face was red, eyes narrowed down and her mouth opening wide as she tore into him. She looked completely furious, almost like she was going to go after him, grab him. Adam walked away quickly, glancing back a few times. She stood there shouting for a bit then seemed to remember where she was. Thrusting her fists into the pockets of her heavy coat she sloped off in the direction of the shopping centre. Her head down as she pushed through the crowd.

I was left looking at where they'd been, at the alley lined with bins, choked with cardboard. I blinked, focused on the glass, fogging with my breath. I was completely thrown off, struggling to regain my mental equilibrium. Adam didn't know Diana, had never met her or anyone from the book club for that matter. They shouldn't have known each other, so why were they having a public slanging match in town? Especially when Adam was meant to be asleep and hadn't said anything about going out. And wasn't Diana meant to be back home, wherever that was? David had seemed pretty sure that she lived quite far off, that she'd had to drive for a few hours to get to Bricknell. She'd told us she was going home, said goodbye and got rid of Marianna's stuff. So what was she doing still hanging around?

Leaving the magazines behind I went outside, looking the way Adam had gone. He'd disappeared into the crowd in the direction of the large park by the river. There were too many shops and branching streets that way to know where he was heading. Why was he in town at all? He'd only just finished a night shift and usually slept until two or three in the afternoon. It was barely noon. Was he there to meet Diana? How did they know each other?

I thought of his new habit of locking his phone. The way he'd lied about working, then sprung a hotel trip on me. He'd been acting strangely but then, things had been a bit strange recently. The emails, the vandalism, his problems at work. Was his odd behaviour a product of stress or was something going on? If so, what?

It felt like forever before the bus came. I wanted to get home, to ask Adam…what exactly? I wasn't sure. But to see how he acted, or if he was even back yet. Everything felt off kilter. Since Marianna's death there had been so much uncertainty, so many weird things happening. I'd thought Adam was apart from all that, separate. That he was the one normal thing in my life, untouched by murders and secrets. Clearly, I'd blinded myself to something. What, I had no idea.

I put my key in the lock and let myself in. On the walk from the bus stop on the high-street I'd imagined Adam asking where I'd been and then laughing, 'Oh, that's weird, I was in town too!'. As for the argument I had no explanation, but maybe he would have. Perhaps Diana had taken something of mine at the café without me noticing, and Adam had seen it? I wasn't missing anything that I knew of, but stranger things had happened. Or perhaps she'd recognised him from somewhere else? Somewhere unconnected. Maybe her husband worked with him? Maybe what with the fog on the window and my own paranoia, it had only looked like Diana with Adam? Maybe it was just some random woman with dark hair that had walked into him?

My hopes faded as soon as I reached the living room and found Adam in his pyjamas. He'd changed back into them since I'd seen him. He was making tea on the gas stove and smiled as I came in, like nothing was wrong.

"You want tea?"

"Sure," I said, putting my bag down. I swallowed and forced myself to ask. "Just got up?"

"Yeah," Adam said ruefully, not quite meeting my eye. "Really long night. Had to stay late to finish unloading some big bastard cases of whisky. All the Christmas stuff's coming in and half the others are sick with flu – or party hangovers more likely. I tell you what, those big tins of chocolate are a pain in the arse. So heavy and awkward to get around."

I nodded. He continued to chat away, telling me about all the stuff that was coming into warehouse. The muscle he'd pulled across his shoulders. How he was getting sick of unloading by hand all the time and not getting a shift doing something less strenuous, like using the forklift. The whole time he was talking my mind spun. *Liar* echoed louder than his voice. He was pretending he'd been at home the entire time. Why?

"So, what've you been up to? Meeting up with David and the rest of the Scooby Gang?"

"I went into town actually, on the bus."

"Oh, right...why?" he asked, and I could see the strain of him trying to remain casual. Adam was not a good liar, so how had he been fooling me so well the last few weeks? Making my suspicions melt away. What had he been hiding, and why?

"No reason, just fancied a look round the shops. Took a little trip to the library, you know, passed the time."

If he knew that his slanging match had been in full view of the library windows he showed no sign. Perhaps he had no idea where the library was, I'd never been with him and he preferred gaming to reading any day. Maybe he thought that because I didn't go up to him, I didn't see him. After all, why would I not approach him? I trusted him, didn't I?

"Cool, next time you pop over there can you get some stuff from the indoor market? I've been craving a proper curry and the spices there are so much cheaper than Tesco."

"Will do," I promised.

"You're out tomorrow right?" He asked as he handed over my cup of tea.

"Book club night, yeah. Why?"

"Just checking," he said, turning away. "Have fun."

CHAPTER SEVENTEEN

Fun was the furthest thing from my mind when David texted me the next day. Adam and I had spent the evening before in tense silence. Mostly tense on my end, but he seemed to pick up on it. He played some games online and went to bed early. I'd stayed up but been unable to face the diaries. For once it wasn't my past making me anxious, but my present.

David's message came as Adam was showing our chosen heating engineer around in advance of a quote. From the amount of teeth sucking going on it is going to be a pricy one, but what else could we do?

I checked the message.

David: Change of plans for tonight. Katrine's not well, so it seems a bit unfair to do her pick when she'll miss it. Who's up to a walk into St. Julien's Woods?

Frowning I opened the app we used for our group chats. I'd somehow been logged out. After a few tries I remembered the password and scrolled back over the last few messages. Two days ago Katrine had messaged everyone.

Katrine: Hi guys, sorry about this but I'm not feeling too well at the moment. Might have to miss Monday's meeting (Sad bat emoji).

Siobhan: Feel better poppet!

Katrine: Thnx!

Then that morning, a string of sad bat emojis, some purple hearts and drooping roses. Followed by another message.

Katrine: Still feeling like death, can't face a meet up. Sorry! If you guys wanted to wait and discuss my book next time that would be great. Sorry for not being able to host. Maybe you could go out to the hide on Monday instead?? I don't mind.

Ricky had responded with a gif of one of Dracula's girlfriends lying back in a coffin. Katrine had heart reacted it. Everyone else wished her a speedy recovery and then David had started a text chain about going to the woods instead of to Katrine's.

Me: As long as Katrine's fine with not going?

Katine: It's OK, I can always go when I'm feeling better.

It was a bit annoying as I'd made the effort to finish her pick in time for the meeting. Not easy as the book was over an inch thick and not particularly well-written. It was on Richard Chase, aka 'The Vampire of Sacramento'. Katrine's tastes ran towards the macabre, and in Chase she'd found a real winner; vampire, cannibal, rapist and necrophile. Somehow the author had managed to make even those vile crimes sound dull.

I found my gym rucksack and packed some tea lights, matches and a miniature bottle of Sipsmith Gin. It was Marianna's favourite and I'd added it to the shopping a few weeks before on impulse. It seemed a fitting memorial gift. David texted and suggested we meet up a little earlier than usual, as it was November and the nights were coming in faster and faster.

While Adam talked cricket with the engineer (a topic he had no interest in but had googled in the name of what he called 'business patter') I went through the box of stuff Diana had passed on to us. It seemed like a good idea to take along something for everyone to have of Marianna's. Digging through the books and DVDs I picked out relevant things for everyone; DVDs for Ricky, the Bundy book for Siobhan, even a Ripperologist book that I was fairly sure David didn't have. Not that he'd complain if he did. David was never one to make a fuss. I dithered a bit over Finn's book but in the end went for a slim paperback called 'Knots, Nooses and Restraints – A Story in Ligature Forensics'. As for the rest of the boxes contents, they could pick over it at the next meeting.

At the bottom of the box, amongst some magazines, I came across a familiar cover. It was the black and white shed drawing I'd seen in the magazine at the library. The self-published Butcher book. Though, seeing it in real life, it was more of a pamphlet. Barely a hundred pages, printed in too-big lettering to stretch it out. It was well put together aside from that, with paragraphs and chapter headings – no sure thing in my experience. A lot of those amateur accounts were walls of text, with only one full stop in two hundred pages. I flicked through it and then put it aside. I'd add that one to my collection.

With the books packed up I told Adam I'd be heading off early and wasn't sure when I'd be back. He seemed distracted, going over the quote. I tried to squash the feeling that he might also be thinking of something, or someone else. The image of him arguing with Diana in the high-street was still fresh in my mind. I wasn't sure what to do about it. The thought of confronting him made me uneasy. I had my own secrets after all.

On the way to St. Julien's woods I stopped at a petrol station and bought some flowers. Bog standard carnations felt disrespectful, so I opted for some slightly wilted yellow roses. I felt a stab of anger as I looked at them on the passenger seat. Ever since Marianna's death we'd all been preoccupied with the creep using her account. Too much so to really honour her properly. That arsehole had a lot of nerve judging us when he was using her death as entertainment.

When I parked up everyone else was already there. We'd agreed to meet at the carpark by the woods, little more than a flat patch of dirt where a handful of people left their 4X4s of a weekend for the hour or so they'd be trekking about in the woods. We were down a narrow lane prone to flooding and the parking area was, this time of year, rutted and full of deep puddles. I wished more than ever that I owned wellies. My boots would be a wreck after five minutes in that wood.

Siobhan had given Ricky a lift and Finn had picked David up on his way from work. Once we'd waited for Siobhan to put wellies on and retrieved our 'offerings' from the cars, we headed into the gloomy woods.

St. Julien's wood was clearly a well-trodden hangout of dog walkers and families with overactive children. The path we took was wide and well-worn, churned up by bikes and buggies, litter caught in the brambles. Above us the ancient oak trees laced their branches together. Ivy clung to their trunks and between the sturdy trees clumps of elder, nettles and fallen logs fought for space. The path was carpeted in a mulch of fallen leaves and acorns already cracked open by boots and half-eaten by squirrels. As we walked towards the centre of the wood I spotted empty bird nests, toadstools and bright holly berries. It was enough to win over even my urban heart.

The hide was in a lesser travelled part of the wood. Steeply uphill from the more family friendly paths and almost inaccessible behind a denser section of newly planted birch and hazel trees. We had to climb over a fence meant to keep deer from snacking on the new saplings. Siobhan struggled and in the end tore her leggings, much to Ricky's amusement.

The sun, which had been a blazing orange eye when we parked up, was quickly setting. It was clear that we'd underestimated the time it would take to walk out to the hide. Under the trees it was already quite dark and most of us were using our phone torches, except David who had a Maglite. I wondered if he'd been in the Scouts as a kid. I could see him running his own troupe in beige shorts with a red hankie tied around his neck. Boring the kids to tears with information on roots and berries.

Ricky took over leading us as he regularly took his dogs near the hide. Having met his two unruly staffies I thought this was likely to avoid other dog walkers. They were sweeties really but Ricky had them in spiky collars which made their big gummy smiles look rather menacing.

Finally, out of the jumble of trunks, bushes and small hillocks, the hide appeared. Ricky had been right, it was just barely holding together. Slightly larger than your average garden shed, with the same weathered board walls and tarpaper roof. The door had rusted off its hinges at some point and was lying on the ground, covered in leaves. Ordinarily the place should have been a magnet for kids building camps and teens getting up to no good, but here there were no signs of disturbance, fires or beers. Even though it was on public land. Definitely the sort of place I would have hung out at fifteen.

I felt a sudden unease, as if we were trespassing. There was something off about the place. I felt as if I were being watched.

"This is where Wayfield hid while they were looking for him?" Siobhan asked, poking her head through the empty doorway. "I think I'd rather be in custody than out here at night."

"He was out here for weeks," Finn said, pulling a camera from his backpack and snapping a few pictures. The flash leapt through the trees like lightning. "There was a bit of a manhunt at the time. They had people watching his house but he must have realised that because he never tried to go back after the bodies were found. He abandoned his lorry and nicked a car to get back to Bricknell, then left that and holed up here."

"Why come back at all?" Siobhan asked, but Finn shrugged.

I had wondered the same thing. Was it to do with my mother, with me? Had he been unwilling to abandon the last connection he had to us? Or was it just about pride and he'd been unwilling to be chased off his patch? Perhaps he hadn't wanted to give up a home field advantage. He knew where all the bolt holes were around Bricknell. Had taken my mother to some of them.

"How did he live out here for weeks?" Ricky asked, pacing around the hide. "There's sod all. Not sure why anyone bothered to build it."

"It's for observing wildlife, not taking a holiday," David remarked. "There isn't meant to be anything other than a roof and a bench."

"There were burglaries at the time, locally," Finn said. "Mostly cars and sheds broken into, the odd remote house, the parish hall. Not much taken except food, some clothes and blankets from the jumble donations, a few tools. He was roughing it. I don't think he really had a plan. He'd have been better off making a run for it and hiding somewhere else. Sticking around here was stupid."

I looked around, regretting this idea. "Shall we find somewhere to set things up?"

I located a tree stump nearby and started to unpack the small candles. The roses I unwrapped and laid against the stump itself. The others began to place their own items beside the small bottle of gin on the stump. Siobhan had more candles and a printed photo of Marianna. David had brought a bunch of lilies and Finn had painted Marianna's name and a short poem on a large stone. A surprising gesture, given how unfanciful he normally seemed. Ricky surprised me by hanging a few small ornaments made of wire and glass beads from a branch overhead. They twirled in the light from our torches; dragonflies and monarch butterflies with glittering wings.

"From the garden centre," he said, seeing my look. I could have sworn he was blushing. "She said she liked them once, when we saw them on Katrine's patio."

It felt very solemn all of a sudden, once the candles were lit. The smoke from them drifted up and the hot air stirred the tinkling ornaments. We stood in a circle around the stump as if preparing for one of the murderous rituals Katrine was always reading about. But instead of a sacrifice we held a moment's silence. When it was done I opened my bag again and passed out the things from Diana's box.

Finn went to snap some more photos of the hide and the rest of us waited. No one said anything about tidying up. I think we were all happy for what we'd brought to stay there. I doubted anyone would notice. My phone had been off for the memorial, but I turned it back on to take a picture for Katrine. She'd like to see it with all the candles lit. After snapping the picture I blew out the candles and the smoke sighed away on the wind.

My phone let off rapid-fire pings as we walked back through the woods, notifications finally able to get through. With my phone already out and acting as my torch, I glanced at the screen to check them, and froze. Siobhan walked into me from behind.

"Jesus Jude! Watch it," she exclaimed.

"Jude?" Finn shone his torch on my face. "Are you OK?"

I held up the phone, unable to speak. On screen was a message from Katrine, sent only a few seconds ago. It read simply, 'Hope you had fun, see you soon!'

Above it, sent around an hour before, was a text from Adam.

'Call me ASAP. Katrine's missing.'

CHAPTER EIGHTEEN

I rang Adam on the spot. The others were clustered around me, whispering, asking too many questions for me to process. He picked up right away.

"What do you mean she's missing?" I asked.

"Her mum's not seen her in three days – she said she was staying with a friend but she was meant to be back today and now she's not answering her texts. Her mum came round with the police to speak to you, since the friend she was meant to be with had no idea where Katrine was. She said she thought maybe she'd misunderstood. That Katrine was with you or someone from the group." Adam sounded freaked out but there was an undercurrent of something else. He was angry, but about what? Me? Involving him in whatever this was? Or did he know something else? Fear seeped through me, making me numb.

"She's been messaging me – messaging all of us," I said, internally screaming at him to tell me what he knew. If he knew the truth about me. About the house. Just to say.

"When?" He asked.

"Last one was a few minutes ago. But, she was chatting with all of us the last few days, about how she's ill and she can't make the meeting." Fear for Katrine won out over everything else. Something was very wrong.

"That doesn't make any sense. The police said she was meant to be at a friend's over the weekend but then didn't come home. But they said this other friend told them Katrine cancelled to catch up on coursework. So...what? She just lied to three lots of people about where she was going to be?"

"Fuck...where the hell is she?"

"You need to get back here and call the police. They want to talk to the rest of your club too. Anyone that knows her." Adam sighed. "Honestly I hope it's just some stupid teenage thing and she's gone off with a new boyfriend or something. But the police seemed to be taking it pretty seriously."

"I'm coming home now," I said, already digging for my car keys.

"I'm going out to help her parents look."

"Are you sure-"

"Yes, I'm sure. You didn't see her mum, Jude, she was in a real state." The anger was more pronounced now. Was he blaming me for not knowing that Katrine was fobbing us off? Or was I just reading into his tone, feeling my own guilt as it started to build? I didn't know anymore.

"OK. Alright...good luck with the search, tell them...tell them I'll be there as soon as I can." I said goodbye and looked at the others. "We need to talk to the police about Katrine. She's been missing since Friday."

"She's been messaging though," Ricky said, waving his phone. "So wherever she is, she's fine right?"

"I don't know. It feels...weird. That she'd lie to us and her mum, and some other friend...she just sent another message through too, like everything's normal," I said, feeling a prickle of unease. Something wasn't right. I could understand Katrine lying to her parents about where she was of a weekend, she was a teenager after all. But she didn't have to lie to us to get out of a meeting. Even if it was her turn. God knew Marianna had flaked out without so much as a text more than once. And why keep messaging if she wanted to ditch us for something, or someone, else? If she was off having fun, why bother?

"Why not just ask her where she is?" Ricky asked. "She's probably down the cemetery with the other vampires, listening to a new playlist of 'music to self-harm to'."

"I am asking," I said, tapping out a message before I strode off, leaving the others to catch up as I hurried back towards the car park.

It was a quick text. I asked her where she was and said her mum was worried, then asked if she needed us to help with anything. Maybe she'd had a fight with her parents and was cooling off at another friend's house. Perhaps she had a boyfriend on the quiet. I tried to put aside thoughts of my mum and Wayfield. How she had been around Katrine's age when she'd started sneaking off with him. Katrine had more sense. She knew what was out there.

We'd just got back to the cars when my phone pinged with a response. I swiped at the screen to see it. Then stared at the two word response as the hairs on the back of my neck prickled and my heart thumped hard in my chest.

The message read simply, 'I'm cold'.

A rushing drowned out the others as they tried to work out if we ought to go to the police station, or home. I typed out a message, my fingers shaking as I tried to stay calm.

'Katrine, where are you?'

This time the answer came immediately. 'In the water'.

Silence surrounded me and I realised I'd screamed for them to be quiet. Finn took the phone when I thrust it at him and read the message aloud.

"What do we do?" David said, in an uncharacteristically shaky voice.

"Call the police," I said, grabbing my phone back from Finn and jumping into my car. "I'm going to try and beat them there."

"Where?" Siobhan shouted, over the roar of the engine as I over revved it, already pulling away.

"The canal!"

*

I'd love to say I was thinking logically. That some kind of Sherlock Holmes-esque brainwave told me that Katrine had to be at the canal – the only large body of water nearby. That I knew the police station was in Newston and I could get to the towpath before they could. I want to be able to say that it came from me. My mind. My logic. But, it wasn't logic or reason that led me to the canal. It was the Butcher.

The canal was one of his places, the scene of one of his kills. That's why it was on my mind. That was the connection that snapped into place when I read 'Katrine's' message. She was in the water. And the only water connected to the Butcher was the canal. That's why I tore over there, my heart racing. Not because of any kind of brilliance on my part, but because my mind brought everything back to him. I couldn't see anything other than Raymond Wayfield.

Just like my mother.

I abandoned my car at the car park barrier and ran for the towpath. My boots, already caked in mud, slid alarmingly on the mulch covered path. With my phone out and shining a cold white light on the water,

I hurried along. I could see almost nothing. It was pitch black and only two streetlights were working, both too far away to be any use.

The night was cold and rain had started to fall in thin, sharp drops. My breath came in white streams of mist. I was straining my ears for a voice, a cry, even a thrashing in the deep water, but could only hear my own blood rushing, my heart thundering. The rain pattering on dead leaves.

"Katrine!" I shouted, then jumped as a pair of ducks exploded from the reeds, rasping their annoyance. "Katrine!" I cried again, my voice a contemptable whinny, high-pitched and afraid.

Panic had seized me well and truly by then. I was shaking, losing my footing on the slippery path. Still I ran, but my head swam with doubt. What if I was wrong? What if Katrine was somewhere else and I was wasting time telling the others to bring the police to the canal? She could be in the river that ran through the nearest town, or somewhere else entirely; a water tower, the coast which was only an hour away by train. Who knew how far she'd gotten in three days. And there I was, wasting time with my Butcher obsession. No wonder Adam was angry with me. I was a mess.

The dark water played tricks on me, stirred as it was by the rain. I kept thinking I saw movement in there, a person struggling, but then I'd blink and there'd be nothing. The wind threw freezing drops of rain like gravel, blinding me. The downpour intensified, deafening me. I slowed from a run to a slithering jog, and finally, to a complete stop.

A burning stitch and doubt started to sober me. My conviction dissolving in a flood of self-hatred. Katrine wasn't there, wasn't answering me. By now she could have gone thousands of miles with god only knew who, for whatever reason. I had no way of knowing where.

I was about to turn and head back to the car, when I looked up and realised where I was. I'd come to the distant streetlight, at the end of the open canal. The black, gaping hole of the tunnel yawned open in front of me, the water vanishing like a snake into the darkness. A spot of deep and absolute blackness which even the electric light overhead couldn't touch. The abandoned workshop looked twice as sinister in the darkness as it had in the day and I swallowed, searching the shadows as my fear screamed that I was being watched. For a moment, it might have been two decades past, it was just as I'd imagined it from the old newspaper clippings. I could so easily have been looking at the ghost of Pippa Grey. Only it wasn't her in the dark water, it was Katrine.

She was bone white in the dark, catching the light from the half-moon. Face down, arms and legs floating out beside her. I thought for a moment that she was naked, but then saw the white fabric ballooning and swaying like a jellyfish in the water beneath her. She had on a white underdress that was stuck to her wet body. The bottom a kind of petticoat, some period costume, swelling and deflating with the gentle lapping of the current.

There is nothing in even the grisliest account that can prepare you for the sight of a corpse. Especially, one that was once someone you knew.

I clutched at my chest, feeling myself start to hyperventilate. The cold air burned in my throat and lungs. Clouds of steaming breath that smelt of the bile I tried to hold back. A weird keening noise came from deep inside me as I bent double, trying not to vomit. Rain ran down the back of my neck, into my jacket.

I dropped my phone on the bank and the torch went out. In the livid orange light of the streetlamp I went to my knees, scrabbling for it. My hands tore at mud and grass until the phone buzzed and lit up on its own. Katrine's name shone innocently on the screen. The message underneath, ending in a sad bat emoji, just like Katrine used all the time. Just like she'd been sending us for the past three days.

'She broke the rules, Judith'.

Then, as I stared in disbelief at the message, the screen went black. I tapped at it but the chat had been deleted. All Katrine's messages gone.

Kneeling in the mud, I looked once more at Katrine's body floating in the water.

I was still kneeling there when the police arrived.

CHAPTER NINETEEN

Sitting in an interview room in a plastic chair I told two police officers about the impromptu memorial, the messages from Katrine and my assumption that by 'water', she had meant the canal. I didn't mention the Butcher, I'd rather they think I was some kind of fantasist playing psychic, than what I actually was. What our mystery messenger had termed us all. A ghoul.

They asked to see my phone and I told them the chat had been deleted. I had no idea how. But if whoever it was had been able to hack Marianna's emails, they could surely erase a chat log. They still took my phone, as evidence. They asked questions until the mud on my jeans was dry and stiff, then they left me alone with a scalding cup of tea.

After a while they came back, this time with new questions. Had Katrine seemed depressed lately? Had she mentioned any problems at home or at college? Had she ever lied about her whereabouts to us before or given us reason to worry for her safety? I answered in the negative. No, Katrine had never lied to us or seemed depressed. Or even worried. She was, despite Ricky's jokes, the happiest out of all of us. As sweet and optimistic as a little girl, despite being dressed up like a Victorian mourner.

Then they showed me a piece of paper in a plastic evidence wallet. A letter Katrine had left on the towpath, weighted down by her shoes and neatly folded outer clothing. Well, they called it a letter, but it wasn't addressed to anyone specifically. It was only four lines.

I'm so lost I cannot find myself.
So broken that my edges cut me.
There is no end to this pain.
But to die, again, again.

I confirmed that it was Katrine's handwriting but told them it didn't sound like a suicide note to me. They exchanged glances at this. They hadn't, after all, asked for my opinion. I explained that Katrine was into gothic fashion and music. A romantic. She wrote poetry all the time, sometimes during book club meetings and quite often about death. As to why this poem had been ripped from her notebook and left with her clothes by the canal, I had no answer. The two officers exchanged glances again. Clearly they thought I was in denial. I said I wanted to go home.

What I didn't say was anything about the emails. I didn't say that I knew the messages we'd been receiving hadn't come from Katrine, but from someone who wanted us to think they were her. Just like that first email had wanted us to think it was from Marianna. Let them think what they wanted. I couldn't risk saying a word.

She broke the rules. That's what the message had said. What the rules were we had not been told, but Katrine had broken them and now she was dead. The only thing she had done that the rest of us hadn't, that I could think of, was sending a message to the police. I wasn't going to take the risk of being next. So I kept my mouth shut about our mystery stalker. The police seemed certain Katrine's death was suicide. If I spun them a tale of mystery emails and murder conspiracies, I would succeed only in making myself look crazy.

Finally I was allowed to leave and found Adam waiting for me by the front desk. He looked terrible; eyes hollowed out by exhaustion and his hair in tufts, like he'd run his hands through it in frustration one too many times. I must have looked equally drained. He pulled me into a tight hug as soon as he saw me. Then gave me his heavy winter coat. My jacket was a soaked bundle under my arm and he took it from me.

Once he'd steered me outside and into the passenger seat he started the car and cranked the heating up. The windows were fogged, rain washing down over the car. It was coming down so heavily I hardly heard Adam when he spoke.

"Are you alright?"

I shook my head, hunched over and began to cry. The numbness that had kept me together at the station abandoned me. The sight of Katrine's body being dragged from the canal flitted before my eyes. She was really dead. Dead and cold, her empty, staring eyes washed over with the rain. Water running out of her mouth. I couldn't understand how it could have happened. There hadn't been any sign of injury, no bashed in skull or bruised arms to explain why she hadn't been able to swim. Had she been drugged, or had she meant to go into the water? I squeezed my eyes shut and hugged myself tightly. Adam put his arms around me and shushed against my hair.

Once I'd stopped sobbing and could breathe again, Adam drove us home. Inside he got me a large glass of neat vodka and I necked it. In my pyjamas I crawled into bed and tried to sleep. Beside me Adam eventually drifted off but I couldn't. Every time I came close to slipping into unconsciousness I'd remember Katrine's face. Her cold, stiff face.

Thoughts kept circling my brain like buzzing insects. I wanted to believe that I was wrong, that this was all just a horrible tragedy. That Katrine really had killed herself. I could almost convince myself. Just as I'd believed that Lara Preston had died in an accident. The poetic note was just Katrine's style, nothing more. Perhaps I was going mad, imagining some killer was responsible. It was just a prank, someone messing with us. Only I couldn't make myself believe it and I watched the shadows in fear. Someone was after us. But the messages sent to us, those I could not explain away.

Standing by the canal as Katrine was dragged out, I'd overheard the two officers talking as they manoeuvred her limp body onto the bank.

"She's not just gone in. Looks like it's been days."

"Smells like it too."

Then they'd glanced around, fearful of being overheard as they struggled to get her on to a plastic sheet. I didn't show that I'd heard. I knew though that they were right. I had the image of her face tattooed on my memory. Katrine had not only just thrown herself into the water. She had been there for a while. Possibly for the entire three day period she'd been missing. Just, floating in the tunnel. Unseen until she was washed out by the rain.

That meant that for three days, certainly the last twenty-four hours, someone had been pretending to be her. They had messaged us just as Katrine would, right down to her favourite emojis. They had messaged her parents and her friend, excusing her absence, so no one would look for her until it was too late.

There was no more room in my mind for doubt. We were being stalked, taunted, by a real murderer. Not some creep playing a sick joke, but someone who was capable of killing. Someone who had killed Lara Preston and now Katrine in the name of their game. A game we had failed to take seriously. That meant we were all in danger, including the victim described in the last chapter. The gambler.

Lying there, I felt more guilt come crashing down. We hadn't even tried to find him. The man at the betting shop. Hadn't even cared enough to check that Katrine's message to the police had been acted on. We'd just gone back to our books. Our club. Without a thought for the man in the 'story'. Who was, if the email was as accurate as the first, already dead.

There was also the question of the rules, the ones that had cost Katrine her life. What were they and how was this killer expecting us to know them? If we were even expected to know them. But, he hadn't been unfair with us yet, had he? The emails were all about giving us a fighting chance to find the victim.

Then I remembered what I'd said about the first email, in all innocence. Why had we not received chapter one? If that file was 'The Second' where was the beginning of the story?

With ice in my chest I slipped out of bed and padded to the living room. Switching on the laptop I poured another shot of vodka and downed it, then typed into the email search bar, 'The First'.

The attachment and its email popped up right away.

It wasn't from Marianna's address. It came from a random string of numbers and letters. A throwaway account. I was not surprised that it predated her death by a fortnight.

Two weeks, to the day.

1

Finally, it begins.

I am not yet ready to make myself known, to bring you into my game, but then again I have no reason to believe you will read this until it is too late. You see, I have already been making moves, taking my turn, before you even realised we were playing.

Still, perhaps I have you wrong? Maybe you will exceed my expectations and burst from the gate, destroying my early lead? I doubt it. But surprises do happen.

I walk in her footsteps and know her routine by heart. It is at home that we are most vulnerable. We believe ourselves to be safe, protected by wood and metal. It doesn't take much to get through a locked door. As with anything else, preparation is key.

And I am always prepared.

A little knowledge is a dangerous thing. I've always liked that saying. I have a little knowledge of a great many things, enough to make me very dangerous. You should remember that.

One of the things I know something about, is pipes. It doesn't take much to loosen this, replace that, make things look worn, damaged. An accident waiting to happen. For extra insurance, sleeping tablets are a good bet. A sprinkling of crushed pills into someone's routine nightcap. A nice, deep sleep. Time for the gas to escape, bit by bit. Breath by breath. Until that sleep drifts neatly into unconsciousness and, finally, death.

By the time anyone knows what's happened I can be miles away.

Or just across the street.

Or right outside your door.

But that's for another day. Perhaps. It depends how well you play, how quickly you learn my rules.

They are simple enough:
1. *Find my chosen victim and send me their name in time to save them.*
2. *Go to the police and I will take one of you.*
3. *Try to run and I will assume you have forfeited. You do not want that.*

I know you won't believe me, so, to demonstrate my seriousness, I am going to take one of you. But I am not vindictive. Their death will be merciful. A lesson to the rest of you so you know what's to come if you fail my challenge.

It should be easy for you, after all, this is what you love, isn't it? Trying to catch a killer?

Or is it different when it's you they're coming for?

The vodka churned in my stomach. I barely made it to the bathroom in time to cast it up into the toilet. Sprawled on the cold floor, forehead against the tiled wall I listened to my own ragged breathing.

He was talking about Marianna, he had to be. The gas leak. It was his first move, a demonstration of his intent. How had none of us seen the email? Even as I shook at the unfairness of it, I knew. He had sent it that way on purpose. The random email address, guaranteed to be caught in a spam filter and spat into the trash. He hadn't wanted us to see, until it was too late. Until he'd had his head start. He was fair, but only to the letter of the law. Send them a warning, yes, but make it one they'll never get in time.

After rinsing my mouth I went back to the laptop. The email was still there, a brilliant white square in the dark room. I read the rules again. They were simple, he was right about that, but each one told me something terrible.

Find my chosen victim and send me their name in time to save them. We could have saved Lara Preston. If we'd taken that first email seriously and thought about it, we could have found her. A woman with a cat, living opposite an elm, by the cemetery. It wasn't outside the realm of possibility. Difficult, perhaps, but we could have found her. Warned her. Sent her name to him and saved her.

We hadn't. Now she was dead.

The same with the betting shop man. If we'd taken the email seriously and tried to find him, we might have. It wasn't impossible. But again we hadn't even tried, hadn't believed. Now he was probably dead as well. Though we hadn't had another message to scold us for failing, had we? Perhaps...perhaps there was still a chance?

Go to the police and I will take one of you. Had we known that, Katrine wouldn't be dead. All of us had decided to contact the police with the second message, but it had been her to send the email. If whoever was doing this had access to Marianna's accounts, and now Katrine's, they were probably monitoring the group chat. They had seen us talking about it. Seen Katrine agree to be our messenger. Why had I not realised they could be spying on us? Why had none of us thought to be worried? To be more cautious?

Because we'd never thought this could happen to us. We were the observers, the armchair detectives. He was right about that. We hadn't been able to see ourselves as what we were; prey.

Try to run and I will assume you have forfeited. You do not want that.

There was no escape.

I opened a new group chat, excluding Marianna and Katrine's accounts. Then I ran off a message, 'Meet tomorrow at mine. We need to talk'.

CHAPTER TWENTY

"You sure you're OK?" Adam asked me, for the fiftieth time.

"Yeah, I'm fine," I lied, also for the fiftieth time.

I'd snuck back to bed shortly before Adam woke up. He seemed to think that the vodka had done the trick and I'd had a decent rest. At some point I had actually managed to sleep for almost three hours. As a result I felt worse, if anything, with a headache pounding at my temples and nausea in the pit of my stomach.

"I won't be out long," Adam was saying, checking for his keys and the list of things he was after at the DIY place.

I watched him, wondering if that's where he was really going. Finding that email had spooked me and now everything that had happened over the past few weeks seemed less and less like coincidence and misunderstandings. The emails, the vandalism and threatening behaviour just after Halloween, Adam's lies and unease. Why was it all happening now? How was it connected? At the back of my mind some remaining rational part of me wondered if I was going mad. If I'd inherited something from Wayfield or my mother that was creeping through my mind, corrupting everything.

I tried to get myself together for when the others came over. Looking at myself in the bathroom mirror was a bit of a shock. I knew

I looked like Mum, but now I looked almost as she had when she died. The dark circles, sickly pale skin and lank hair. I could have been her ghost. Avoiding my reflection I scrubbed my face pink and put my hair in a ponytail. I had no energy for concealer and lipstick, but to be honest they'd have only made me look worse.

Siobhan was the first one to arrive, straight from the school run. She had on purple plaid pyjama bottoms, Uggs and a hoodie. She looked like she'd had even less sleep than me. Shortly after her, Ricky and Finn turned up, then David. I made coffee and we perched on the limited furniture. Siobhan took the desk chair and Ricky sprawled on the beanbag, leaving some as yet unpacked boxes for Finn and David. I perched on the bed.

Never had the absence of Marianna and Katrine felt more obvious.

"What happened after you ran off?" Ricky said, voice even louder and more obnoxious than usual, like he was compensating for the absence of the others.

"I found Katrine at the canal, phoned the police. Which I guess you'd already done, because they showed up right after that. They asked some questions while they…dealt with things at the canal. Then took me to the station to ask some more questions. Then Adam picked up the car, waited for me and brought me home."

"But how did you know she was there, in the canal?" Ricky said.

"I didn't."

"But you went straight there, like you did know," Ricky pressed. "Like you knew she was there before you got there."

I looked up sharply. "You think I had something to do with this, is that it?"

Ricky met my eye. "I don't know. Did you?"

There was a sharp silence. No one leapt to my defence. I felt singled out again, the new girl, the weird one.

"I mean," Ricky continued, flushing an angry red. "None of us really know you, do we? You've only been around a few months, moved into the Butcher's house out of nowhere. And now the two people who first met you here are dead. What is it that you're hiding from us?"

"I haven't done anything. But if you're so concerned I might? Maybe you should leave," I ground out.

"Maybe you should answer the fucking question; why are you here? What the fuck's your deal?"

"I don't think this is helping," David said quietly. "Should we not just get on?"

"Not 'til she comes clean," Ricky insisted. "There's something she's not telling us. It's happened too often, we'll all be chatting and she'll just go quiet. Like there's something she's hiding."

"Ricky, for fucks sake –" Finn started, I held up my hand, mind whirling. I had to calm this down and I had to do it without revealing anything. If Ricky was this suspicious of me now, how much worse would it get if he found out who I really was?

"No, I'll answer – You want to know how I 'knew' Katrine was in the canal? I didn't. It was common fucking sense, alright? I got that message saying she was in the water and I just assumed it was the canal, you know, because it's the only major water source in Bricknell. But I don't know Ricky, maybe it was witchcraft or ESP. Would you like to test me? I've got some playing cards around here somewhere."

I was blustering too hard, unwilling to admit anything else about my history or the Butcher, the skeleton in my family tree. I wanted them to trust me, needed it, because I didn't fancy taking my chances alone. But this was private. I wanted to keep it that way. Fortunately Ricky seemed cowed by my explosion of sarcasm and let the matter drop with only a muttered swearword.

"I have something to show you guys. Go into your emails and search 'the first'."

I waited for them to fumble with their phones. All aside from David, who leaned over Finn's shoulder, ancient mobile still in his pocket. It was obvious when they'd found it; one by one they went completely still. David's lips were pressed hard together, almost invisible and Siobhan's mouth hung open like that of a discarded puppet.

"When did you find this?" Finn asked, in the crisp silence.

"Last night. I asked myself how Katrine was meant to know if she was 'breaking the rules' and then I realised there must have been a first chapter to this…story. One we all missed. One we were supposed to miss."

"Jesus," Ricky said. "How is this fair? Playing this game without knowing what the rules are meant to be?"

"It's not fair, that's the point," Finn said. "He's a murderer. He's not going to give us a real chance at stopping him, he's playing with us."

"But why us?" Siobhan blurted. "We haven't done anything!"

"To him, we have," I say. "Remember the last email – he called us ghouls, said we thought we were amazing detectives when really we're just…sickos, who like this kind of stuff," I waved the book I'd taken from Marianna's stuff.

At the mention of the last email David sat up straight. "That man from the betting shop. We have to find him, if this is real, if we really are in this game, we have to save him."

Finn nodded and even Ricky muttered in agreement. They turned silent when I shook my head.

"I think, if the pattern is the same...he's already dead."

"How can you know?" Siobhan asked in a small voice.

"He sends the emails a few days after a meeting, and then the person is killed before the next time we meet. He sent the email about Marianna's murder two weeks before she died. Then the next email just after that – two weeks before Lara Preston's murder. Which happened the night before our next meeting."

"It's already been two weeks since the third email," Finn said numbly. "That was the meeting before last night, the memorial. So this guy in that message, you reckon he was killed in the last two weeks?"

"But he killed Katrine," Ricky said. "She sent that email right after the second, or third email, whatever. The one about the old guy. So...is that not a change in the pattern? What if he replaced this guy with her to teach us a lesson? That man might still be out there somewhere."

"Maybe," I said. "Although it doesn't seem likely. Either way, I do agree we need to find him. It's evidence of a pattern. We'll have two emails, both of which predicted a murder. Three if you count chapter one, which suggests that Marianna was the first victim. The police didn't seem to act on the email Katrine sent, but if we go to them with three murders...suggesting Katrine was also murdered, they'll have to listen. Have to offer us protection so that what happened to Katrine won't happen to us."

"I can't believe Marianna was murdered...and we could have stopped it," Finn said. "If we'd seen the email..."

"He made it so we wouldn't," Siobhan said. "We're not to blame for him killing people."

"But Finn's right...we don't know if we could have stopped it, because we didn't even try," I said.

Silence followed my words as we all digested this. Then David spoke up.

"I think we need to try and find this man. Dead or alive...we need to know and we need proof of what's happening."

"What, so we can go to the police? No thanks," Ricky snapped, leaping up from the beanbag. "You saw the rules. You know what happened to Katrine. If he can get one of us he can get all of us."

Siobhan started to cry, audibly. Looking around I saw none of us had it in our hearts to comfort her. The danger was real for all of us. In Ricky's eyes I saw a shadow of my own thoughts. We were being targeted as a group, but really, was it not every man for themselves? After all, we were being punished as individuals. Having all agreed to contact the police, it was Katrine that had done it. Katrine who had been killed.

"How are we going to find him?" I asked, trying to squash the idea that we were all alone in this. I didn't want anyone doing something reckless and paying the price for it.

Finn looked over the email on his phone and David read over his shoulder. "It says he goes to a betting shop every day. He wears musty clothes, he isn't a good gambler...lives alone?"

"Not much to go on," Ricky muttered, but Finn was looking at the email himself and I could see the ideas flying behind his glasses. Finn, our forensic whizz, our calm and collected Sherlock. If anyone could work out the riddle, it was him.

"OK..." Finn murmured, "I think it's an older guy. Betting in a shop instead of online, that sounds like someone not great with technology, plus this says his body's 'gnarled' so, likely over middle-aged at least. Sounds like he wears a tweed jacket and visits a betting shop within walking distance of a pub, and his house." He looked up and pushed his glasses up his nose. "It's got to be round here, right? I mean…everyone else he's killed has been from here."

"Only there's no betting shop in Bricknell," Ricky said scornfully.

"There is over Newston town centre," I said, thinking back to my trip out, when I'd seen Adam arguing with Diana. Should I mention that? Was it connected? No, I'd sound paranoid. Adam wasn't a murderer, even if he'd lied to me. I wasn't my mother; if he was that evil, inside, I'd know.

"There's lots," Siobhan sniffed, wiping her eyes with the sleeve of her hoodie. "Three on the high street and some others down the side streets by the market."

"And there's pubs there too," Ricky sighed. "The George, Crossed Keys, Pig and Whistle, the Wetherspoon and Yates – they're all in that crappy new build bit. Cheap too. Exactly the kind of places this guy would hang out if he goes drinking every day on a pension."

"So we go and ask around," I said. "We check out the betting shops and the pubs and ask about their regulars. Someone has to know this guy if he's in there every day. The message says he's obsessed with history programmes, right? Maybe he's the type to talk people's ears off about that stuff."

"And what if you're right, and he's already dead?" Ricky demanded.

"We'll keep an eye out for anything in the local news. They said they'd put him in the bath when he was passed out right? Drown him? So any news story where it's an old guy that died at home. And if we go to these betting shops and ask around, they can tell us if he's been in recently," I said.

"And when the next email comes?" Ricky asked. "What then? Are we going to keep doing this forever, or just until he gets bored of the rules and kills one of us to spice things up?"

He had a point. That was the annoying thing. I'd been focused on tracking down the betting shop man and not on the game overall. What was the end goal of the killer? Did they have one? Were they just going to toy with us until they got bored, then kill us too? Why had they chosen us to begin with?

"If we can find the man from the third email, we can start trying to work out how he's choosing who he kills. Maybe how he chose us, out of everyone else who likes true crime. The more we can work out about him, the sooner we can find out who he is and lead the police right to him without worrying about any 'rules'," I said.

There was silence, then David nodded. "I think you're right, Judith. It's our only option at this stage. The police ignored us before and we lost Katrine. Marianna's death and that poor Lara woman's, they were both dubbed accidental. We need more concrete proof of intentional murder if we want them to listen to us."

Finn met my eye and inclined his head as well. Ricky sighed, but didn't disagree.

"Where do we look first?" Siobhan asked.

CHAPTER TWENTY-ONE

We agreed to split up. Two pairs to go round the betting shops and pubs. Siobhan was given the job of checking local news and Facebook gossip pages for any deaths in the area. She grabbed the opportunity with both hands. I figured she was feeling the loss of Katrine quite strongly. They'd been close. Ricky, with his crush on Katrine was also showing signs of stress but Siobhan appeared closest to breaking point. I thought it was best to keep her out of the way.

David chose Ricky to go with him, I assumed as some kind of noble sacrifice. I didn't mind. I was getting distinctly aggressive vibes from Ricky. He wasn't going to let the subject of my secret drop. I could only hope he'd be distracted for a while. Predictably Ricky insisted they take the pubs. I could hardly blame him, it was only my nausea that had me avoiding a double vodka myself. I left a note to Adam to say I'd gone out with the others and not to worry. Then Finn and I took his car and went to check out the betting shops.

It had started to rain on the drive over and the high street was miserable. The outdoor Christmas scenes had started to look bedraggled, listing under the barrage of rain. We had, if anything, underestimated the number of betting shops. In addition to the three on the high street there were four more down side avenues. There were also two more in the form of 'casinos'; shopfronts with blacked out glass through which the blinking lights of slot machines could only just be seen.

"We should split up," Finn said, upon realising how many there were.

"I'll take the side streets," I said.

He went off to the first chain shop and I hurried towards the back streets. I passed a shop selling bongs and resin gothic ornaments, a second-hand record shop, a chippy. The bookies on the end had a window plastered with A4 printouts advertising odds and popular races. I went inside.

I'd never been in a betting shop before, but it reminded me slightly of a high street bank. The same bland cream walls and nylon carpets, the plastic furniture and plastic plants. The same scent of money and nerves in the air. The only real difference was the lack of a long queue and the fact that the wall mounted screens showed horse racing instead of adverts.

There were only three people in the shop, one man on the counter and two punters by the screens. Both were older men in anoraks and one had a steaming Styrofoam cup in his hand, the teabag deposited on the table in front of him. I approached the counter, the guy behind it was younger than me. He had on a t-shirt bearing the name of the place 'Rich's Bookmakers' and an open plaid shirt over that. He stopped scrolling through his phone as I approached.

"Hi, I hope you can help me. I'm looking for someone who might be a regular here."

"Owes you money does he?" It seemed to mostly be a joke, but I sensed a faint undercurrent of suspicion.

"No, I'm just worried about him. Haven't seen him around in a while," I improvised. "What's his name?"

Why hadn't I thought about how awkward this would be? I felt so stupid, standing there, grasping for inspiration.

"I only really know him to look at. He's an older guy, history buff, comes in every day for a few hours before going to the pub…" I trailed off when he laughed.

"That could be any of my regulars," he said, glancing pointedly at the two blokes by the screens.

"He wears a tweed jacket," I said, determined not to give up. "Lives alone, probably talks a lot, really bends your ear about history."

"I'm sorry love, even if I did know who you were talking about I couldn't give out their name or anything. Data protection, all that shit. Where is it you usually see him?"

"The pub." The lie came so smoothly I didn't have to think about it, I'd pushed the nerves down. After all, I lied to everyone. Even people I loved. I was good at it.

"I'm sure he'll turn up there then," he said, then reached for his mouse and keyboard. I was being dismissed.

"Sounds like Howie," one of the customers called.

I glanced at the cashier, his neck had turned pink under his tattoos. I turned, managing not to smirk, and addressed the pair of anoraks.

"Is Howie a regular?"

"Not in here, but at Lucky's on the market. He only came in 'ere when they closed for a bit a while back. They 'ad a break in."

"Have you seen him recently?"

His friend chuckled. "No, thankfully. He's a bit of a gas bag. If he's not talking about some documentary he's always going on about his ruddy books. Not sure how successful they can be though – he's always borrowing off people. In fact, if you see him, he owes me forty quid."

"And me twenty-five," the original anorak put in.

"Do you know whereabouts he lives?" I asked, crossing my fingers in my coat pocket.

"Nah, sorry. But if you ask about at Lucky's they might know. Sian that works there, she had to drive him home once after a bit of a session at The Millpond."

"The Hay Wain," his friend corrected.

"No, it was The Millpond."

I muttered a quick thanks and hurried out, heading for the market. Held daily on the bottom level of the multi-storey carpark, I'd gone there a few times since moving, for spices and cheap coconut milk. Aside from the specialist food stalls the market had a jumble of other things; carpet sellers, 'real' leather handbags, mobility scooters, a butcher and cake designers. I'd never noticed a bookies in the area though. As I scoured the aisles I began to think the two old blokes had been having me on. Or that they were remembering something from fifteen years back.

It turned out to be right at the back, just before the optimistically named 'food court' which was a few tables and a café selling baked potatoes. Lucky's was sandwiched between the side of the café and a barbers. The back area smelled of chip fat and comb dip, the sound of razors mixing with that of a coffee grinder.

There were five people at the counter in Lucky's and I had to wait my turn. Clearly business was better here than at the last place. A good location to get a short back and sides and gamble away your pension money over a baked spud. Behind a thick pane of security glass sat a woman in her sixties wearing a Christmas jumper. A name badge pinned to Rudolf's left eye said 'Sian'. Flashing LED Santa earrings jostled with heavy gold hoops for space and her frosted blue eyeshadow reached her wire thin eyebrows.

"Hi," I said when it was my turn at long last. "I'm looking for Howie, have you seen him around recently?"

"Owes you money, does he?"

"No, actually, I owe him," I said, hoping that if Howie was used to dodging creditors, the promise of receiving money for a change might make him a little easier to get hold of. "He gave me a tip and I've got fifty for him."

"Oh, right," Sian said, clearly only half believing me. "Well he's not been in for a while. Have you tried The Hay Wain?"

One of the anoraks was right at least. "Not yet. I was hoping he'd be around. Doesn't he come in every day?"

"Usually. But it's that time of year isn't it? Everyone's sick at home or off visiting family."

I nodded, internally willing her to give me the information I was about to request.

"Do you know whereabouts his house is? Only I'm going away for a week and I did say I'd pay him before then. I can pop the cash round to him this afternoon."

She regarded me with slightly narrowed eyes for a moment and my heart flipped as I waited for her judgement to be made. Then Sian sniffed and pulled a post-it pad towards her, scribbling something with a miniature biro.

"He's on High Elms – here."

As I took the post-it she kept a firm hold on it and looked me in the eye.

"Now, I've got you on CCTV my darlin' so don't be doing anything stupid – you get me?"

"I won't, don't worry," I said, not sure what she thought I was going to do. Maybe rob him if he wasn't home. Whatever it was, my stammered promise seemed to satisfy her and she let go of the paper. I hurried away and went to find Finn.

After grabbing Finn outside a Ladbrokes and rushing back to the car I messaged the others to see if they had any leads. They didn't. I sent them the address we were heading to. It was on the other side of town to where we were. If Howie was the man we were looking for he'd be the first victim outside of Bricknell. Was the killer becoming bolder or did we have it wrong?

As Finn negotiated the post-lunchtime traffic I tried to make sense of things. Why were these people being targeted? What did a habitual gambler and a single cat owner have in common? Was there any reasoning to how these people were being chosen, or was it simply about ease of access – single people meant a quiet home in which to stage these 'accidental' deaths.

"This it?" Finn asked as we pulled up.

I checked the address Sian had written down, then checked the sign outside. Apparently Howie's flat was part of an assisted living complex. A red brick warren of individual flats and postage stamp sized gardens littered with gnomes and wilting pot plants. I got out of the car and waited for Finn to park up, then we followed the sign that said 'Visitors This Way'.

Arriving at a reception area I rang a doorbell taped to the desk and we waited. A woman in a lavender blouse with a pair of glasses perched on her hair stuck her head around an office door.

"Are you delivering something?"

"No...we're looking for one of your residents?"

I heard the rattle of a protesting wheelie chair and she exited the office.

"Sorry about that, we've had so many packages showing up recently I've quite lost track, Christmas eh?" she smiled and quickly swept a pile of leaflets back together. "I'm Maureen, the day manager, how can I help?"

She looked quite harried; her lipstick smudged off and a coffee stain on her blouse. She had also neglected to slip her shoes back on and stood there in tights, one big toe poking out through a hole.

"We're looking for someone called Howie," I said, seeing her blush as she noticed the direction of my gaze.

"Howie..." she tapped at a long out-of-date beige keyboard. "Oh...Mr. Stepp. May I ask what this is regarding?"

"He's an old friend of my Mum's and they lost contact for a bit. I was just hoping to arrange a visit if that's OK?"

Maureen rubbed her lips together contemplatively. A few crumbs of dark pink lipstick disappeared into her mouth. "Perhaps you ought to come into the office, would you like some tea?"

"We're fine," I said, a sick feeling building in my stomach. "Is something wrong? Is Howie not well?"

She swallowed and twisted her hands together. "I'm afraid Mr. Stepp recently passed away."

"Oh...that's...I'm sorry," I said, scrambling. "Was it...sudden or had he been ill?"

"Quite sudden, I'm sorry I can't really go into detail," she seemed flustered now.

How could I find out if he'd drowned without setting off alarm bells? I glanced down at my hands, stalling for time. My eyes strayed to the leaflets that littered the front desk. Feeling suddenly cold I swallowed my exclamation of shock and quickly slipped one from the pile. With an effort to control my face I smiled ruefully at Maureen.

"That's alright, I'll have to break it to Mum…thank you for your help."

Nudging a confused Finn into motion I strode towards the door. My legs felt weird and rubbery, not quite my own.

"What was all that about – we still don't know if he's the right guy," Finn said as he caught up with me.

"We don't know for sure, but I'd be surprised if he's not the guy."

"Why?"

"Because, 'Howie' is Howard Stepp," I showed him the leaflet, a cheaply printed A6 flyer probably ordered online. "Marianna had his book. A book on the Butcher."

CHAPTER TWENTY-TWO

With the knowledge that the killer was targeting us, a group of true crime buffs in the Butcher's locale, and had killed an author who'd also written about him, it didn't take me long to find a connection to Lara Preston. I didn't know her, but I did, I realised, as we drove, know *of* her.

I wasn't one for remembering the names of authors or individual musicians. But 'Late Night Investigations' was my favourite true crime podcast. I'd listened to every episode dozens of times, but especially to the one devoted to the Butcher. How many times had I heard that intro? *Hello everyone and welcome back, I'm Lara and today...*

She'd never used her last name, but it was in the description on each episode. Narrated by Lara Preston. I must have seen it dozens of times, but never taken it in. Not really. She'd also never said she lived in Bricknell. I guessed because giving that information out to the internet would have seemed incautious in the extreme. Not that keeping her address a secret had helped her much. Somehow the killer had found her anyway.

It was odd to think that this woman who barely existed to me as anything other than a voice on a podcast, had lived so close by. I had no idea what she looked like, yet, if she'd chanced into a conversation with one of the group members, we might have become friends. The world felt very small then. Online, Lara Preston, podcaster, had seemed so far away. In reality, she was less than a twenty minute walk from my house. I shivered, looked out of the car window. The killer, in his emails, had also felt removed from my reality. Now I knew he'd killed two of my friends, and two strangers. He was in the town I lived in, stalking the streets. I wanted very badly to go back to being ignorant of that. Not that I'd be any safer.

Finn pulled up at David's and I saw that the others had already parked on the street. They were waiting inside, the atmosphere tense and miserable like a dentist's waiting room. Even David, ever the host, hadn't so much as provided a glass of water. I took a seat and let Finn explain the events at the supported housing office. When he was done, all eyes turned to me.

I produced the leaflet and explained about poor Howard Stepp, his self-published account of the Butcher's crimes, and Lara's podcast. Only Finn and Siobhan were familiar with it and neither of them had made the connection either.

"You think that's why we're at the heart of all this," David said when I was done. "That this is about the Butcher? And because we know about him and have talked about him as a group, we're the focus of this person's obsession?"

"I'm not sure," I admitted. "He calls us ghouls and says we're sick for being interested in this stuff. It might be that he's trying to punish us just for being interested in crime. The Butcher connection might be part of why he's angry, or it might just be a local thing he's picked up on as part of his signature. A way to choose his victims."

"But at the same time he's the one killing people all over the place – so maybe he isn't so much angry that we like murder stories, as pissed off we're not talking about him," Ricky said.

I'd not considered that but it did make a warped kind of sense. Perhaps there was a serial killer operating under our noses, eclipsed by the local notoriety of the Butcher. Our group wasn't public knowledge, but then again we hadn't made a secret of it either. Anyone might have overheard us at the bar in the Highwayman, or had the group mentioned in a casual conversation with any one of us. Even Katrine's parents, Siobhan's husband or someone else might have mentioned the group to someone. That was how most of us had found the group after all. I was even living in Wayfield's house for fucks sake, anyone watching it would have seen me, perhaps found the others by following me. The idea made me feel exposed, vulnerable.

Had he been watching the house? What if that was how it had started; stalking the new residents of Wayfield's bungalow? Had he noticed us the few times we'd met at mine? Followed us? It was scarily possible. Had I seen him, thought no more of him than any other punter? Was this why he was playing this game with us – because he had seen us, but we had not seen him?

"What do we do now, can we go to the police?" Siobhan asked.

"We still have no idea who it is," Finn said. "Howard Stepp's death seems to be looking like the others; an accident. What if the police can't find whoever it is before they get one of us? I mean, they can't lock us all in a cell together and keep watch, can they? I doubt our local nick is running witness protection."

"But they could do something," Siobhan insisted.

"You think they can keep us safe?" Ricky demanded. "You'd bet on your life, your kids' lives, would you? Is it worth the risk if this arsehole decides to burn your house down or gas you all?"

Her silence said quite clearly that no, it was not worth the risk. Even if the police did believe us, this guy had a way of getting to people; tampering with gas pipes, perhaps even drugging poor Marianna's evening drink so she couldn't wake up and escape. I felt a crawling dread. He could already have been in our homes, sneaking around, setting traps for us. The police couldn't protect us from that.

"But we know his type now," I said, trying to escape the feeling of helplessness that threatened to overtake me. "He's after people who've done something to increase the Butcher's fame, or people who have tried to profit from or exploit that fame. People that pay attention to killers. We can narrow down our victim lists."

"You think we can find the next victim based on that? Beat him at his game?" Finn said.

"It's worth a try. I mean...we're not in danger if we play the game, right? If we don't break the rules, he won't hurt us. And if we can save the next person, we win...right?" I said, trying to believe it, trying to convince myself that there was a way to win against this psychopath.

"We don't know how to win," Ricky said, not buying it. "Or what he'll do if we manage to beat him. He might just get crazier."

"I know that, but it at least buys us time to work out who he is. Then we can send the police after him and it'll all be over," I said.

"So we could maybe work out who a likely target is?" Finn said. "That might actually work...especially if we're right about him fixating on the Butcher and people that've studied him. Not many people have done stuff specifically on the Butcher. He was a flash in the pan, caught too quickly to gain a lot of fame."

"Can anyone think of someone off hand? Maybe another author or maybe a vlogger, something?" I asked.

"Caz is a Youtuber, he does videos on niche British killers," Siobhan offered.

"He lives in Copenhagen now, you twat," Ricky snapped.

Siobhan huffed.

After a few minutes we still couldn't think of anything. Most of my information on the Butcher came from newspaper archives, history websites and my own independent research. If the killer was targeting local people it was unlikely he'd go after journalists based in London or website admins who could be anywhere.

"We can narrow it down when we get the next email," Finn said, after a while, tacitly admitting defeat.

None of us questioned whether there would be a next email. Whatever this was it was in full swing now and there would be no stopping it. Not until whatever goal the killer had in mind had been reached.

We agreed to check through our Butcher collections to see if we could identify anyone local. Once everyone left I went out for a walk. I needed to get away from the house, clear my head.

On the way around to the park I found myself passing by Mum's old school. It was a primary only now, the upper years having been swallowed by a nearby middle school. The black hairpin fence was cold under my fingers as I peered through at the playing fields and large sycamores. I could imagine Mum and her poor friend Elaine sitting in the shade of those trees, making daisy chains on lazy afternoons. Perhaps Wayfield had come to watch her, just as I was looking through the iron fence now. The idea chilled me.

I'd gone back to the diaries the night before, after asking everyone to meet. I had no idea why. Perhaps some instinct to try and seek comfort from the familiar, and what could be more familiar than my mother's disdain for me?

There must have been a gap in entries, but without the dates it wasn't obvious. There was a change though. The entries had mostly been devoted to Wayfield and furious denials of his guilt. Her hatred for her parents, her aunt and the situation she was in. Then came the shift, and I stopped being a bit part in her saga. I guessed that this was the point of my birth, when she could no longer ignore me.

Aunt Jill came today. She says they'll be up from Bricknell soon to take me home. 'Soon' is her favourite word. Soon I'll be going home. Soon all this will be behind me. Soon arrangements will be made. I feel like time has stopped. There is only 'before' and 'soon'.

They keep bringing the baby out and trying to get me to feed it. I don't want to. I see the other women on the ward doing it and they disgust me. I want to stay looking good for when I see him again. I don't want saggy awful boobs. It cried and cried, and eventually they let me use a bottle. I look at it and try to find anything of Ray but it's hard to tell. It looks like literally any other baby I've ever seen, pink and wrinkled and screaming like a kicked cat. The only way I know it's the same baby each time is the scabby rash on it, the skin all peeling like a snake. I shudder every time they make me touch it.

With time not passing I make my plans. I am not going back to Bricknell with them, that's for certain. They'll take the baby away from me. It's Ray's and I refuse to let go of it until he's back with me. So I'll have to get away somehow, before I have to leave the hospital. I can't do much, it hurts to move around and I'm tired a lot. But I've been watching everyone else, all the women here and the nurses. I know where they keep their spare change for the shop downstairs. I know where their going-home clothes are put away. I even managed to get Jill to give me some money herself, for some socks and things from the little shop downstairs – though of course that's not what it's going on. She seemed too misty eyed over the baby to be a bitch for once though. Gave me an actual fiver. It's the least I'm owed, after all the cheques Dad's sent her.

The nurses haven't asked what I'm going to call it. They know I'm meant to be giving her up. Everyone here knows. It's obvious what's going on. It's so old-fashioned, like I'm being shipped off to a nunnery. But I don't care what they think of me. I have someone that loves me, who's going to marry me. I don't need their pitying looks and I don't care about their glares. I hate each and every woman on the ward. It gives me a little bit of pleasure to know that it's their stuff that will allow me to escape.

At some point either before or shortly after her escape, my mother did name me. I hadn't thought of my old name in ages – I'd seemingly always been Judith Broch, though not even my mother called me anything other than 'Jude'. Only David, with his teacher's dislike for nicknames.

In stolen clothes, with stolen money in her pockets, Mum hitchhiked from Liverpool to London. She had a suitcase with her, also stolen, containing some nappies, someone else's baby clothes and her diaries. She was on her way back to the capital, where Wayfield's trial had already begun.

I got a ride with a lorry driver yesterday. I didn't ask if he knew Ray. It would be too dangerous. He's still in the papers, not on the front page, just little bits further back about the trial and how he's being held in London. Ray in prison. It makes me want to cry.

The driver asked me where I was going and I said my boyfriend had put me out and I was going back to my parents. He asked the baby's name and I said Julie without thinking. It's Raymond's mother's name. That makes the baby Julie Pike. But as soon as Ray is out and we can get married she'll be Julie Wayfield, and I will be Eleanor Wayfield. I like the way that sounds. Eleanor Wayfield.

I've been looking for any mention of me in the papers, in case they've reported me missing. Nothing has shown up. They must be looking for me in Liverpool, or expecting me to go back to Bricknell. They still have no idea that it's Ray I was with, Ray who's the father of this baby. I can tell them they have the wrong man, and they'll have to let him go. To be with his baby, and me.

She's been quite quiet since we left the hospital. Maybe she isn't such a pain after all, it was just that place getting to both of us. Soon though, it won't matter. He'll be with me. To help, to have and to hold. Soon.

I was sickened by how grateful I felt for the acknowledgement of my existence in those pages. For the tiny amount of satisfaction I got from being referred to as anything other than 'it'. I knew that Mum's feelings for me had always rested at around 'indifference' but to consider that a relief from her total disgust made me feel worse than I ever had before. I'd put the diaries away and gone back to bed.

I called out for Adam as I came in through the front door. There was no answer but the car was outside. I felt guilty for having vanished with no note left behind. The search for Howard Stepp's identity had overridden every other concern. Given what had happened with Katrine he was probably frantic. Yet another selfish thing I'd done. It seemed that whatever I tried to do, I ended up hurting someone. And that someone was usually Adam.

"Adam?" I tossed my keys onto the box of Marianna's remaining books. I had to remember to move it at some point. It really was in the way.

"Oh, hey," I said, when Adam came out of the bedroom. "Sorry, I had to…"

I trailed off as I saw what he was holding. My mother's diaries.

CHAPTER TWENTY-THREE

For a moment we just stood there staring at each other. I looked at the cluster of dog-eared notebooks in his hands and he looked at me. I felt the house yawn around us. Suddenly it felt too big, too much. I wasn't afraid, but I felt lost, swallowed up. As if suddenly it was unavoidable that my whole life had been about this place and the man who lived there, rather than anything I had felt or seen or done. And now Adam knew it.

"Jude," Adam said, clearly trying hard to keep his voice level. "Can you explain this to me?"

I shook my head, unable to speak. How had he found them? How much had he read?

I tried to remember putting them away last night. I'd been scared, exhausted and drunk. Washing my pain away with the vodka followed by several glasses of red wine. Had I just left them out somewhere and forgotten?

"I was worried when I got back and you weren't here," Adam said, and I snapped back to attention. "But I thought maybe you were with the others. Grieving. I thought I'd get some stuff done, a nice surprise for you when you got back...and then I decided to start taking the vent covers off – for the plasterer...and I found these." He held up the books, each one held shut with fraying ribbons or perishing elastic bands. The cheap decoration on their covers flaking off. They looked small and incomplete in his hands.

"And I thought," he laughed bitterly, "I actually thought you'd be so excited, because I'd found secret diaries in the Butcher's house. I thought you'd be impressed. And then I started flicking through and I found this," he held up the piece of card I'd been using as a bookmark; my bus ticket from when I'd been to town. Dated.

"You already knew about them. And they're not his diaries at all, are they?" He said, flicking to the inside cover. "Eleanor Pike," he read, from the first diary. "Who's that?"

I thought, for one wild moment, that I could deny everything. Tell him it was some other woman's diary. Wayfield's mother's perhaps. But if he'd read even a little bit of it, seen the dates, that wouldn't wash. No, now was not the time for more lies. It was, finally, time to tell the truth.

"Eleanor Pike, became Eileen Brock...my mother," I said.

Adam didn't look satisfied with that, not that I'd expected him to be.

"I guessed. Flipped through one and it talks about her daughter, born the same month as you. Not likely to be a coincidence, was it? So I was thinking, why would Jude hide her mum's diary from me? And why would she hide the fact, that her mum grew up in Bricknell." He was getting angrier, his words punching out of him, speeding up, like he was running me down in a car, barrelling towards me.

"Because she knew him. Well, judging from what I've seen in here. And there's a picture too. Of you Jude, only you're not Jude, are you? You're Julie. Julie Pike."

It wasn't a question, but I nodded anyway.

He held up his other hand, in it was a photograph Marianna had printed for me. One of the better shots from Wayfield's trial. She'd got it from a friend who had access to newspaper pictures, even those unprinted, kept on archive digitally just in case. I'd tucked it into the diary to keep it hidden. Stupid of me. I should have kept them apart. Together they were damning evidence.

The picture showed my mother at the courthouse, clearer than any blurry black and white ink page could have shown her. In it you could see her face fully, in all its painful yearning. She was wearing a stolen coat too big for her, carrying me in her arms. Adam had never seen pictures of her in her youth. The woman in the old picture however, could have been my twin. And there was no hiding the placards in the crowd, which marked it as Wayfield's trial. Adam wasn't stupid. He'd put it together; Wayfield, Mum and me. The way I looked, and the way some people in Bricknell had reacted to me. To us. The ones who'd known her. The ones who remembered what she'd done.

"This is why everyone's been so agro about us being here...isn't it?"

I looked away.

"Isn't it?" he repeated, not shouting, but raising his voice and taking a step forward.

"Yes," I croaked.

At my admission he tossed the diaries onto the box of books by my feet. He threw the picture sideways, but it sliced through the air and drifted to the floor between us. It sat there, face up, my mother's eyes burning their love and devotion into the ceiling.

"You let me think it was because of me," Adam said, eyes holding me to the spot, the betrayal in them so sharp I could hardly breathe. "That they hated, me. You let me think we were being targeted, that you might be in danger, for being with me."

Tears started to blur my eyes. Each word from him tore into me. What had I done to him? To the kindest, most loving man I'd ever met? Hurt him, lied to him, and betrayed him. I didn't want to cry, didn't want him to think that I was sorry for myself. I couldn't care less what happened to me, but Adam... I wished I could take it all back. Never get involved with him. Never let him get close, open up to me, just to have me do this to him.

"Why the fuck would you do that, Jude? Why would you lie to me? Ever since we met you've been lying to me – about who you are, your Mum, your...Dad. Did you not trust me? Did you think I would hold it against you? That's how little you think of me?"

I couldn't look at him.

"How could you let me think this was about me? Let me feel as shit as I have been? How the fuck do you justify that?"

My words came out as a thin whisper.

"What?" he said sharply.

"I can't." I said. "I won't insult either of us by trying."

In the silence that followed, I choked back tears, feeling cold all over, watching him stand there with so much hurt and anger in his eyes, his breath coming quickly as if he was trying to hold himself together. I realised he was moments from crying. I had done that to him. My heart broke, knowing that I didn't deserve any of the love he'd shown me since we'd met. Not one single bit of it. He loved someone that didn't exist, someone I'd pasted over my twisted heart with lies. I was a feeble con of a person and now he knew. I wanted to reach out to him, to try and hold him together, but I couldn't. I was the last thing he needed.

I was the evil bitch that had done this to him. Evil. Just like my Father. Selfish, just like my mother.

"I've booked off work and I'm going to stay with Mum and Dad for a bit," Adam said at last. "I think we need some time – I need some time. Then we can start sorting this out, this," he gestured to the walls around us, "mess we're in." He turned away, towards the bedroom, I guessed to pack, then he froze, turned stiffly back to me with new horror on his face.

"This place...did he really leave it to your Mum?"

The instinct to lie was there, if feeble. I squashed it. "He...he gave it to me. It was never hers. I think he wants something from me. A visit a...relationship. But I don't want that. I just...we needed somewhere so badly."

"Don't you dare try and turn this into some...noble sacrifice," Adam spat. "You didn't do this for me."

"No, I didn't," I admitted. "I told myself having a home was what was important...but I wanted to be here. To try and...to find out about what happened. I hadn't read those," I pointed at the diaries. "I didn't know about them until after she died. And then I felt like I needed to know, about everything that happened."

"But you already knew he was your father," Adam said. "You knew and you kept it from me."

"I've never told anyone. I wanted to tell you."

"Just not enough to actually follow through and tell me the truth."

I knew he was right. If I'd really wanted to tell him, I would have. The truth was I hadn't ever planned to come clean. I'd lied to myself every time, just so I could live with myself.

"Adam," I said, and he half-turned back to me. "I...I'm so sorry. I wish...I wish I could take it all back."

"Yeah, well...you can't."

"I know. I don't expect you to forgive me, but, please don't go away thinking that I wanted to hurt you. You're the last person in the world I want to hurt," I felt tears start to drip down my face and quickly turned so as not to hurt him further. I didn't deserve his pity.

I stood in the living room while he packed. The monitor and his gaming PC were already gone, he must have already put them in the car. His car. All kinds of thoughts were running through my mind. I wanted to beg him not to leave, to keep apologising. I wanted to cry. I was thinking about how I'd sell the house and divide the money. Pay him back everything he'd spent on doing it up. Wondering how much he'd read of the diaries, how much he knew about Mum and what she'd done. By the time Adam wheeled a suitcase out of the bedroom I was coming apart.

"I'll let you know when I'm coming back, to work, alright? Until I can get transferred back to London," Adam said awkwardly, standing in the doorway. I could only nod. If I opened my mouth I knew I'd start to cry again and he didn't deserve that. I'd done enough to make his life difficult already.

When the door shut behind him I just stood there. I felt like all the life had gone out of me. I was all alone and it was all my fault. Adam was hurting, destroyed, and that was my fault too. I didn't even want to be with me.

I didn't want to go back to the diaries, but something pulled me to them. They had cost me the one person that had ever loved me. I had to finish them now. I had to know if it had been worth it.

I'd almost reached the end now. The entries, when they came, were shorter. She had been writing to him then, at the prison, and had probably had little use for writing anywhere else. Still, I made myself read the entries from the trial.

Arrived in London yesterday. Very cold out. Julie very quiet which is a blessing. The last driver to give me a lift gave me ten pounds to get her a winter coat. I've added it to my store of money from the hospital, and what I've pinched on my way south. It's enough to get us into a B&B for a few days. Not a very nice one, but at least it's a bed. I've spent so long half-sleeping in lorries, watching out for creeping hands, I can hardly think straight.

I know where Ray's being held, and which court he's going to. It's in the papers and I've been collecting them, ripping the pages out and keeping them in my diary. He looks thinner, so pale. I can't imagine what he's going through in prison with murderers and other hardened criminals. He's suffering while they put him on trial for something he didn't do.

*

The old bitch that runs the B&B puts us out in the mornings. I've been taking Julie out to the courthouse to look for him, but they seemed to be taking the people on trial in through a back way. Then today I caught a glimpse of him. A bad accident blocked off the back road and they had to bring him around the front. He was in chains. Like an animal. I was wishing so hard that he'd look up and see me, and then he did! I held Julie up and looked right at him. He misses me, I know it. I could feel how much he wants to be with me.

I have to do something for him, to get him out of there. No one knows the kind of man he is, but I can tell them. I can make them see he can't possibly have done what they say. I've spent what little I have left on some paper and stamps – I barely need to eat, I'm so excited to be near him! – I'm going to write to his solicitor, to the papers, the police, someone has to listen to me.

And listen they had.

I'd found the news stories from that time, though I knew already what had happened. It had impacted my life since before I could remember. My mother, a flash-in-the-pan newspaper headliner. They painted her as a combination of Myra Hindley and Eva Braun; a deluded girl either complicit in or unbothered by his slaughtering of young women. Her testimony was not made on the stand but was heard widely in the tabloid press. Every. Deluded. Word. Signed with her real name. She considered Raymond Wayfield's arrest a miscarriage of justice and begged for the father of her child to be released. The public reacted as could be expected; with anger, shock and ultimately, hatred.

Once her letters were printed in full, Mum was recognised everywhere she went. Her school picture had been in the papers and she was unable to find anywhere to stay. By then she was also afraid that 'Ray's baby' would be taken from her. Worse, that her parents might find her. Though I had to assume they had no wish to be any more associated with her than they already were. According to my research it looked like her father had taken early retirement right after she went to the papers. Her parents moved to Spain shortly after that. They'd stayed out there until they died, leaving her nothing.

Her diary contained few clues as to where she had ended up, but I thought it sounded like a shelter of some kind. She was going by the name she'd use for the rest of her life 'Eileen Broch' and had dyed her hair from blonde to brown. She was dressing me as a boy and called me 'Jude' as part of her disguise. Her diary entries were few and far between, but ached with loneliness and a naïve sense of persecution. I think her vilification in the press came as a complete shock. One she debatably never recovered from.

I felt sorry for her, despite myself. She'd never loved me but, had anyone loved her? Maybe her parents had tried but they'd treated her harshly, pushed her away. She'd been groomed and exploited and they'd left her to fend for herself. Even if she'd been naïve, foolish, hadn't they raised her to be that ignorant?

Mum remained in London for the rest of the trial. Whether she was moving around to different shelters or refuges, or in one place, I had no idea. On the day of the verdict she wrote only, *Today my life is over. I will never know happiness again.*

She was still a teenager, yet her words proved prophetic. Until her death I never saw Mum happy at all. The next time she'd left London, it was as ashes, packed with the rest of my stuff.

She gave no details on how she was able to survive. Perhaps she found a job, paid under the table, where she was able to hide her identity and make steady money. Perhaps she took to the streets, easy enough to do in London. So many lonely men around. That was, funnily enough, something I wouldn't judge her for that would have been pure survival, for her, for me. However she made money, when she wrote the next entry, it appeared she had found a place to live.

We moved in today. Not much to move. The room is furnished, but barely. At least I'll have a bed of my own and a place to keep my things safe. Better still, an address to write from.

I think the landlady felt sorry for me. She gave me some tins and packets of cereal to be 'getting on with' and brought up some blankets and old toys for Julie. Action Men and a plastic tank. I've cut her hair and with some old jeans and jumpers from the shelter on, she looks like a little boy. I wanted to call her 'Ray' but don't dare. So it's Jude. No one can know who we are.

I am writing daily letters to the governor at Belmarsh. They have Ray locked up there as a 'danger to the public' should he manage to escape. He has no family to visit him and they will not let me go. We weren't married, but that shouldn't make a difference. I am trying to persuade them that I should be allowed to see him with Julie, so that she will know her father.

She is not sleeping and is no longer quiet. She cries all the time and having to find money for her milk now that mine's dried up is exhausting. At the shelter they helped me to apply for money to keep her and myself – but it's so little. If I didn't need her I would have left her there.

I'd always known it, but to see it written down was something else. If she hadn't needed me as a way into the prison to see Wayfield, I would have been left behind like an old coat.

I couldn't remember the early visits to HMP Belmarsh. Newly opened in 1991 I supposed it might have been less foreboding then. But then, how much less horrible could a prison be, just because it was new? My first memories of going there start when I was about six or seven. We could visit only once or twice a year and sometimes these were cancelled. Wayfield was not a model prisoner. He got into fights and attacked people as payback. Even though he wanted us to visit, it seemed he couldn't stop himself from being violent. Mum blamed everyone else, of course, when his visitor privileges were taken away. Even after the guilty verdict, she never stopped believing in him.

On visit days Mum would dress carefully and wear makeup. We would take the train and then walk what felt a long way, on my little legs. At the prison we were searched and ordered about. I always found it scary and felt as if I was the one who had done something wrong. Then we'd be put in a room with him. He was always in handcuffs and there were guards there to stop him from getting up or touching either of us.

Mum would sit there and stare at him as if she was trying to memorise his face. As if she was trying to fill some tank inside her with fuel for their months apart. He never really spoke to her, she just poured out information about what we'd been doing and how I was getting on. Dreams and plans for after his release, which she seemed to think was coming but which never arrived.

Through it all he would stare at me. He was thin, his light brown hair cut short, but still springing with curl. Eyes like coffee – so dark brown they were almost black. My eyes. He had long fingers with yellow ends, from smoking. Mum sent money to him for cigarettes and anything else he wanted. Money we could have used at home. His skin was very pale, almost grey and his mouth was thin and thoughtful. I was never frightened of him. I didn't know enough then to be frightened. To be horrified. He was just that weird man we went to see, who she called my Dad. But there was a calm in him that even as a child I found strange. He reminded me at the time of one of the teachers at school who taught the upper classes. Soft spoken and very passive, but who I'd once seen burst into red-faced, spitting rage at some boys who'd started a glue-throwing fight. Later I'd be able to assign names to the impression he gave off; stern, calculating, explosive.

By the time I turned sixteen Wayfield had earned the privilege of solo visits from Mum. His 'good behaviour' came about after he was stabbed and lost half a lung. After that he wasn't so aggressive. Or he got better at hiding his retaliation.

By then I was old enough to refuse to visit him and stayed with friends or mooched around town to get out of going. I don't think Mum cared. She didn't need me to get in to see him anymore. She only kept me around for the benefit money by then. But he must have wanted me there, because he got Mum to try and make me go. She confiscated my CD Walkman and stopped paying for anything beyond school dinners; no new clothes, trips out or money for shopping. It didn't make any difference. I didn't go to school much, and anything she took, I went out and stole a replacement. I didn't need her.

Then he started to write to me. In these short messages he would tell me how proud he was of whatever accomplishment Mum had told him about. He'd say how sad he was that I didn't visit him anymore. Reading them made me feel guilty, a sick, twisty kind of guilt. Still, I refused to visit the prison. Mum took the letters from me and read them herself, desperate for any little crumb of him she could hoover up. It made me hate him more. Hate both of them.

At eighteen I went to university. Not a good one. My marks were middle of the road. The degree didn't matter, I'd only chosen to study History because I was good enough at it to get in. I just wanted three years of student loans and bursaries, a way to escape Mum and our tiny flat. After uni I took whatever jobs I could to afford a place of my own. That's how I met Adam.

I was training to be a driver for London Transport and he was getting a special licence for warehouse machinery. We met at a testing centre and when he offered me change for a vending machine I was struck by how warm and unshuttered he was. There was no calculation in Adam, nothing hidden. He smiled like a kid, big and carefree. There wasn't a violent thought anywhere in him.

I put the diary aside. There was nothing more it could tell me. I already knew the rest. Mum had visited Wayfield for the next few years. I had avoided her. Then, after one meeting, she'd left the prison and stepped off the kerb in front of a taxi. When I spoke to the governor he was cagey, but said Mum had been 'upset' following the visit. Wayfield had apparently said some 'unpleasant things' to her. I could only imagine what, but, given his apparent hatred for women, it wasn't hard to picture the scene. Wayfield, scornful and mocking of Mum's puppy love, her aging appearance and poverty. Mum, tearful, begging him to stop, to not say such horrible things. Wayfield laughing, taunting her.

I could imagine Mum leaving the prison, walking down the street. Had she had some clarity in those moments? Had she realised what kind of man she had devoted her life to? Perhaps it was the loss of his love that had driven her to step out in front of the car. Perhaps it was the knowledge that she'd never had it to begin with.

CHAPTER TWENTY-FOUR

The chiming sound of an email hitting my inbox woke me up like a gunshot. Even after crying myself to sleep, my stomach churning with vodka and regrets, I snapped awake before even sitting up properly.

With my phone still with the police I'd left the laptop on and plugged in beside the bed, sitting on the box of books. Dimly, I'd hoped for a message from Adam, though I had no right to expect one.

Rolling over the empty space where Adam should have been, I swiped at the mousepad. If I'd thought I was too numb to be afraid, that idea was put to rest. The sight of the subject line 'The Fourth' filled me with instant dread. I clicked it. There was no time to waste; we had already cost two people their lives.

4

Do we understand each other yet?

Katrine didn't have to die. If you had all only stuck to the rules, she would have been fine. But no, you all thought yourselves too clever for me and you had to prove it. Too special to obey the rules of my game. Now a young girl is dead and it is your fault.

I feel you haven't been taking me seriously, so here is a new rule for you. Hopefully it will sharpen your minds and bring the stakes home to you.

> 4. If you fail this time and I reach my target, I will take one of you.

Maybe now you'll try harder to save her.

I've been following her for a few weeks, not as closely as Lara and Howard, but close enough. Keeping an eye out for changes in her routine. There have been none. It's sad. The more I look at people the clearer it becomes that we all run through life on tracks, on rails. We do not veer from the expected, the normal.

Normal is what she likes. Net curtains, shoes off at the door, wicker shopping trolley in the hall. A new bunch of carnations on the dining room table every other weekend. Her children visit, but never think to buy flowers before driving over. Petrol station carnations, every fortnight. She pretends to be delighted every time.

I've trailed her as she shops, finding the cheapest options and going out of her way for them. Topping up her electric meter key at the post office and getting her weekly supply of gossip at the same time. Picks up romance novels from the free book trolley and takes them home in her stout, reliable M&S handbag. Two cups of tea and a shortbread finger, two Mills and Boon a week.

I am going to stab her.

As she walks home from coffee morning this Friday, mind on getting home and starting on a new book, I will walk up to her and smile. Before she can smile back, I will push a knife into her. Through the anorak and sensible cardigan. I will open her up and let your failure spill out.

I will be out in the open, visible, vulnerable. It's a risk I'm willing to take, to give you a chance. No not waste it.

Find her. Save her. Or one of you will die with her.

I'd hardly finished reading when another email pinged my inbox. It is David, summoning me to his house for a meeting with the others. I dashed off a reply and tried to scrape myself into something resembling a stable adult. With my hair twisted into a bun and my puffy eyes dabbed with cold water, I went to put on my jacket hoping to block out some of the chill. My hand found only empty space on the hooks in the hall.

Frowning, I checked the bedroom, the living room. My jacket was missing. I realised I hadn't seen it since the night at the canal. I remembered Adam giving me his coat on the way home. My jacket had been wet through from the rain, he must have put it somewhere, or had it been forgotten in the car? I checked the house over again and decided it must still be in the car, only now it was back in London with Adam.

Shaking off fresh tears I picked up Adam's winter coat. He'd taken his jacket but not the bulky parka. The scent of his body spray clung to it, along with a subtler smell that was uniquely him. I told myself not to be so maudlin and put it on. I quickly left the house, letting the cold wind snatch that comforting, heart breaking smell from me. As I started walking I stuffed my keys into the pocket and felt something through the lining. There was something hard in one of the internal pockets.

I fumbled it out and found a small black box and a tiny envelope. A jewellery box. With a sick feeling I opened it, already knowing, in a far off, resigned way, what I'd find. It was an engagement ring, silver, an emerald surrounded by tiny diamonds. Adam must have been saving for it for a while. Inside the envelope I found a neatly printed receipt. I checked the date. The day he'd lied to me about going to town.

I'd only known Adam to lie to me twice. Once when planning the hotel surprise, and again to buy me an engagement ring. I closed the box. That ring wasn't for me. It was for the person I'd allowed him to think I was. I retraced my steps and let myself back into the house. I stashed both the ring and the receipt in a bag containing the rest of Adam's as yet unpacked clothes. I wasn't about to risk losing it. He'd either find it there, or I could hide it in the coat again once I got home. Adam never had to know I'd found it.

Having to walk meant I was almost the last person to arrive at David's. Even Finn who'd had to pull another sickie from work had beaten me. Only Siobhan wasn't there yet, probably still outside the school gates, oblivious to the latest message.

In David's brown-on-brown living room there were signs that he'd been fretting just as I had. There was a pile of Ripper books on the table, with several empty mugs and a half-gone bottle of whisky. A rumpled blanket and pillow were stuffed behind an armchair. He hadn't yet shaved and was wearing yesterday's creased up clothes.

"We need to form a plan," David said without preamble. "He's sent this email later than the others. We only have a week. That's half the time he's been giving us. But this time we know what's going on, that it's real, and we have to stop it."

"How?" Ricky asked. "We have no idea who this person is. What are we meant to do, stalk every biddy in Bricknell?" He was jittery, one knee bobbing up and down as he sat, tapping a lighter against the other thigh. It was the first sign I'd seen that he was back to smoking. Now the going was tough, vaping didn't seem to cut it for him. I was a hair away from asking for a cigarette myself.

"Not just Bricknell," Finn said gloomily. "Howard Stepp didn't live here, or die here. Whoever's doing this has already branched out to the neighbouring towns."

"Exactly, we'll never track this bitch down." Ricky said. "We're fucked."

"We are not," I said, as David cringed. He was not someone who appreciated course language, or raised voices. "We found Stepp, just slightly too late. Which, given that we started looking late anyway, means we stand a chance of finding this woman before something happens to her."

"There's not much to go on," Finn said, looking at the email on his phone. "Even less than last time I think. An older woman with a shopping trolley, living alone like the others, in a house with net curtains and who goes to coffee morning every Friday."

"And she has children that visit every fortnight," I said. "I know, it doesn't tell us much."

"The coffee morning's probably our best bet," Finn said. "It gives us her whereabouts on a specific day and time at least."

"Do you know how many places do coffee mornings in Newston?" Ricky snapped. "Probably twice as many as there are schools. You got parish halls, scout huts, youth clubs…they all do stuff for old people during the week. Not to mention, she could be going to someone's house. Like we do."

"There's at least two on Friday that I've found in Bricknell so far," David said. "The old Salvation Army hall on the high-street and the St. Julien's church annexe. There are more but those are the wrong days."

"Alright so we just need to find out which places in Newston also have coffee mornings specifically on Friday and then we can split up and try and find this woman," I said. I felt a tiny sliver of hope start to take root in my chest. We could do this, it wasn't impossible.

"Fuck," Finn said, glaring at something on his phone and prompting another purse lipped expression from David. "You've got to be kidding me."

"What?" I asked.

"This Friday is 'The Big Coffee Morning'. It's a charity thing. I've just googled a couple of places in town and they're all participating. Café's, pubs, even some shops."

"OK, but, where normally has it on a Friday?" Ricky said.

Finn was shaking his head before Ricky finished speaking. "Read the email again. It doesn't say what day she normally goes. It just says she will be killed *this* Friday, after a coffee morning."

There was silence as this sunk in. The hope in my chest faded. Of course the killer wouldn't make it that easy. Of course there would have to be a trick, a trap. However much they might talk of levelling the playing field this game was still rigged. Half the time and double the work. They wanted to win, to reach whatever end goal they had in mind. We could not be allowed to outmanoeuvre them.

"We'll need to split up, try and cover as many of these meet ups as possible and hope we find the right woman," David suggested.

"What, an old woman in an anorak, with a wicker shopper? Like there aren't hundreds of them out there," Ricky muttered.

"Do you have any suggestions, or are you content to be a waste everyone's time with sniggering and backchat?" David snapped, voice raised in an unmistakeable 'teacher on the edge' tone. This triggered some kind of response in Ricky, who instantly shut up as if afraid of getting detention.

"Someone needs to tell Siobhan," David continued in a calmer voice. "We only have a few days to work out a plan of who is going to which community centre. We need to be methodical about this to stand any chance at all."

"We might be able to get to her before Friday," Finn said slowly, as if still thinking. "If Jude was right and the people he's choosing are related in some way to the Butcher, that could give us a way of finding her without going to the meetups on Friday."

"An older woman who's written something or done something regarding the Butcher story," I said. "Someone who would fit the pattern."

"What about where this is happening?" Ricky said. David turned, seemingly ready to snap again, but Ricky held up his hands. "I'm being serious – if this is about the Butcher somehow, isn't it a big coincidence that Katrine ended up in the canal, where one of his victims was? What if this old girl's going to get stabbed somewhere to do with him too?"

"Perhaps, but the other murders don't –" David began.

"The cemetery," I interrupted. "Lara Preston's house bordered the cemetery. That's where one of Wayfield's supposed victims died. Not a canonical one, but the one you told me about – the assault...there is a link."

"A tenuous one," David sighed. "As Lara Preston wasn't actually in the cemetery."

"And Howard Stepp?" Finn asked.

"That sheltered housing development is fairly new," David said. "I can't see how it would relate to him...unless..." he seemed to focus inwards, dredging up a memory. "Before they built it there was a row of shops there, an off licence, a hairdresser and..." his eyes widened. "A massage parlour."

"A massage parlour, or a '*massage parlour*?" Ricky asked, with air quotes.

David reddened. "It was not, I think, a legitimate establishment."

"Perv," Ricky snorted, seemingly finding comfort in the familiar ritual of embarrassing David.

It clicked. "One of the three bodies in Wayfield's garden was meant to belong to a local girl, supposedly working as a prostitute, though her family denied it. That's only a rumour, from Lara's podcast, but what if that's the reason the killer staged Stepp's death at home? It fell into their lap, that he happened to live there, maybe that's why they took the risk of killing him near all those other residents, the carers and all that."

"What about the other two bodies in the garden, where did those girls come from?" Ricky asked.

"I think he was meant to have picked them up hitchhiking. I'm not sure where. There was less CCTV around then, their last movements weren't certain. Could have been on the motorway for all we know."

"But he said he's going to stab this woman in the street," Finn said. "Not on the hard shoulder."

I shrugged helplessly. "Then I don't know. Could be that one or both of them were picked up somewhere else, on a street. Maybe he offered them a lift? Or maybe it's nothing to do with those girls and the location will be somewhere else the Butcher went or was thought to have attacked."

"You're meant to be his biggest fan, or whatever," Ricky snapped. "Why don't you work it out?"

I glared at him. "I am not a 'fan'."

"Well out of all of us, you're the one with the real boner for him. Living in his house, always asking questions about him."

"Ricky," David said, warning in his tone. "Please leave Judith alone. We're all trying to work this out. We're all somewhat invested in the Butcher killings."

"Not like her," Ricky muttered, then fell into mutinous silence.

"We'll have to work on finding the right coffee morning, and trying to work out the link to this woman. We can't reliably guess where he's going to attack her. Wayfield lived here, most places are going to have meaning," Finn said, breaking the tension.

I nodded, still a bit shaken by Ricky's outburst. He seemed more erratic than usual. Not surprising, given our circumstances. "Alright. Who's going to ring Siobhan?"

Ricky took out his phone, already rising, ready to storm off. "Got it."

David rubbed his face with both hands and let out a long sigh. Tension still filled the room and he looked older and more tired than I'd ever seen him. I reached over and patted his knee. David looked up and offered a small, unconvincing smile.

"It'll be OK," I said, trying to sound sure. "We'll get there."

"How are you holding up?" he asked.

For a moment I thought he was talking about Adam, but then I realised he meant about Katrine. I'd found her body after all. I thought briefly of telling him that Adam had left me, but then I'd have to explain why. I'd never revealed to any of them that I was Wayfield's daughter. They knew, obviously, about the woman who had so provoked the public with her letters. They knew she had a child by Wayfield, but there were no records to show where that child was now.

My birth had never even been properly registered. Back then paperwork got lost all the time. It was easier to slip through the cracks, blur the truth, and finesse the details. To invent a life. Everything about me was a lie.

I knew in that moment that, even if we got through this, found the killer, escaped the game he was playing with us, I'd still lose everything. Already I felt things breaking down to nothing. Adam was gone. The truth was already leaking out, contaminating everything. Already I could feel my ties to the others fraying. Too many lies to sustain. How long before they found out? I'd been a fool to think they wouldn't. To think that what I had could last. I'd have to disappear, just as my mother had done all those years ago.

I was spared having to lie to David's face when Ricky emerged from the kitchen, yelling into his phone.

"You stupid bitch! Do you have any idea what you're doing?"

David jolted in his seat and even Finn looked shaken by the sudden outburst. I felt a deep pit of fear yawn open inside me. Now what?

"Turn the fucking car around, turn it – Siobhan! Don't you dare!" Ricky tore the phone from his ear and glared at the screen as he stabbed at the redial icon. "She hung up on me....great, now her phone's off."

"What is she doing?" Finn asked, but I think we'd all guessed.

"She and Tom have packed the kids up and she's taking them to her sister's in Essex. For a 'holiday'."

"But...she's coming back?" David said incredulously. "She has to, we all saw the rules. We know what happened to Katrine. Running is against the rules."

"Try telling her that," Ricky spat, waving his phone. "She says she's 'sorry' but she can't stay here and put them in danger, or leave them without a mum. So she's off. Stupid bitch!" He was furious, but his hands were shaking. He cared about her, maybe more than I'd realised.

"He's going to kill her," David said, with such certainty that I winced, glancing at Ricky, who'd gone grey. There was no hope in David's voice, only anger and exhausted resignation. "We can't let her do this."

"We can't stop her either," Finn said. "None of us know where he sister lives, right? So it's either try and find Siobhan or try and find the next victim."

"But we can't just leave her…" Ricky said, trailing off when he saw my face. He looked to the rest of us, but I knew Finn was right. And so did David, looking at his grave face.

"I don't want to choose," I said, trying to sound calm when inside I was sickened. "But Siobhan is putting herself in danger, and this next victim doesn't even know what's coming. It's not fair to let her die, when Siobhan knows the risk she's taking. And if we fail, it's one of us who dies," I said. "If Siobhan wants to run, she can. We can't waste time trying to help someone who just left us to face a murderer without her."

For once, Ricky was speechless. He just stood there, pale as a corpse.

I grabbed Adam's coat, not wanting to look Ricky in the eye. "David, you and Ricky work up a list of community centres we need to check on Friday. Finn and I will work on a connection between the Butcher and any local elderly women." Looking back at them, I tried to force some authority into my voice, quelling the tremble I felt in my lips. "And nobody runs, OK? Or they're on their own."

CHAPTER TWENTY-FIVE

I felt guilty as I walked home that day. Siobhan was part of the group and a friend. Leaving her to fend for herself felt wrong, mercenary. I tried to remind myself that she had left us first, but it made little difference. I couldn't convince myself that we were doing the right thing. Fair and good were not the same. Fair was like justice, cold and calculating. Good was infinitely harder, and sometimes made mistakes. Mistakes we couldn't afford to make.

At home I found another letter waiting for me. This one was marked 'Urgent' on the envelope, written by hand in red ink. I opened it, skimming it angrily, then stopped. This was not the usual letter, asking me to visit as soon as possible. This time they'd apparently decided to be more direct. Now, at last, I saw what it had all been about. The house, the move, everything that had helped to tear apart my fragile existence. It was obvious in retrospect really, that it would all be about him.

Dear Ms. Pike,

I have been instructed by your father (Mr. Raymond Wayfield) to contact you once more in the hope that, with some additional information, you will see fit to contact me. With his permission, I am now able to reveal details of his situation, as outlined below.

Mr. Wayfield has, as you may know, sustained injuries in the past which have resulted in the loss of part of his lung. He has been living with this injury for some time, however, last year he was hospitalised with breathing difficulties. Following some tests, it was revealed that he had the early stages of lung cancer.

Since being diagnosed, Mr. Wayfield has undergone treatment, first with radiotherapy and chemotherapy and later, a surgery to remove several tumours. Recently however, his condition has worsened and, with further loss of lung function, he requires a donor. Due to his poor health and current situation, he is not a priority candidate. Your mother, before her sad passing, underwent testing but was, unfortunately, not a viable match. Therefore, I am writing to convey his wish that you consent to testing, to see if you would be a suitable match.

With time advancing, I must convey the seriousness of Mr. Wayfield's condition. He hopes that, now you are installed in your new property, you will be able to undergo the procedure and recuperate in comfort.

Yours sincerely,
Martin Lancaster

I stared in disbelief at the printed words, so cold and calculating. So that was what it had all been about. He wanted my lung. He'd taken my identity, my childhood, the man I loved and now he literally wanted blood. I crushed the letter into a ball and dropped it on the desk. I had already lost everything. They could send a hundred letters, call every minute, knock on the door forever, but I wasn't going to do a thing for that man. Ever.

I went online to try and find any leads that would take me to the killer's next victim. I had a few books that featured chapters on the Butcher, but none with local authors. Similarly, none of the few podcasters or youtubers that had mentioned him lived anywhere near Bricknell. As I hunted for a book, podcast or even a poem about the Butcher that I'd not yet read, I couldn't help but think of my mother and finally, of Wayfield.

Was I becoming like her, like him? Both had been calculating in their own way. She had used me to get to him, to hold his interest. Stolen and lied just to follow him. At the same time blindly falling into the role of his victim, over and over again. Letting him take and take from her until she was empty of everything but despair.

As for Wayfield himself, he had apparently convinced everyone around him that he was a normal, innocent man. While inside he had a hunter's ability to find those he could manipulate and victimise. To know just how to lure and dispatch them.

Now I was in my mother's role; victim of a killer, scrambling to meet his demands. Yet also making the same kinds of unfeeling decisions Wayfield had excelled at; about Siobhan, about the hunt for the killer, deciding who was vulnerable and who to pursue. Who to leave behind. I tried to shut out the thoughts. I wouldn't let myself be like them. But how? How could I escape it? I was trapped between them, neither one nor the other. Some unholy mix of predator and prey.

I'd forgotten about the plasterers. After I'd been researching for a few hours there was a knock on the door. As soon as I opened the door two of them trooped in with their dust sheets, buckets and ladders. I couldn't find the words to turf them out again. I sort of wanted company. Anyone to distract me, though soon I couldn't think with the noise from them and their radio. I ended up on the back step with a mug of coffee and my laptop.

Compared to most serial killers, there had always been a dearth of media relating to Wayfield. Mention Bundy, Dahmer, the Zodiac, and everyone knew who they were. As in all things, America dominated through sheer volume. Even the most notorious killers from the UK, like Fred and Rose West, had far less media attention than their US counterparts. Fewer books, lesser TV series'. That was taking into consideration the fact that the Wests killed for over ten years, a whole decade of material. It was no wonder then that the Butcher had gone mostly unnoticed in terms of wider media, having only been actively killing for a few months. Of course coverage at the time had been quite wide, but not sustained. There was no mystery to his story and, despite his effect on my mother, no charisma to his presence. His name did not sell books or bring in ratings. He was not marketable, as serial murderers went.

I was scanning the pages of Amazon, trying to find any new titles that mentioned Wayfield, when I realized I was being watched. Keeping my head down towards the screen I glanced sideways. There, looking over the fence, was number twelve. She was holding some kind of garden tool, the long handle in both hands. I felt my low level anxiety flare, heat burning over me. Who the hell did she think she was, watching me like a zoo animal? What had I done to deserve her hatred? Absolutely nothing. Yet how superior she could feel looking down on me; the bastard of a murderer's groupie. Inside, I felt something spill over, my anger getting the better of me. I needed an outlet for all the fear and guilt boiling away in my chest, and she was it.

"Can I help you?" I snapped, turning to her suddenly. I was gratified to see her jump. "Or is it that you have nothing better to do than stand and gawk?"

Her mouth pursed up like the arse on her little dog. She sniffed, nostrils wide and quivering as if scenting the rotten parts of my past. Still she seemed set to ignore me. It was this that finally broke me. I left the laptop on the step and strode over to the fence. My sudden approach seemed to startle her. She froze to the spot.

"What exactly is your fucking problem, eh?" I said, both hands grasping the top of the fence, shaking the desiccated wood. "Cat got your tongue? Or do you just like to watch?"

"You have no business being here," she said all at once, the words flying over one another like hailstones. "Shameless, that's what it is. Shameless."

I glared at her and her pouchy, whiskered cheeks quivered. Watery blue eyes moved over my face quickly as if hunting for a way in, a gap to exploit in an upcoming attack. I refused to back down.

"I've got nothing to do with him. I didn't know him, I wasn't even fucking born. But somehow it's my fault just for being here, right? Even though any one of you could have pulled your heads out of your arses and realised what was going on right next door. Could have stopped him. Maybe it's you who should just fuck off!" I shouted the last part, saw her flinch as I unloaded all my frustration on her.

Number twelve's eyes darted behind me and I turned to find one of the plasterers there. A cigarette hung limply from his hand. Clearly he'd come out for a smoke break and found me, going nuts at the neighbour. Embarrassment burnt up my spine. A slamming door and irate barking told me that number twelve had made her escape. I was glad. I didn't want to face her again.

With my cheeks flaming I gathered up my laptop and went inside, shutting myself in the back bedroom. There I put my face in my hands and cried. Everything from the past weeks came crashing down about me; Marianna, Katrine, the emails, Adam, the murders. As I had done my whole life, I wished I had a mother there to comfort me. And just as every other time, I was disappointed.

*

The next four days reminded me unpleasantly of exams. Trying frantically to work everything out in time, only to end up with a confused mess that even I couldn't understand. Everything I tried to find the killer's next victim lead to a dead end. I was putting in hours upon hours of work but moving no closer to success.

Having found no local authors or podcasters or anything else I'd started trying to find out where anyone who had done something on the Butcher would be on Friday. Maybe they were in the area for an event or to visit family. It was a slow process, checking blogs, social media timelines and sending emails. I amassed a list and kept it updated, but responses were slow in coming and some people had used pennames or no name at all.

The others were also working hard. Between them they'd identified at least twenty community centres with a weekly coffee morning, plus more with a one off event on Friday. The list was being divided between the three guys as, without a car, I could only cover the ones in Bricknell. Finn had expanded his search from authors and creators to those involved in Wayfield's trial. From journalists to jurors. Still, he'd found no one who might be our mystery woman. None of us were any closer to working out a location and we'd largely abandoned that avenue of investigation.

Ricky had also been trying to get in touch with Siobhan, but she had her phone off. I had given in and emailed her twice. The first message just asked her to come back, the second was to remind her of the danger she was putting herself in. She didn't reply to either, though I got read receipts for both. I began to worry that she was already dead. Only, surely the killer would have rubbed that in our faces already? Or was he waiting for the right time, already devising new ways to fuck with us. Just in case, we'd created a new chat without Siobhan in it, so he couldn't spy on us if he had her phone. Slowly, we were learning. Too slowly to be much use.

I heard nothing from Adam. In the interest of giving him space I'd sent him only one email to make sure he got to London OK. I'd also apologised again. Though I knew I could ever apologise enough. He hadn't replied and I regretted sending the email as soon as I'd done it. What I'd done was unforgiveable. I had never wanted to hurt him, but that of course didn't matter. I had hurt him all the same.

On Friday morning I woke and felt as if I was facing execution, which I was, in a way. If we failed to save this woman, whoever she was, one of us was going to be next. Siobhan was also in danger, but I wasn't going to rely on the killer counting her as part of the forfeit. They had not shown an abundance of mercy so far.

I put on Adam's coat and headed to the first of the two local events. I'd bought myself a pay-as-you-go handset to replace my smartphone and we'd agreed to call in if we found anything. The bulky plastic phone rattled in my pocket. All the way to the Salvation Army hall I was waiting for it to ring. Nothing.

Inside the red-brick building around twenty people were already seated. A steaming tea urn took up most of the space on a Formica counter. Two older women were doling out biscuits on paper plates and there were buggies and walking frames everywhere. A quick check of the room later and I had nine suspects. Everyone else was either a man or a young mother. Looking at the nine possible victims, the hopelessness of our task almost overwhelmed me. How were we supposed to narrow it down? I still had another meeting to go to.

What else had the email said? I checked the piece of paper I'd scrawled clues on. M&S handbag, stout and reliable. Not hugely helpful, most of the women had large, plain handbags. The only other identifying information was her penchant for book sales and her drink order; two teas and a shortbread finger. But how much of that was poetic licence? It was impossible to know.

I checked my watch; twenty minutes until the other coffee morning started. Only an hour until this one was over. We were running out of time.

Getting up I did a quick circuit of the hall. I disregarded a woman with no anorak, because I had to start somewhere, no matter how flimsy. With a cup of tea in one hand I watched the other women, one at a time. Three were drinking coffee, one hot chocolate. If the woman I was looking for was actually a tea drinker, that brought the suspects down to four. It didn't exactly feel concrete.

Of the remaining four one had no handbag, just a purse in her pocket. Three left. This was hopeless. How could I really discount any of them? It all felt so circumstantial. Which was probably why the killer had included those details in the email. They were next to useless.

I looked around for a book stall, even just a shelf of old books, but there was none. Hard to tell if that was normal though, it might have been put away recently. What now? Sidle up to each one and ask what they were reading at the moment? Romance novels weren't that niche. My phone rang, startling me. I pulled it from my pocket and saw Finn's number on screen.

"Have you found her?" I asked.

"Maybe." I could tell from his breathing and the wind rushing that he was walking fast, outside. "Older woman with a wicker shopping trolley. She's around the corner from the youth centre in Newston. Topping up her electric."

That had been in the email, hadn't it? Part of her routine? My heart leapt in excitement.

"Keep on her, have you heard from the others?"

"Not yet. Ricky rang in when he got to town but David's MIA."

I swallowed. "You don't think…"

"We haven't failed yet though. He can't take one of us…can he?" Finn said. "Hang on, she's on the move. I'll ring back." The line went dead.

I tucked the phone away, flooded with relief and anxiety in equal measures. Finn had someone, but where was David? Had he been taken, or just forgotten his ancient mobile? What to do now? I looked at my three potential candidates. They were all deep in conversation, well stocked with cake and tea. Another glance at my watch. I could make it over to St. Julien's and see if anyone there matched the description, then come back if not. I had time.

Outside I walked quickly around the corner and started up the hill towards the church. It was an old flint-studded thing and the location of the new churchyard, as the cemetery was no longer in use. Here the graves were modern slabs of granite and marble, still shiny as glass. Flowers, statues and toys brightened up the well-kept grass. I'd only been once before; to scatter Mum's ashes. She hadn't said where she wanted to go, or even if she wanted to be cremated. I'd had to decide. She had no other relatives that I knew of then, having not read her diaries. I doubted 'Aunt Jill' was still alive. If she was, I couldn't see her fighting me for Mum's remains. The ashes had come with us to Bricknell and I'd had to put them somewhere. I suppose she would have liked to be scattered at Wayfield's house, or outside the prison. I wasn't about to facilitate either.

The church annexe was invisible from the front, reached from a gravel path that snaked around behind the yew trees. A 1970s prefab with grey vinyl flooring and light green walls, it smelled of antiseptic and public toilets. My footsteps echoed but other than that there was dead silence. I paused when I got to the empty hall.

"Hello?" My voice bounced around but no one answered. The hall was deserted. Stacks of plastic chairs lined one wall and on the other metal climbing frames were folded flat to the plaster. My neck prickled. I'd double checked the date and time. There was even a poster about the coffee morning on the front door. Where was everyone?

"Oh!" Someone exclaimed behind me, followed by a crash.

I turned around and found a woman in her fifties standing there, one hand clutching her chest. On the floor several buckets rolled around.

"You startled me," she said, bending to pick the plastic buckets up.

"Sorry."

"Isn't there meant to be a coffee morning today?" I asked, checking my watch. Not much time.

"Oh, I thought Pam had put it on Facebook," she pulled an apologetic face. I noticed for the first time that she was wearing wellies with tights. Odd. Seeing my look she glanced down at the wet boots.

"We've had a bit of a leak through the church roof – stolen lead! Again! Would you believe? – anyway the electrics are completely scuppered. Can't turn a single light on, health and safety and all that. So we've had to cancel."

"Right," I said, already turning when my eyes fell on something across the hall. Half hidden by an ancient and very battered upright piano, was a wheeled trolley of books. I noticed a whole shelf of those distinctive pink and navy blue covers; Mills and Boon.

"It's on Facebook? That it's cancelled?" I asked.

"Yes…" she was looking at me strangely. "Sorry…you're not a regular are you?"

"No. I've got to go though, thank you."

I managed to walk to the door, then broke into a run. If one of the coffee mornings was unexpectedly cancelled we had potential victims loose and no idea where they might be. I pulled out my phone. Finn picked up on the second ring.

"Was it her?" I asked.

"She went to a coffee morning. I'm waiting there now – getting some funny looks, but if it is her I'm sticking around."

"Stay on her. Anything from the others? David check in?"

"David's texted, he's found two likely ones and he's keeping an eye on them. Nothing from Ricky yet. You?"

"Found out one of my meetings is off. Unexpected leak."

"Shit."

"Yeah, if she was coming here she could be anywhere now. But it's on Facebook. I might be able to find the people that said they were going."

"If she's even on Facebook. She might not be tech-savvy."

"That's why I said 'might'," I said, hurrying through the graveyard. "Hopefully it's your woman or one of David's, but I'm going to double back to the Salvation Army just in case, then go check online."

"Catch up later."

"Will do." I rang off and half-ran back to the first meeting. My three ladies were still there and I parked myself in a corner to watch them, wishing I still had my smartphone. Feeling impotent I could only wait and see. And hope.

CHAPTER TWENTY-SIX

After the coffee morning ended my three suspects took different routes. I had to choose between them and ended up freezing, not knowing who to go after. Thankfully two of them headed into a café on the high-street. They seemed to be friends. If they stayed together they'd be unlikely targets. I followed the lone woman until she rounded a corner and got into a waiting car. The woman inside looked like her daughter and gave her a warm greeting.

Satisfied that all three were out of danger and therefore not the killer's target, I hurried home. I didn't even bother taking my shoes off, just grabbed the laptop and searched for the St. Julien's page. At the top of their wall was the post about the coffee morning. Underneath were around fifty comments, one of which was from 'Pam Stokes' telling everyone about the leak.

Annoyingly it had been put on as a post rather than an event. There was no list of attendees. I went through the comments anyway but none appeared to be from anyone old enough to be in our target range. Mostly it was young and middle-aged mothers.

I checked my phone. Nothing from Finn or anyone else. What was happening out there? Not knowing was driving me crazy. I checked the local news sites and social media groups. No reports of a stabbing or any other kind of death. Had we stopped it? Or was it still too early for it to be online? I gnawed at the skin around my thumbnail, wishing someone would call.

If one of the others hadn't found the woman and prevented the attack, or sent her name to the killer, one of us was slated to die. Unable to sit still I got up and went to check the back door. It was locked. The windows that had been broken just after Halloween were secure. I went to the front door and locked it, then put the chain across. I still wasn't safe, I knew that. A gas leak, a fire, he could still get to me. My heart was drumming crazily, as if it was ready to go into arrest at any moment. Feeling sick I sat down and tried to breathe calmly, slowing my pulse. I had to stay alert.

When my phone did go it made me jump. It was David. I answered and could tell immediately from his tone that he'd struck out.

"Judith? It's me, David...I'm afraid I didn't find anyone. The two women I was following both got home without incident."

"Right...Finn said he had someone with a wicker trolley – has he called you?"

"No. I've not spoken to him since I sent a text over."

"And Ricky?"

"Texted to say he was 'surrounded' at his first meeting. There were so many women it could have been any of them."

"I know," I said. I had after all only had to cover one meeting in the end, and even then my list had been hard to narrow down. For the others, rushing all over town to multiple locations, it would have been impossible. Any number of women could have come and gone before they'd arrived at each location. Any one of them might have been the killer's target.

"Do you think we ought to have gone to the police?" David asked, reading my mind.

"If we had, one of us would be dead, in addition to Siobhan being in danger and one of us being on the chopping block for failing," I said, though there was no way of knowing what the killer would do, how the rules would be enforced. They changed them at will, toying with us.

"I'll wait for Finn to call," David was saying. "And Judith?"

"Yes?"

"Be sure to lock your doors. If we have failed..."

"He's going to come for us."

David was silent for a moment. "I hope Siobhan's alright. He won't be able to find her, will he?"

"I don't know...but, it's us in the shit right now. She knows she broke the rules. She can look out for herself. We need to focus."

"Tell me if you hear anything," David said, and rang off.

It was over an hour before Finn called. He sounded equally dejected. He'd followed his woman from the coffee morning to a luncheon club and then the supermarket. At that point she'd noticed him one too many times and had a security guard accost him. He'd lost her while trying to excuse himself. Worse, he hadn't heard from Ricky. I'd tried Ricky a few times myself and got no answer. He was either busy, or in trouble, and we had no idea where he'd ended up.

All I could do was sit tight and see what happened. One of us would be the one to pay. The sky outside had gone dark grey, the threatening gloom of rain slowly edging towards nightfall. I couldn't relax, didn't want to. In between refreshing the local news pages I made preparations. I balanced empty bottles on the back and front door handles to alert me to any movement. Lined more of them up with some empty jars on the windowsills of the boarded frames, in case anyone came climbing in.

As a last ditch precaution I took the big kitchen knife to bed. I still wasn't sure I'd actually be able to use it, but the threat of it might be enough to ward someone off with. I hoped.

Of course none of my precautions would help if the killer had already been in the house, a small voice whispered in my head. What if there was already some kind of sabotage in place to kill me? The boiler or the electrics? What if I went to sleep with my knife within reach and woke to a fire? Or didn't wake at all?

I found our kitchen fire blanket and put it by my bed. Then, feeling foolish, I put a bucket of water there too. The carbon monoxide alarm was already in the living room, but I checked to make sure it was working. Unease crawled over my skin.

When Ricky called, the sound made me jump. Trembling, I picked up the call.

"Alright," he said, sounding slightly slurred. "Take it you never found nothing?"

"Where are you?" I demanded. "Why didn't you call sooner?"

"Home. Didn't think I had to ring if I didn't see anything. And I didn't."

He'd been drinking, it was obvious. Though I couldn't blame him. I was moments from hitting the vodka myself. The whole day, the waiting, the search, had left my nerves frayed. I felt like I might cry or throw up at any moment.

"We couldn't find her either," I said quietly. Hating to admit that once again we had fucked up. Once again we were going to cost someone their life.

"Well then...one of us has had it. That's how it works right? One of us has to die now?"

"That's what he said. Have you locked up, got something to protect yourself with?"

"Not that there's much point...but yeah. I do. Might be our best chance you know, take him out when he comes for one of us."

I'd not considered it, having had tunnel vision on finding the victim, but he was right. If the killer was coming for one of us and we were ready, we might have a chance at stopping this. For good.

"Siobhan had the right idea," Ricky said, jolting me from my thoughts. "If it's not me, I'm going – tomorrow. You should too."

"I can't," I said, not sure if it was the thought of other innocent people dying, or my own warped need for closure that made me say it. Either way it was true. I couldn't leave Bricknell. Not now. My past was all I had left.

"Then I guess this is goodbye, either way," Ricky slurred. "Bye Jude."

"Bye Ricky."

He hung up and I was left alone, staring at the phone's tiny display until the light died. I went to the freezer, poured myself a double vodka and hunkered down in bed with the laptop.

Nothing left to do but wait.

*

I didn't sleep. It wasn't really a surprise. How could I when I expected an attack at any moment? Would it be me or one of the others? Which was better; escaping death or being free of the game we were all stuck playing?

I kept my phone close and even thought I heard it ring a few times. Once or twice I jumped, thinking I heard the sound of glass tinkling on the wooden floor. Each time I sat, straining my ears, but no sounds followed. The vodka had if anything made me even more tense, imagining noises and flinching at shadows.

I spent my time drafting and deleting emails to Adam. I poured out my history, the diaries, even the events since Marianna's murder. If I was going to die I wanted him to know the truth, at last. He deserved that. Even so, I couldn't get it right. In the end I gave up trying to explain myself, set the latest draft on delayed send for two days in the future and shut the laptop off. At least if I did die, he'd get some kind of closure.

It was dark outside. No sign of dawn yet. My watch confirmed that I was stuck in the interminable witching hour – it was almost one in the morning. This time of night belonged to insomniacs and serial killers. I squeezed my dry eyes shut for a moment. Exhaustion weighed on me almost as much as my guilt. Even the low light of the one lamp burned my eyes when I forced them open again.

Was one of my friends already dead?

The urge to call them was unbearable. We should have stayed together. It was stupid to be facing this alone. Still, our enemy had seemingly unlimited patience to stalk and strike at just the right moment. If he wanted one of us dead, we would be, eventually.

Where would the bodies turn up I wondered. The motorway was too far removed from Bricknell itself. Not to mention all the traffic cameras and constantly passing vehicles, not the safest place to leave one body, let alone three. The thought that I was waiting for three bodies to be found chilled me. One victim, one forfeit, and one who had broken the rules.

I hoped that Siobhan was hidden well. She'd taken a big risk. I thought of her husband and kids, caught in the crossfire. What had she told him? Anything at all? Did he just think they were away for a little break, or was her behaviour cluing him in that something sinister was going on?

My eyes started to droop again. I downed the last of one of Adam's energy drinks. I'd taken the gas canister out of the stove for safety and didn't dare put it back just for a coffee. The caffeine wasn't doing much to keep me awake, fear was doing that just fine, but it had shaved off the fuzzy edges of the vodka and made my heart race. I'd been stupid to start on the booze. Aside from how easily it could be tampered with, I needed my edge if the killer came for me.

Case in point, it took several long minutes for me to work out what was bothering me. It was needling away at the back of mind. Something I'd thought, or said, or seen. Some idea rolling around in my exhausted brain. A rule breaker, a forfeit, a victim...three bodies...

When the thought finally solidified I felt my whole body got stiff. Three bodies. In failing to find the old woman one of us was forfeit. The old woman herself was a victim and Siobhan had broken the rules. Rules that said she had to die. In total, three people had to die today. And if the killer was leaving his kills at Butcher specific locations, there was one place he could leave three bodies where it would have meaning. The place three of the Butcher's victims had ended up. Right at the bottom of my garden. The place where Wayfield had dug his corpse pit.

My breathing became shallow, panicked. Was he already coming for me? Certainly I was closest, most convenient. Did his mind work that way or was there some other logic he was following? Some other goal in mind? I picked up the knife and held the plastic handle so tightly that my fingers ached.

The time ticked on and I sat there, burning with the need to know but too afraid to move. But slowly, surely, my curiosity began to win over my fear. The idea that curiosity could kill a cat, much less an intelligent person, had always struck me as ridiculous. But at that moment, desperately wanting to run out in to a night that contained a serial killer, I could see how one might end up literally 'dying to know'. The sooner I checked, the sooner I saw, the sooner the nightmare could end. I would know, one way or the other, if I was going to be targeted.

It was like a mild out of body experience, watching myself unlock the back door. I'd not taken off the bulky coat or my boots on arriving home, but the night air still stung my cheeks and hands. I kept the knife in my grip as I locked the door behind me and stepped onto the grass. I felt it crackle like broken glass underfoot. Frost and mist hung about, smelling like sharp pines and eighty proof alcohol. Like Wayfield.

I had no torch, but walked in a straight line over the uneven ground. With every step I swivelled my eyes left and right, trying to force the shadows that leered from the fences to make sense. When my outstretched hand found the back fence and its clinging ivy, I took a deep, shaky breath. Nothing. I turned and looked back at the bungalow. Nothing there either. All was still and quiet.

I'd taken one step back towards the safety of home when I remembered the division of the garden. The actual pit site was behind me, over the fence, in a public carpark. My breath streamed up, white and whirling as I sighed. To get round there I'd have to go down the street, turn left and go all the way along. A fifteen minute walk there. My nerves couldn't take it. Looking along the fence I found the outline of the pile of rubbish we had yet to dispose of. I made my decision and tucked the knife into the waist of my jeans. Using both hands I pulled myself up onto the icy washing machine and hooked a leg over the fence.

Slithering down on the other side, I wiped my hands on my jeans. Looking around I found the carpark unsurprisingly deserted. There was however a large wheelie bin I could use to get back over, that was something. Several streetlights also helped me to feel more secure. Their bright, white light pushed the darkness back. It also reminded me that there were businesses and CCTV on that street. Although most were likely shuttered, there could still be a few pub customers around. I wasn't completely alone. At least, that's what I told myself. The frosty silence whispered otherwise.

I took a few steps and began a circuit of the carpark. It was split into two large rectangles on either side of a bit of grass and trees. The trees themselves had lights strung in them for Christmas. Underneath them the bushes were around knee height. Not impossible to hide in but you'd have to lie on the ground and stay very still. I kept my eye on them and didn't see any movement at all. No so much as a twig snapped. I didn't have the sense of being watched either.

When I completed a circuit of the carpark I stood by the fence and listened. Still nothing. The cold was starting to seep through the thick coat now. There was nothing there, time to give up and go back inside. Perhaps the killer had yet to take his victims, or he was going somewhere else with them. Perhaps he'd somehow been caught. I put one had on the frost-covered bin and prepared to climb up.

Almost as soon as I'd lifted myself up off the ground, a horrible shriek came from behind me. I turned so fast I nearly fell. A low, dark shape shot across the tarmac and under the trees. I let out a shocked laugh. A fox. A fox had almost scared me to death. Jesus. I needed to get hold of myself.

I was about to climb the bin again when the fox left the little thicket, this time carrying something in its jaws. I froze, staring and staring, waiting for the shape to make sense. To be anything other than what I told myself I could not be seeing; a human arm.

The fox, sensing me, dropped its ungainly load and ran for it, slithering out under the fence. I walked over as if in a trance, knelt and reached out, lightly touched the stiff, cold flesh. Under my fingers the light hairs and goose pimples rasped. On the middle finger was a ring I knew well; a blue stone with an insignia, a replica from one of her favourite shows. Siobhan's ring. Siobhan's arm.

The scream ripped out of me. It seemed to belong to someone else, though it was my breath streaming out with it, my throat tight and raw with horror. I snatched my hand back so quickly I overbalanced. Clawing my way to my feet I ran to the trees at the centre of the carpark, the place the fox had come from with the limb that now lay on the ground, beckoning at me. I had to look. It was a compulsion too strong to resist.

The plants were not bushes at all, they were reeds. Under the trees was a tiny pond, mirror still and dark. Half sunk in the shallow water were shapes, pale and fungal, disarticulated and strange.

Number twelve's wrinkled face glared up at me, her mouth full of mud.

I turned and stumbled away, retching onto the concrete.

CHAPTER TWENTY-SEVEN

Sitting at the table in the interview room for the second time in as many weeks, I felt the fight drain out of me. If I'd had any chance of escape the killer it was gone now. Without even intending to do it, I had royally fucked myself over. I was with the police – a violation of the rules. I was a dead woman.

It hadn't taken long for the police to show up. My scream must have been heard by the whole street. One good citizen had run to the phone and I'd been found in the dark, by another body. Bodies plural. In pieces.

This time the mood was different. Once was an unfortunate accident, and they still thought Katrine was a suicide. But finding four bodies in less than a fortnight? Three of them in chunks? Suspicion was thick in the air from the moment the blues and twos made their presence known. This time no one was rushing to comfort me, but they did shut me in the back of a police car.

I hadn't been arrested. That was something. I was however being interviewed under caution, albeit 'voluntarily'. As if I could have declined. I had however decided not to wait for a duty solicitor to be found. I wanted to get out of there as quickly as possible, in the hope that somehow I could escape the same reprisal Katrine had met for just sending an email. I knew that trying to tell them anything was a waste of time. The entire story was incredible, a wild fantasy, and I was not the one to tell it. I'd already shown myself to be hysterical, when the house was smashed up, and suspicious, in finding Katrine's body. No one was going to believe a word I had to say. Even if I told them the truth – which just flat out wasn't going to happen.

The interviewer was a woman in slightly mumsy clothes, accompanied by a balding man in an ill-fitting suit who didn't speak. I'd forgotten his name and rank as soon as he'd been introduced. Her name was DS Sutton. Sutton, like the prison.

"How did you come to be in the carpark so late?"

We'd gone at this three different ways already. My answers remained the same. "I climbed over the fence."

"Why?"

"I thought I saw someone run across my garden and over the fence. I thought they might be a burglar or something."

"And you decided to chase them?"

"I wasn't thinking properly. I'd had a drink and it seemed like the right thing to do, to try and catch them. Obviously I wouldn't normally chase a stranger alone at night," I said.

I'd chosen my story based on the facts I couldn't deny. There wouldn't be any CCTV of me walking around to the carpark the normal way. It would be obvious I'd come in over the fence. An imagined criminal however, they couldn't disprove – what I *thought* I'd seen wasn't up for debate. They could find it unbelievable but they couldn't outright prove I was lying. I was just grateful they hadn't found the knife. I'd had the presence of mind to fling it over the fence into my garden when I heard the sirens.

"And once you got over the fence?"

"I thought whoever it was might be hiding. I took a look around and decided they must have run off, or I'd seen a shadow or something. Then when I was climbing back, I heard a scream. It scared me, but then I realised it was a fox. It was going into the bushes – what I thought were bushes. Then it came out with the arm."

"The arm," she repeated, glancing at her notes. "You identified it as belonging to Siobhan Cotton, one of your friends?"

"Yes." My throat was dry. It'd been days since I'd slept properly and all I wanted was to lie down and let go of all the awful goings on of the past few weeks. But I had to stay alert. I couldn't lose the thread of my own lies, or I'd be done for.

"You told myself and DC Bailey at the scene that you recognised a head found in the pond – that it belonged to your neighbour at number twelve Julien's Crescent? Mrs Sybil Barker?"

"Yes, that's correct." I'd never known her name. Sybil Barker. The Butcher's neighbour. She'd been right there the whole time. Next door. She was connected to him, no matter how distantly. Perhaps, given enough time, we might have found an interview from her in the papers, a ten second spot on the news. Something. Too late now. Far too late to save her, or the others.

"The third body, Finley Shaw, another one of your friends?"

"Yes, Finn was a member of the same book club as Siobhan and me."

"The same club as Katrine Reynolds?"

"Yes."

"Do you see how that might look – you discovering the bodies of four people you know, three of them dismembered behind your back fence? And in such a short space of time? Would you like to comment on that?"

"Seeing as I'm the one that discovered them, it looks like someone's trying to frame me, or frighten me," I said.

DS Sutton shifted, cocking her head to the side. "And who might that be?"

Fuck, I'd slipped up. No conspiracy shit.

"I've no idea."

"Hmm…is it correct that you argued with Mrs Barker only a few days ago?"

How did they know about that? "We had a disagreement. It wasn't an actual fight."

"A 'disagreement' that led to her calling the local police station and making a complaint?"

"Not so serious that one of you lot came round to see me though, was it?" I pointed out, then immediately regretted it. I did not need to aggravate this situation any more than I already had. "It really wasn't anything. I just told her I was sick of her spying on us. She's been watching our house since we moved in. Looking over the fence. It was inappropriate."

"'Us' meaning you and your partner, Adam?" DS Sutton asked, checking her notes again. "He's mentioned in a report about vandalism at your property. Where is he now?"

"London. Visiting his parents."

"I see. And did he also feel harassed by Mrs Barker?"

"He thought she was being weird, yeah."

"Did either of you have any idea why she was acting in this way?"

Now was the time to decide. Tell a lie, a half-truth or admit to everything. She was good. I almost wanted to tell her. Almost.

"Adam thought she had a problem with us being together, living there. He...uh...he said he was having trouble with some racists at work."

I felt sick just saying it. How had I ever thought it was OK to let him believe that?

"Did you agree with Adam, about the reason for Mrs Barker's actions?"

My mouth was dry. "I don't know."

DS Sutton regarded me for a long moment. I tried my best to look suitably innocent and traumatised. It wasn't too far of a stretch. I felt traumatised, felt battered and bruised inside and out. I'd taken as much as any reasonable person could, and more since Marianna's death. I was exhausted.

"You've had a very fraught time of it lately, haven't you?" she finally said. "The vandalism, finding your friend Katrine's body, and now this. That's quite a lot of bad luck for one person."

"Some people are unlucky," I said, inanely. What else could I say?

"Some people make their own luck," DS Sutton sighed, closing her notebook. "Miss Broch, I'd like to be honest with you, as you've been so forthcoming with me."

Was that a dig? I looked closely but her face betrayed nothing. Perhaps she did really believe me. I was after all quite an accomplished liar. Even my name was a lie.

"Sure," I said.

"It seems that you believe, given the personal connection you had to the three people found dead by your home, you may be the target of someone's obsessive behaviour. That is certainly a possibility. One we'd like to look in to. If this act was, as you say, meant to frighten you, maybe even punish you, can you think of a reason why anyone would want to do that? Or of anyone you have reason to believe would be stalking you, and those around you?"

It took every ounce of hard won lying skill I had to meet her eye and shake my head.

"No...I have no idea."

DS Sutton nodded sagely, before getting to her feet. Her male shadow muttered to the tape recorder and then turned it off. DS Sutton opened the door and held it for me.

"Please make us aware of any strange occurrences, no matter how harmless they seem," she said, signalling that I was free to go. I almost tripped over my numb feet hurrying to the door. "A car will drive by your house to check up on you. Don't hesitate to contact the station if you feel under threat."

"I will," I said, already looking past her to the front desk.

"And Miss Broch? Please don't leave Bricknell without informing us of your whereabouts," she added, somewhat coolly. "We may have more questions for you once we have results back on the remains."

"I won't go anywhere," I said, then took my leave quickly. Whatever she was thinking, I wasn't in the clear yet. I'd have to be careful. As if being stalked by a murderer wasn't bad enough, now the police were on to me. How long before they connected the murders to the house, to the Butcher? How long before they started asking me how I'd come by the place, what my connection was to Wayfield? It would only take a search through my records or one DNA test to land me right in it.

Outside it was bright, the midmorning sun glancing off the windshields of several parked police cars. I'd been in the station for hours, waiting and answering the same questions over and over again. Plenty of time to decide what to do next.

Only Ricky, David and myself were left. Ricky had told me he was planning to run. I wondered if the police had contacted him about Siobhan yet? I'd given them the numbers of the remaining book club members, as well as Adam. If Ricky knew she'd been killed would he still try to get away? I hoped not. But then maybe he'd think himself cleverer than Siobhan. Able to escape.

I headed back to the bungalow. The first step in my plan was to delete the delayed email to Adam. Then I'd get hold of David and Ricky, fill them in on everything and invite them to stay with me. We had to stay together. It was our only chance. A united front. Between us we might catch the killer unawares when he came for us. Though Siobhan had been killed despite being with her family. How had our stalker managed that? Lured her away perhaps? Or waited until she was alone? The police hadn't said anything about her family being injured. That was something.

There was a police car outside number twelve when I got home. I guessed they were in there looking for evidence of how the killer managed to get to her. I had my own theory on that. Ten to one she was meant to be going to the St. Julien's coffee morning. It made sense. Then, that when it was cancelled the killer had to change tactic. They couldn't just stab her in the street, they had to get to her at home. How had I not made the connection? The net curtains, the carnations on the windowsill. Just like the email said. I saw them so often I'd become blind to them. He'd bet on that and won.

I put the key in my door, still cursing myself. Then I frowned. It was unlocked. I'd left out the back last night, thinking the house was locked up behind me. Had I accidently unlocked the front door instead of locking it? As I opened it I remembered the balanced bottle too late, flinching in expectation of a crash.

None came.

As I stepped onto the pebbles of broken glass I felt my heart hitch in my chest. Someone was already in my house.

CHAPTER TWENTY-EIGHT

I was frozen in the entryway for a long moment. Then I felt automatically for my mobile, remembering with a dart of frustration that for the second time my phone had been taken by the police. Shit.

Only two people had keys for the bungalow aside from myself; Adam and David. I'd left the key with David as a spare. He was the most reliable new friend I'd made, and we needed someone to have it. It wasn't like I could trust it to one of the neighbours. Had someone stolen it from him? My heart leapt; was Adam back?

Then I heard David's voice, coming from inside.

"For God's sake can you –" followed by a crash.

I strode down the hallway and found David and Ricky in the living room. The crash could have been any number of things; stuff was strewn everywhere. Books, CDs and the contents of the desk drawers littered the floor. Ricky was pawing through what looked like one of the boxes of Wayfield's stuff, scattering mouldy maps and cassette tapes. He and David both snapped to attention when I came in. David looked like a startled rabbit, Ricky like a dog about to go for the neck.

"What the fuck are you doing?" I said.

"Judith, I'm so sorry – he took the key from me. I couldn't stop him."

"Oh shut up," Ricky snapped. "Don't apologise to her, she's been lying to us."

Anger turned to fear in an instant. "What do you mean?"

"Don't 'what do you mean' me," Ricky sneered. He kicked aside a drift of old bank statements and picked up one of Mum's diaries from underneath, waving it at me. I'd stopped hiding them after Adam left, just left them out. Now I cursed myself for being so stupid. In his other hand was a letter with a familiar header, the solicitor's urgent message, left out on the desk.

"You know exactly what I mean. I knew you were hiding something, that you were too into the Butcher to be normal – now I know why."

As if he wasn't also 'into' the Butcher, into far worse killers. People who'd mown down whole nursery classes with an AK-47. But no, here he was pointing the finger at me. The full weight of my exhaustion hit me. I wanted to be angry, to fly at him, but I was so very tired. Bone tired; of keeping secrets, of failing to keep them. It was so hard and all of a sudden I just wanted to be done with it all. I didn't care. What was there to care about? Adam was gone, most of my new friends were dead, those left didn't trust me, and I was being investigated by the police. How much more could I lose? My life? Did I even want it anymore?

My lack of reaction only seemed to make Ricky angrier. "You're Wayfield's fucking daughter and you didn't think to mention that to any of us? When he's the one thing connecting us to a murderer?" Ricky shook the letter at me, David looked miserable and trapped beside him. "Your *Dad*, wants to see you. It's you isn't it? And this is why you've been doing all this. For *him*."

"It's not me!" I snapped, realising what was going through his mind too late. "Jesus! You know me! I was with you when we found out about Katrine. How could it possibly have been me?"

"You planned it. Kill Marianna, kill Katrine, then meet up with us and act all shocked when they're found," Ricky said triumphantly, having cornered me. "Who else could get close to Siobhan when she was so scared, get at Finn too – by knowing them. They let their guard down and you stuck the knife in, didn't you?!"

"That's insane," I shook my head. "I didn't do this. Any of this. I hate Wayfield more than anyone else. I would never kill for him. If anything I want him dead."

"I think we should all take a seat and try and calm down," David said, reaching for Ricky's shoulder as Ricky heaved in a breath and seemed ready to attack me again.

In response, Ricky whirled and shoved David away. Any hope I had of convincing him quickly drained away. Ricky stood there, breathing heavily for a second, before turning back to me, his face red. David stayed where he was, wide eyed and pale.

"You're the one that magically knew where Katrine was," he said, now sounding deathly calm. "You're the one living in the Butcher's house, obsessed with him, just like this killer is meant to be. You're the one who was in Bricknell all yesterday while we were off running around like blue arsed flies. And you're the one," he shook the letter again, "that's been lying to us, about your *dad*."

"Ricky..." I began, trying to keep my voice level. "I have lied, and I'm sorry. My mum was slated for revealing who she was, I was just trying to protect myself. And as for Wayfield. He's not anything to me. If I could wipe him off the face of the earth, I would. I certainly wouldn't kill for him, or for his memory or anything like that. I am just as scared and confused as you are by everything that's been going on."

Ricky shook his head. "You're lying. You knew Siobhan was running, your fucking neighbour is the one that's been killed, why else would she be a target?"

"She knew him though! She knew the Butcher from before. That was the connection. I didn't even think about it before I found her body."

"I don't believe you. And the police won't either once I tell them everything," he waved towards me. "David, get that gaffer tape and tie her up."

"What?" David blurted.

"Tie her up, so she can't try anything before the police get here."

"I don't think that's really necessary," David said. "Judith, you're not going to do anything are you, if this is a misunderstanding?"

I shook my head quickly. "No. I'm not going to do anything. Because it's not me doing this."

"For fuck's sake, David! Tape her up, or are you with her?" Ricky snapped.

"Richard, I think you're being a little bit extreme," David said, "I hardly think Judith is capable of –" he was cut off when Ricky's fist hit him square on the jaw.

For a moment it seemed as though he'd shake it off, continue his teacher-esque sermon, then he keeled over. David hit the floor hard, lip split and bleeding. I waited for him to move or get up, but he didn't. He was out cold. I turned to Ricky, speechless. He too looked in shock at what he'd done.

For a moment neither of us moved, then Ricky leapt at me and I turned and ran for the hall. I got maybe three steps before his full weight hit me in the back and we both went sprawling to the floor. I felt a horrible grinding in my wrist as I landed on it, the full weight of both of us sending white hot pain through my whole arm. I twisted and kicked out, throwing elbows and trying to shake him off, but Ricky was bigger and stronger. Pinning me down he managed to pull the belt dangling from Adam's parka and tied my wrists together, making me yelp in pain as the bones grated again.

After he got to his feet, Ricky dragged me up and knotted the ends of the belt around one of the radiator pipes that ran up the wall. Then he stood there, catching his breath as I struggled, electric shocks of pain radiating from my wrist. I was fairly sure it was fractured, if not broken.

"Ricky, I haven't done anything wrong. I haven't killed anyone," I hissed, tears of pain rising in my eyes. "This is nuts. Can't you see that?"

"If it's not you, who is it, huh?" Ricky said. "Who else is as mad about the Butcher as you?"

"I don't know," I snapped. "If I knew who it was I'd have told the police. I don't want to die, Ricky. I didn't want any of us to die, and if I could have stopped it I would have. I don't want you to get hurt now either, and that's what's going to happen if you break the rules and tell the police all this. We are all going to get it."

I was thinking of the police car outside, trying to see past him and through the window. Was it still there? Would they hear me if I screamed? Would it be worth it, outing myself as Julie Pike just to get away from Ricky? What if this was an act? If he was the one behind all this? I couldn't think straight anymore.

More than anything, I cursed DS Sutton for confiscating my mobile as evidence. If I'd had it on me I could have called for help the moment I saw my door had been unlocked. None of this would have happened if I just had my phone.

"I really liked her, you know?" Ricky said, voice cracking. "Katrine was...she was so funny, and really she got me, you know? I always thought I ought to ask her out, but she was too smart for me ..." he swallowed. "Too good for me."

I held my breath, afraid to say anything that might upset him further. He'd already knocked David out just for questioning him. What would he do to me now he was convinced I was a murderer? I spared a glance in David's direction. His eyelids flickered, forehead creasing. I tensed, willing him to wake up and get behind Ricky, do something to subdue him.

"She never would have killed herself," Ricky said.

"I told the police that," I said, stalling. "I told them that the note was just one of her poems. We know she didn't kill herself."

Ricky nodded. I took a breath and caught a whiff of beer on my clothes. Was he still pissed from last night? Looking at him I noticed the puffiness in his face, his red eyes. I'd assumed he was sleep deprived, but no, he was drunk. Or at least, not entirely sober. Ignoring the roar of pain that went through my wrist I started to wriggle my hands, trying to get free. The belt wasn't well made, I could feel the cheap fabric stretching as I pulled.

"The police didn't believe me," Rick was saying, wiping his nose on his sleeve. He looked like a beery, overgrown schoolboy.

The belt gave a millimetre. The buckle end clanged on the heating pipe and I went still, but Ricky didn't seem to notice. Just a little more. I pulled my wrists apart, biting my lip to keep from crying out in pain.

"It has to be you," Ricky said, focusing on me again. "Don't you see? There's no one else. We're running out of time. Just us three left now and...just admit it. Admit what you did!"

Stitching snapped and I threw myself at him, catching him off guard and knocking him back. He tripped on the loose CDs and fell. This time I had the advantage of being on top. I acted on base instincts, grabbing his hair and knocking his head on the floor, once, twice. My wrist bones grinding in protest. He wasn't unconscious, but the hit to the head, combined with the alcohol, seemed to have him stunned.

I grabbed the gaffer tape. Before he had time to regain his senses I'd taped his wrists and ankles, ripping the role free with my teeth. He managed to kick me with his joined feet, sending me sprawling. But it was too late. I'd won. He was helpless, like a turtle on its back. I pulled off a final piece of tape and stuck it over his mouth as he snapped at my hand, accusations frothing on his tongue.

"I'm sorry, but I can't let you go to the police," I said. "I'm not responsible for what's happening, but I need to find who is. I can't do that if I'm locked up for trying to keep my secret. And I won't let you risk your life on this, I'm sorry."

Ricky's eyes widened, the whites showing all the way around. I had a second to wonder why, before something heavy made contact with the back of my skull.

CHAPTER TWENTY-NINE

When I opened my eyes, colours swam and spiralled in front of me, light and dark flecks spinning together like snowflakes. I struggled to steady my mind against the concussion that was probably already in full force. It took me a moment to realise that I'd been blindfolded.

Blinking against the soft fabric over my eyes, I tried to sit up and cracked my head on something hard.

Pressing my cheek to the carpeted floor I heard the rumble of tyres and the hiss of puddles splashing. The roar and cough of other engines. I was in the boot of a car. Blindfolded.

I tried to wriggle my way into a more upright position, but my wrist sent such a spike of agony through me that I quickly gave up. My hands were taped behind me and I could feel the pressure in my swollen wrist. My legs were free but there was tape over my mouth. Breathing through my nose was making me lightheaded. I tried to twist my mouth and jaw to loosen the tape but it was stuck tight.

What had happened? I remembered Ricky knocking David out, me subduing Ricky in turn. Then...my head throbbed, someone had hit me with a bottle, or something else hard that had sprayed broken glass over me. Even now I could feel sharp bits of it in the collar of my coat, slipping down my back like bits of ice. Someone knocked me out and put me in the boot of a car.

I couldn't force the jagged bits of memory together in a way that made sense. Ricky had been suspicious, violent, but I'd been looking at him when I was hit from behind. David was the one I had my back to. But David was only there to stop Ricky smashing the place up? He'd tried to talk him down. It didn't make sense that David was the one who'd been after us, stalking us. That he was the one who'd killed our friends and sent those insane messages.

David was the father figure of our weird club. Old and soft and worn out like the knees of his cord trousers. A fusty former teacher, collecting his Jack the Ripper library with care. The only one who could get Ricky to behave, who could get Siobhan off her phone. Who always asked how I was and who was the only one so terminally polite as to use my full name.

My thoughts stuttered to a stop. My full name.

In my head I was back by the canal, rain falling, blinding me. Katrine's body in the water like a strange, pale, fish. The wet screen of my phone showing a last taunt from her killer; 'She broke the rules, Judith'.

David and the killer had something in common. I felt my insides go cold. More than one thing. In that moment I saw it all. David, with his Ripper fascination. Jack the Ripper, most famous British serial killer, who had never been caught. The Ripper, who had sent messages to the police, taunting them. The famous 'From Hell' letters. The emails from our stalker. The way the killer had called me by my full name. David's disappearance during our search for the latest victim.

How he'd insisted I take the box of Marianna's books, with the Howard Stepp one inside. He'd been the one to bring up Evelyn Scott, the cemetery attack, prompting me to link it to Lara Preston.

David had knocked me out, put me in his car and was taking me somewhere. Panic seized me. What was going to happen to me? Where were we? Was Ricky already dead? Had David planned this, egged Ricky on? I fought to regain control of my breathing. I had to try and get free. That was my only chance. Get free and be ready when the boot opened. Surprise him and get away.

Bracing myself for the pain, I moved my wrists experimentally. The tape was tight, so tight that my fingertips were going numb. There was no wriggling out of it. I felt around but there were no handy pieces of jagged metal to try and cut it off with. Nothing at all except rough carpet and the smooth plastic lip of the boot hatch. As I shifted my butt to feel underneath I felt glass shards slither around under the coat. Sharp glass.

I lost track of time as I shifted and wriggled my shoulders, trying to get the glass to fall out onto the floor. The first few bits were tiny, seed like, and when I felt for them I couldn't find them on the rough carpet. They cut my fingers well enough though. The larger pieces made maddeningly slow progress. I bucked and shook, scared that they would get caught in my jumper and stick there. Then, finally, a sliver of glass the size of a scrabble tile dropped onto the carpet. I snatched it up, cutting my fingers again, then twisted it around to get the sharpest point against the tape. Slippery with blood, it was hard to keep hold of.

The sudden rush of icy air made me cry out against the tape on my lips. I'd not realised the car had stopped, but it had. Now the boot had been thrown open. I curled my numb fingers around the slick glass and hoped it was hidden. David grabbed me, pulling me to the lip of the boot and rolling me out of the car. I fell onto the ground. It was muddy, soft. I'd expected the road or pavement. Where were we?

Hands hauled at me and I struggled to my feet. I was almost panicked enough to run, blind as I was, when something sharp was pressed under my chin. A knife, colder than the wind. The message was clear. Don't try anything. A hand on my shoulder turned me around, then pushed the small of my back. The tip of the knife poking my shoulder.

With David behind me I couldn't cut at the tape. I had to wait. How long I'd have when the moment came I had no idea. So I walked as I was told, over the muddy, uneven ground. It was only when I heard the sighing of trees and the creak of branches that I realised where we were; St. Julien's wood. The Butcher's hide out. Last stop on the killer's tour of Bricknell. This was his end game all along.

I shivered, wondering how long he'd been planning this. Had it always been a lie? His friendship, his interest in crime. Laughing at us all along? Hating us, waiting to strike. Was this why he'd started the group, recruiting first Finn, then Ricky, letting them bring others in? Why was he doing it? I thought of his near religious devotion to the Ripper's lore. The most famous killer the UK had to offer. Was this his attempt to replace him in history? Surpass even the Ripper's fame?

Walking in complete darkness with no idea where I was going, or what was about to happen to me, was the single most terrifying thing I'd ever experienced. My mind was consumed with the knowledge that I wasn't going to leave the woods alive. He had brought me there to kill me. Could I reason with him, trick him somehow? Was he too far gone even for that? My heart was like a hot coal blocking my throat. I couldn't breathe for panic.

Adrenaline kept me going. Despite my exhaustion, the freezing air that I could only breathe in through my nose, the cramp in my legs, the throbbing of my wrist, I kept walking. Every time I slowed even for a moment the knife point was pressed between my shoulder blades. It had cut through the coat already and I felt it draw a bead of blood each time he prodded me with it. The cloth over my eyes was wet with tears, the trails on my cheeks and under my nose freezing and burning with cold.

I began to think we'd walk forever. Then he grabbed my shoulder and pulled me to a sharp stop. Fresh terror burst in my veins. As long as we were walking I had time to think. Now that time had run out. We were at our destination and I had no idea what he might do next. What he had in store for me, but I knew I wouldn't survive it. I'd walked to my death.

My legs were kicked out from under me and I fell, hard. I felt the leaf litter under my cheek, sharp with frost. We were still in the woods. A fox's lone bark sounded in the distance and I shivered, afraid to move. Footsteps moved away from me. I heard a metallic rattling, then the splashing of liquid on the ground. The night breeze carried a sharp smell to me; petrol.

He was going to burn me alive.

I forgot everything, any hope of escape, any thought for Adam, Ricky or the others who'd already met their ends. I was blindly, primitively, terrified. All I could see was my own agonising death ahead of me. All logic and thought fled, leaving me like a rabbit in a trap. I gulped sobs against the tape and wriggled helplessly on the ground.

Then the glass cut my fingers, and the pain sharpened my mind.

I had to do it now. Cut the tape, get away. This was my one chance.

Holding the glass in my numb fingers I scratched blindly at the tape. It was thick, the adhesive strong. The glass shard was slick with blood and I couldn't stop shaking. I tried to block out the sounds of petrol being poured, heavy footsteps. The tape gave a little as I managed to cut into it. My hands moved a little further apart. The glass slipped and nicked my swollen wrist. I yelped against the tape but kept going.

A little more and I could move my hands, free them. I could remove the blindfold and see to run away. It wasn't much; David still had a knife and whatever else he'd brought, but it was as fair a fight as I could hope for. No matter how sadistic and calculating he was, he was still an old man. I had a chance against him even if he had a knife.

When David grabbed my shoulders I screamed. It came out wet and garbled against the tape. I was hauled upright and pushed back against a tree. The chunk of glass shook free of my grip and fell amongst the leaves. Lost. All hope lost.

I twisted my wrists, ignoring the pain. Half the tape holding them together was cut through, the rest clung stubbornly. I pulled them apart, trying to rip them free. My injured wrist screamed with such pain that I thought I was going to be sick. Blood flooded my mouth as I bit my tongue. White spots danced before my eyes in the darkness of the blindfold.

Then a hand ripped the tape from my mouth. I let out a cry; half the skin on my lips and face went with it, leaving behind raw patches that burned in the cold. Before I could begin to plead with him, the blindfold was torn off and a blinding light shone in my face.

I coughed, bloody spittle running down my chin. Squinting I sucked down a lungful of air, thoughts clearing. A shadow moved away from me and retreated into the dark. He had a torch, a bright beam that cut between the trees. Other lights danced behind him. Flames. As my night vision returned I saw the red plastic petrol can on the ground. It was on its side, empty. The stink of it was everywhere.

I twisted, spat onto the ground and gagged on the smell of fuel and coppery blood. This was it. My last moments on earth. Despite my fear I felt strangely calm underneath, as if, deep inside, I'd always known this was coming. With my parentage I'd been fated to turn murderer or victim. It was destiny, and I'd tripped right along as intended. Following the path laid for me.

"Hello Julie," said a soft voice, so unexpected it made me freeze in place, all thoughts of my parents forgotten. I squinted into the darkness, finding the shadow where it sat on a stump. I swallowed a metallic mouthful of my own blood.

"Marianna?"

CHAPTER THIRTY

For a long moment we only stared at each other. In the shadow of the woods, sitting on a stump and lit only by the candles on our makeshift memorial shrine, she looked like a faerie. There was something about her that didn't look quite real. For a wild moment I thought she might even be a ghost.

Then she laughed, a sharp, cruel sound, and I was back in reality. In one gloved hand she held a lighter, in the other, a long kitchen knife. My knife, from beside my bed.

"Go on then," she said, impatience clear in her cultured voice. "Ask me."

"What?" My mind was struggling to catch up with everything I was seeing. She looked put out. Like I was a particularly stupid pupil and she was my long suffering teacher.

"How I did it? Why I did it? Come on Julie, this is what you've always wanted, isn't it? You and the others? To get as close to the story, the action as possible. Well," she waved the knife to indicate the clearing, "this is as close as you can get. The cutting edge of true crime. So ask me. Interrogate me."

She sat there, watching me, as poised and unaffected as a cat watching a mouse come and go, waiting to pounce. I swallowed, wetted my raw lips.

"You didn't die in the gas leak."

She laughed. "Oh dear, I hit you quite hard, didn't I? Yes, Julie, obviously I did not die in a gas leak. That was the easiest thing actually. You'd think faking one's own death would be difficult, but if you're only trying to fool a handful of self-absorbed idiots, it's quite easy. They'll believe anything you tell them, because they only care about themselves."

I struggled to understand, mind working with no fuel other than fear. "We all heard it from David, and he got it from Diana...she was lying."

"There you go, warming up. Diana's not her name of course. She's just some homeless junkie who looked like she could be my sister, sort of," Marianna wrinkled her nose in distaste. "If I got the good genes and she spent five years living in a mine. I did try to clean her up but, well, it worked, didn't it? Anyway, I paid her to drop the bombshell on David and meet with you – spin you a line that I was being cremated."

The image of Adam and 'Diana' arguing in town came back to me. I already knew he hadn't lied for any other reason than to surprise me when he proposed. Was it just a coincidence that he'd stumbled upon Diana? A homeless woman, maybe harassing him for change, or drunk and spoiling for an argument?

"It's quite easy to follow people when they think you're dead," Marianna said conversationally. "A wig helps. And of course you kept using the group chat, keeping me updated on everything. So considerate of you. I hadn't even planned for that. But it certainly helped."

I felt sick. She'd been watching us react to her own death, the random email. Watching as we freaked out, as we discussed Katrine going to the police. She'd been keeping an eye on all of us.

"I couldn't bank on which of you would break my rules though, had to change a few things along the way. Improvise. I think it was kind of a masterstroke, luring Katrine to the canal by spoofing your number. Catching her unawares. Siobhan made things a little tricky by running off but I knew she'd do anything to save her kids. Even put herself in harm's way if it meant I left them alone. It was all going well until Ricky had to go and fuck everything up." She sighed as if greatly put-upon. "Honestly, one more round and I'd have had all of you up here. I planned it. You and whoever was left. Then I'd kill them, and save you for last. Only Ricky had to get ideas in his head and go after you. If I hadn't been following him and David he might have robbed me of you entirely. But here you are – the Butcher's daughter. The best and the last."

"What've you done with them?"

"Oh, they'll be gone shortly," she said airily, waving the knife. "I thought I'd make it a fire as well, so you could all go the same way. And your place was quite a tinderbox, all those magazines and papers. I left a candle burning, bit of petrol to be sure things go with a bang."

"Why are you doing this?" I asked. "They were your friends, you–"

In two seconds she had crossed the clearing and slapped me across the face. The cut in my lip re-opened and the lighter in her palm scratched my cheek.

"We were not friends," she hissed. "I always knew what you were, all of you. Vultures. Ghouls. A sick little cult." She pressed the tip of the knife under my chin, against my fluttering pulse. "I always knew who you were, Julie."

I stared at her, afraid to say anything, to ask the question burning my tongue. But she answered it just the same.

"Of course it wasn't until I let myself in to your place and found the diaries that I found out your name. Your real name. My Mum kept a scrapbook on the Butcher of Bricknell too. She had it all. All the newspaper articles, the photographs."

"Your Mum was obsessed with the Butcher?"

"Not in the way you are. Your mother was. I think she just wanted to understand the man that took her daughter away."

I felt a shiver pass through me. That was what this was about. Marianna had lost someone to the Butcher. To my father.

"That's where I got the picture from, her collection. Did you like that picture? It's a good one, isn't it? Easy to see the likeness between you and your mother. Though it was still quite a shock the first time I saw you in the flesh. I honestly couldn't believe my luck. There you were, the perfect final piece." She clicked her tongue. "I'd already met the others, from a distance. I go to the cemetery quite often. One of the reasons I've stayed close to Bricknell over the years. And who should I find there one day, David and his motley gang of ghouls? Taking pictures of Pippa Grey's grave." She came alarming close then, pressing the point of the knife under my jaw. "Her grave! Like she was a tourist attraction, or a wax dummy in a museum. Taking pictures of the place her parents buried their only child."

"So you decided to kill them?"

"Well, they were no better than the killers themselves. Taking pleasure in other people's suffering," she sniffed. "Besides...I had to do it. For my sister."

"I don't understand. Why kill them, us, because of what Wayfield did?"

"Because you don't care," she said, pressing the knife harder. I felt it break the skin. "You barely talk about the women he killed – Pippa Grey, Emma Diggory, Katie McCleod, Georgina Franklyn. My sister." She punctuated the last words with two jabs of the knife. "How often have you said their names? Not just 'the victim' 'the canal body' 'the dismembered corpse'? She doesn't even get that! No one cares who killed her. Why is it that you know everything about him, about all the sick fucks like him; collect their pictures, their headlines – but the people they killed are just meat to you?"

I swallowed. Madness sparkled in her eyes, her teeth white and sharp, bared as she ranted. Yet she was right, in a way. We knew their names, the killers both famous and less renowned; John Wayne Gacy, Ted Bundy, Jeffrey Dahmer, Richard Ramirez, the Wests. How many people would recognise the names of those they'd killed? Janice Ann Ott, John Butkovich, Mei Leung? Their names were not on book covers or Netflix menus. They were played by unknowns while Hollywood actors scored the parts of their killers. They were remembered by only a few, their families and friends, while their murderers commanded legions of fans from jail cells.

Marianna wasn't right about us though, she wasn't right about me. I knew the names of Wayfield's victims, not only those that had died, but those that had lived. Carol Marks, Joyce Everett, Phillipa Dent, Marcy Crosby...every assault, even the ones he had never been charged with. The ones where the only link was a route he may or may not have taken in his lorry. I'd made it my mission to know, to torture myself with that knowledge. To add fuel to the fire that burned in me; my hatred for the man who had cast a long shadow over my life.

"He beat her and left her for dead in that cemetery," Marianna said, voice cold and monotone. "They said it was lucky someone found her before she choked to death on her own blood. But it wasn't lucky. They had her in hospital for months before they told us she'd never wake up. That her brain had bled and swollen and she was basically dead already. They were just keeping her warm. Only by then no one cared about some girl getting beaten up in a cemetery. It was all about him. The Butcher. The manhunt. The pit of bodies. No one even mentioned her name, but we knew it was him that did that to her. No one would listen. They had the only victims they cared about, and she could rot."

"He was never charged for her death," I said, beginning to understand. "She wasn't part of his story."

"Not charged, not even considered," she spat. "Police tried to pin it on some secret boyfriend she was out meeting. Basically called her a stupid slut to my Mum's face. I heard the way they talked about my big sister. Saw what it did to my Mum. The drinking, then the drugs. She never got her answers. It's still unsolved. Never going to be solved. And not one of the pathetic parasites clinging to the Butcher's legend could bring themselves to even say her name."

The podcaster, the writer, the neighbour. None of them had included Marianna's sister in their stories, and so they had been punished. Our group had chased his myth, giving him attention, remembered him, so we had to be punished too. It made sense in a warped way. Almost.

"Why are you doing this if you know how much it hurts? Killing people who knew about him, putting their bodies in places he made famous...that's just adding to his notoriety."

"Because he took my sister, and my Mum, and now I'm taking you away from him. This is the only way people will care about me, about my sister and what happened to us," Marianna hissed. "Everyone will know my name now, and they'll forget his. When I tell my story people will listen. They'll write it down in their little books and talk about it on their podcasts and everyone will know about Evelyn Scott and her sister, Marianna – the real Butcher of Bricknell."

I saw the shutters come down in her eyes and knew this was the moment. She was going to drag me to the hide which stood in shadow behind her. Lay me there, in Wayfield's hiding place and set the whole thing ablaze. Already I could imagine the flames eating through my clothes, melting them onto my skin. The fire devouring my hair, roasting my eyes and warping my flesh. I had to do something, distract her, escape. Anything. Even being stabbed as I tried to run would be better than burning alive.

"I can help you."

The words leapt out of my mouth, leaving my brain to catch up. Marianna cocked her head, dark hair falling from her face in a wave.

"How the fuck, do you think you can help me?"

"I can give him to you – Wayfield. I can help you kill him."

My words hung between us, spelled out in wintery white breath. I eased my wrists behind me, pulling slowly, trying to rip the tape further. I didn't dare look away from Marianna's face, from the calculations going on behind her eyes. Finally she poked me with the knife again, eyes narrowed.

"And why would I want him?"

"Because then you'd be the person who avenged her sister. You wouldn't just be a better killer...you'd be a hero. If you kill me, he won't care. He doesn't love me. He can't love anyone other than himself. If you kill him, you'll be an inspiration to everyone who's ever lost someone to a monster like him. They'd remember you long after someone else committed a new crime, because you'd be special."

Another long, charged silence. I gritted my teeth against the pain and pulled more firmly against the tape, trying to part my wrists. I could run with them still tied if I had to, but would stand a much better chance with both hands free. If I fell or had to fight, I'd be fucked.

"How can you give him to me?"

I had her. I just had to keep her calm, reel her in. I had to do what I'd been doing all my life; lie.

"There's going to be a hearing. A special hearing. He's served nearly thirty years of his life sentence, and now he's ill, very ill. It's why he signed the house over, trying to get me to see him before it's too late. He wants see me after he gets transferred to a hospice...you could go, in my place."

I watched the idea enter her mind, take root there. I hardly dared breathe, just kept pulling against the tape, ignoring the pain. Now or never Julie.

"I could kill him," Marianna said, slowly, as if tasting the possibility in the words. "Kill Raymond Wayfield."

I nodded, afraid to speak in case it burst the fantasy she was creating for herself. The tape pulled wider, almost there.

Then the knife was back, pressing into my throat.

"You're full of shit," Marianna snarled. "If they were even thinking of letting him out it'd be in the papers – you guys would have known, talked about it. It'd be a wet dream for you all – the Butcher, free at last."

"Well," I said, feeling the last fibres of tape pull apart as the knife poked me and blood ran down my neck. "It was worth a try."

In the split second that confusion registered on her face, I brought my arm up and knocked the knife away. My bloodless limbs were awkward, the blow mistimed. The knife dragged along my arm, piercing the plush coat and my flesh in a jagged sewing-machine line. In and out. Pain flared and I screamed, the sound mingling with Marianna's cry of rage.

Ducking away I stumbled to my feet and ran. She tackled me as I passed the hide, flinging me against the wooden wall. The acrid smell of petrol rose up. I heard her flailing with the knife, catching it on the planks, screaming like a fury.

I kicked out, forcing her back. Twisting away I saw the blade flash past, narrowly missing me. It bit into the wood and she pulled it back with a shriek. Again I tried to make a break for the woods but she slammed into me, driving me sideways. I fell to the ground in the hide, sprawled on petrol soaked leaves.

Marianna stood in the doorway, the silver rectangle of the lighter in one hand.

From her coat pocket she pulled out a small bottle of lighter fluid. Without looking away she pulled the cap off with her teeth and poured it over herself. I just lay there, the pain in my arm and wrist receding in the wake of my horror. She was really going to do this. One look at her face told me all I needed to know – if she had to, she would burn us both. The patience, the methodical effort she'd put into stalking us, that was not in play right now. She was just like me; a cornered animal ready to do anything.

"Are you ready?" she asked, breathlessly, reaching her hand towards the wooden walls, glistening with fuel. "Shall we do it?"

"Don't!" I shouted, pointlessly. I cast about for any idea, any thought that might save me. "You won't be able to tell anyone about your sister!"

"I've written it all down, even made a nice little video for them to show on the news," she laughed, a genuinely delighted laugh. "It was you lot that gave me the idea - books, podcasts, telly. I've left something for everyone."

While she'd been speaking I'd pulled my feet in. As she clicked the lighter and a torrent of flame leapt up the doorframe, I ran at her.

She let out a great howl of rage as our bodies collided. The force of my tackle brought us down a foot or so from the entrance to the hide. Marianna's coat was burning, bright yellow flames turning dark blueish green as they devoured the material she'd drenched in lighter fuel. I felt the fire catch my jeans, racing up my leg where the petrol had soaked in.

While she raged and struggled I grabbed handfuls of wet leaves and dirt, smothering the flames on her. I kicked my legs on the ground, rolling them as I crawled away from the fire, dragging Marianna with me as she screamed and clawed at my face. I rammed my forehead into hers to keep her from gouging at my eyes, then staggered to my feet.

Stumbling away from her dazed form, I found the knife in the light from the fire. The whole hide was now ablaze, flames crackling greedily through the petrol and into the worm-eaten wood below. Smoke belched up through the trees as the damp wood sizzled. I turned my back to it, pinning Marianna down with one knee on either side of her. She looked up at me, glittering sloe eyes over a bloody nose.

"Do it then," she spat. "Kill me."

"I'm not going to kill you," I panted.

"Afraid you'll enjoy it?" she grinned, teeth bloody. "Afraid you'll find out that after all this time, you're Daddy's little girl?"

I said nothing. It was true. I was afraid. Not just of what would happen if she got free, but of how it would feel to drive the knife into her throat, end her life. Even if it was in self-defence, even if she deserved it for killing all those people…I was scared that in that moment I would feel whatever it was that made my father a monster. The joy of killing.

But if I let her up, did nothing, wasn't I just like my mother? Naïvely placing my trust in the hands of a maniac?

Marianna began to laugh, a long, gurgling laugh. I felt the hairs all over my body lift as the sound went right through me. It was a crazed sound. Unnatural. Overhead an owl screamed in dismay.

"What's funny?" I said, at last, afraid she was going to keep going until she choked.

"My phone, is over there," she jerked her head towards the little shrine we'd set up for her. For poor, murdered Marianna. Our friend. "If you want to call for help, you have to let me up, or kill me. And if you won't kill me, I'm going to kill you." She laughed again, though it sounded more like sobbing. "You can't run either – I'd catch you," she said in a singsong voice.

I swallowed, looking at the shrine. She was right. I had to get up if I wanted to get the phone and call the police. Once I did, Marianna could get to her feet and attack me again. We were evenly matched, but I was injured and had only narrowly managed to best her. If we struggled again she might well overpower me. Then I'd be dead, for sure.

"What's it going to be Julie? Are you a murderer, or a victim?" Marianna said, through the blood trickling over her lips. "Are you Daddy's little monster, or Mummy's little fool?"

My hand tightened around the knife handle. I was fairly sure one of my fingers was broken. I hadn't even felt it happen. Adrenaline was still pumping through me, blotting out the pain. I felt almost unreal, invincible in that moment. The fire on my back, my heart a battering ram in my chest. Was this how he'd felt, every time he'd taken a life? Was this how my mother had felt, flinging caution to the wind, ready to follow him anywhere?

"I'm not a killer," I said, bringing the knife down. Marianna shrieked as it went through her shoulder, into the soft earth beneath. Pinning her down.

Her eyes widened as I pulled back my arm and clenched a fist.

"But I'm not a fool, either."

The punch connected with her nose and I felt her go limp.

Staggering a little, I made my way to the shrine and scooped up the phone. It was a relief to see that it had a bar of signal. I dialled and waited for the line to connect, listening to the roar of the fire.

*

I was not as surprised to see DS Sutton as she was to see me. Even without the pain slowly impinging on my adrenaline soaked brain, the look on her face as she entered the clearing, made me realise how battered and beaten I must look. DS Sutton arrived in the last of three parties of police. Most of the others were trying to cordon off the smouldering hide.

An ambulance crew had already arrived and dressed my wounds. They were loading Marianna onto a stretcher to get her down to the carpark. She was still unconscious but handcuffed and escorted by two police officers. I watched them go, feeling exhaustion starting to claim me. I was starting to shake uncontrollably. I hadn't slept properly in so long. Unless you counted being knocked unconscious, which I personally didn't.

"Miss Broch," DS Sutton said, coming to a stop where I sat on the tree stump that had once been a memorial, a blanket around me. "You've had quite the time of it, haven't you?"

"It has been an unusual night," I said. I wasn't sure what was going on with me. I felt...light. Despite of or because of my tiredness, a bubbly state of glee was overtaking me. The relief of being surrounded by high-vis jackets and witnesses almost intoxicating.

Of course the painkillers might have also had something to do with it. God bless the paramedics.

Sutton removed a packet of cigarettes from her pocket and offered me one. I shook my head, I'd inhaled enough smoke for the time being. She shrugged and lit up.

"You'll be pleased to know we've been round to your bungalow and found your friends."

"Are they OK?" I'd had to insist to the operator several times that I wasn't drunk, or joking. I had actually apprehended a serial killer, and there were two unconscious men in my house, who were about to burn to death.

"They're a bit shaken but aside from concussion there's nothing wrong with them. The fire never got a chance to start." Sutton said. "One of them corroborated your story – says he saw Miss Scott arrive via the unlocked front door and attack you from behind. She must have been waiting outside, keeping watch. We've found her vehicle, a rented car parked just outside the woods. The two men at your home said they'd been trying to get loose for hours, then the police arrived. Both seemed quite worried about you – one especially, almost looked guilty."

As well he might. I'd not yet forgiven Ricky for attacking me and David. Though if he hadn't shown the diaries to the police there was perhaps a little room in my heart for reconciliation.

"I'll be escorting you to hospital to have that wrist looked at," Sutton continued. "Then I'll be taking a statement from you."

"Alright, thank you."

"You know, my boss thought you looked familiar in our interview. He said you looked just like a girl he went to school with, back in the day. Eleanor Pike?"

"Oh, really?" I said, a tingle of unease spreading over me.

"You must get that a lot, especially round here."

"It's come up."

"Hmmm," she said, an unreadable expression on her face. "Might be a good idea for you to relocate, once this business is all cleared up."

Relief flooded through me like morphine. "Probably."

"Wouldn't want something like that following you around, while you're trying to make a home for yourself."

"No, I wouldn't. I suppose I just need to…move on." I said.

"Is that going to be a problem for you?"

"No," I said, truthfully. "There's nothing keeping me here. Not anymore."

Seemingly satisfied that I wasn't going to be her problem for much longer, DS Sutton escorted me through the woods to her car. On the way to the hospital I put my head against the window and dozed.

CHAPTER THIRTY-ONE

It was almost dark again by the time I returned home. DS Sutton drove me from the station, where I'd given my statement. My wrist was in a dayglow-orange cast and I had stitches all up one arm, under a thick dressing. The burns on my legs itched, but weren't too serious. I was coated in ointments and had been given painkillers, antibiotics and a tetanus injection. Now all I needed was sleep.

Sutton offered to come and 'settle me in', which I think was code for 'check under the bed for serial killers'. I refused. There was nothing scary in the bungalow. It was just a house. No matter what the locals thought.

Inside, with the door locked behind me, I took in the mess. Everything was still where Ricky had thrown it, CDs, papers and books on the floor. It looked like the police had stomped all over everything and there was a whiff of petrol about the place. The belt from my coat was still knotted around the heating pipes and there were scuffs and scrapes on the floor where Ricky and David had clearly tried to kick their legs free. I wasn't in the mood to clear up.

I found the diaries under the beanbag. At some point Ricky or David must have realised that I wouldn't want the police snooping in them, and had hidden them as best they could. It was a gesture I appreciated. They were private and I had no wish for them to be pawed over by Sutton. Or anyone else for that matter.

With the diaries in my arms I went to the bedroom. My clothes had been collected as evidence. I was wearing an oversized sweatshirt and jogging bottoms supplied by Sutton. I was grateful, as I fell asleep almost as soon as I hit the mattress.

In the morning, stiff and swollen with fresh bruises, I set the bungalow to rights. It looked almost like a proper house since the plasterers had been. With a new fitted kitchen it would make someone a lovely home. Not me though. Whatever pull Bricknell had held for me, it was gone now. I had no desire to see Wayfield in the flesh, I'd been mad to think of even trying. There was no reasoning, no winning, with someone like that. I'd learned as much from Marianna. Some people were beyond logic, beyond reason. You could never win against them, only escape.

I'd read the diaries and they'd given me no comfort. I would probably never get the closure I wanted with my mother, but I'd seen what that kind of resentment led to. I had no desire to end up like Marianna, filled with blame and grief and hate.

It wasn't until the afternoon that I checked my messages online. I had new emails from both David and Ricky. They were pretty much identical; how are you? Can't believe Marianna would do something like this. If you need anything...etc. Ricky added an apology for good measure. It was a nice gesture but I wasn't planning on trying to patch things up with them. My time in Bricknell was over and there was no way to salvage what was left of my relationships there.

There was also a message from Adam. Apparently Marianna's arrest had hit the news cycle. It wasn't a long email but each word made me tear up more. I could almost see him writing it, sitting in his bedroom at his parent's house. All the old football posters still on the wall with his Action Men looking down at him. I could imagine his face as he tried to find the right words for the bizarre situation we were in. I wanted to hug him.

Hey,
Saw the news, are you OK? Shit's crazy.
I'm sorry I wasn't there. Not sure what good I'd have been but, I hate thinking of you facing that alone. Let me know if there's anything I can do.
Adam

I wanted to call him, to see him, but that wouldn't be fair. Despite the awful events of the past few days I had no illusions about the state of our relationship. What I'd had with Adam was broken beyond repair. I'd been the one to destroy it. The fault lines in our relationship, which had been there from the start thanks to my lies, had cracked wide open. None of it was forgivable.

Had it been worth it, to get to Bricknell, to confront the events that had haunted my childhood? Not really. I hadn't really found anything that helped me, in all the time I'd been there. Since Marianna I certainly felt lighter, freer, than I had in years. Determined to change my ways and not follow her example. How I'd feel a week, a month down the line, I had no idea. I hoped it would last.

I almost felt like I owed Marianna. She'd forced me to see myself as I really was; not a victim of my parents, or a copy of them, but a survivor.

I still hoped they threw the book at the bitch.

I deleted the delayed send email that I'd written to Adam while waiting to be attacked. Everything I'd written, every excuse and reason, had been for my benefit, not Adam's. Instead I typed a short message back, telling him I was grateful for the concern but that he didn't have to worry. I wanted him to know he didn't owe me anything. That he could put me out of his mind for good. I wished him all the best and told him I'd pay him back for what he'd spent on the house. I told him I was sorry, but knew that didn't change things.

Then I put the laptop away and fetched out Marianna's box of books, taking it to the garden. I piled up every letter from the solicitor I could find along with some dried weeds. With the books on top and the whole thing drenched in white spirit, I lit the fire and watched the pages go up in an almighty whoosh of flame. I added more books, one after the other, not just Marianna's but my own, making trips to and from the house. Everything I had on the Butcher; my journal, newspaper cuttings, photos, articles. All of it. At last I was left before the dying fire, the diaries stacked in my lap.

I tore them apart piece by piece. It was awkward with only one hand, the cast only useful for holding the books down as I ripped at them. The paper was so dry and brittle that it seemed to burn before it ever touched the flames. I fed the fire my mother's pain and triumphs, her fantasies and terrors. I let it all go and watched it be consumed.

It was in her final diary that I found the card. I'd only flipped through that one, hadn't bothered to read very far into the more recent entries. It was a stupid thing, something I'd clearly coloured at school.

A tulip for mother's day, scribbled over in purple and dark blue. What surprised me what that she'd kept it. Had pressed it into the diary as she had Wayfield's rose. Only mine still clung on, pasted in with glue turning gummy and brown. As I ran my fingers over the thick, crayon lines, the card slipped an inch and I saw that there was writing underneath.

She'd done this once before, hiding her pregnancy fears under something she'd stuck in, seemingly afraid that her parents might stumble on her secrets. But this was her adult journal, the blank pages at the back a testament to her sudden death. Under the card she'd written from margin to margin, cramming the words in so closely that they ran together. The letters were sloppy, scrawled fast as if she was thinking through the pen, pouring out the words from some hidden place.

Judith hasn't visited in ages, not that I blame her. She has a life and I am very much not welcome in it. She made that clear when she left for university. I'm the one that shut her out first, held her at arm's length. I didn't understand then what it was like to be a mother. I don't mean that some magical change overtook me when I gave birth, it would have been so much easier if it had. No, I felt nothing change then. I didn't want her when she was inside me or when she was finally born, screaming. I only wanted him. I only wanted us to be together. Me and him. She was just something else that I could offer him. Something he might want. Then later, a way for us to be together, even if it wasn't for long. Never enough time.

It took me so long to realise that he didn't love me. To see that he's not capable of loving anyone. But for him I threw away anyone who did love me; my parents, who cared in their own, starchy, middleclass way, my friends wherever they are now, and my daughter, who loved me best of all, with all the innocence and completeness of a child. I ignored that love and pushed it away, until it withered. Now, it's the only love I would kill to have back.

He wants to see her. Keeps asking me for details, anything about her. Anything he can use. To get to her, manipulate her. Like he did me for so long. He's dying and he needs her, wants her cut into pieces like the others. The women he killed. I never wanted to see that part of him. Pretended it wasn't there. But he's a user, a killer. He'll tear into anyone to get what he wants.

He's wearing me down like he always does. He gets into my head like a worm, seeking out the little gaps and weaknesses he can slip through. Talks and talks and then gives me silence, silence in which I will tell him anything just to have him look at me, say anything kind. Eventually, he will get it out of me; where she lives, what she does, what she fears and needs and wants. Everything he can use to manipulate her into saving his life.

As long as I'm alive, he has a way to get to her.

A gap followed by several lines. Then, in a firmer hand and different ink, she continued. Each line written as if for a teacher's approval, the letters perfectly formed and spaced. It looked like an exercise in handwriting, considered to perfection.

I will do this for you, Julie.
Love, Mummy.

I stared at those nine words for a long time. Never had she called herself 'Mummy'. The phrase 'I am your mother!' was used a lot when she wanted to make me do something, but never that. Even on Christmas presents and cards she'd never said it. Not even 'love' just, 'from Mum'.

I didn't have to wonder what it was she'd done. Through a film of tears I looked into the fire and heard again the voice of the police officer. He'd called while I was at work. I'd been waiting to take over a route when I answered, half paying attention. 'I'm sorry to have to tell you that your mother has been in a road traffic incident…'

Was that the only thing she thought she could offer me, in the end? A firebreak between me and Wayfield? Severing that tie to keep me safe, knowing that as long as she was alive, she'd go back to him? That as long as he could reach her, he could get to me, eventually.

I smoothed the page with my fingers, feeling the hurt engraved in every pen stroke. The scent of her perfume rose up, mixing with that of the fire and the wax crayons I'd used on her mother's day card. I reached for the last thing beside me, a folded sheet of paper.

It was the final letter. The urgent one that Ricky had shaken in my face. The one that outlined Wayfield's dire prognosis. That letter was proof that without me, he was already dead.

I balled the letter up and tossed it into the fire. It burned along with the remains of the diaries. Then I took the tulip card and its hidden page and held them, re-reading my mum's final message even though each word was burnt into me already, stored away where it would never be forgotten. Then, one after the other, I laid the card and letter in the flames. I would always, in some hidden part of myself, know that however much she'd failed me, Mum had loved me, in her own way, at the end. That would have to be enough.

It was time to let her go.

OTHER BOOKS BY SARAH GOODWIN

For more novels by Sarah Goodwin, try these recent releases from Avon, available in paperback, ebook and as audiobooks.

Stranded

You'll want to stay. Until you can't leave...

A group of strangers arrive on a beautiful but remote island, ready for the challenge of a lifetime: to live there for one year, without contact with the outside world.

But twelve months later, on the day when the boat is due to return for them, no one arrives.

Eight people stepped foot on the island. How many will make it off alive?

Buy 'Stranded' on Amazon

The 13th Girl

'Because he chose you. Out of thirteen girls. You were the one. The last one.'

Lucy Townsend lives a normal life. She has a husband she loves, in-laws she can't stand and she's just found out she's going to be a mother. But Lucy has a dark and dangerous secret. She is not who she says she is. Lucy is not even her real name. Twenty years ago, she escaped something terrible. Something she has tried to put behind her.

Someone out there knows all of her secrets and has been biding their time to come back for her; the thirteenth girl, the only one who managed to escape.

Lucy was lucky once. But now it's not only her life on the line. Will she be so lucky this time?

Buy 'The 13th Girl' on Amazon

The Resort

It was a safe haven, until it became a trap...

Mila and her husband Ethan are on their way to her sister's wedding at a luxurious ski resort. As they drive through the mountains, surrounded by snow covered forests, Mila feels like everything is finally going to plan. When the car engine suddenly stops and won't start again.

Stranded, with night closing in, they make their way on foot back to where they saw a sign for some cabins. When they finally reach them, they find the windows boarded up and the buildings in disrepair. They have the eerie sense they shouldn't be there. With snow falling more heavily, they have no choice but to break into one to spend the night.

In the morning when Mila wakes, Ethan is gone.
Now she is all alone.
Or is she?

Buy 'The Resort' on Amazon

The Blackout
Coming in September 2023 – Pre-order now!

When Meg and Cat arrange a night out in Bristol, it's the perfect distraction from Meg's grief over her brother. But, after accidentally spending their cab money on drinks, they must walk home all the way across the city. Hungry, exhausted and barefoot, they decide to take a shortcut along a dark canal path.

That's when they notice the two men silently following them.

Suddenly forced to run for their lives, Meg and Cat scramble into an abandoned house and hide for hours before eventually the police show up to rescue them.

But then the night goes from bad to worse...

Pre-Order/Buy on Amazon

ACKNOWLEDGEMENTS

Thanks as always goes to my family for their support during the writing and editing process. As this book was self-published they also provided a sounding board for creative decisions, gripes, tears and recriminations.

Thank you to Vander, who provided input on the cover, title and the decision to publish this book at all. Thank you for promoting my work for years now and for supplying free feedback and cover art when I first started trying to get my books out there. Every writer needs a friend like you (so basically, a friend who is also a writer but who has about a thousand other talents). Vander is a very talented EVERYTHING and is a professional drag artist. Everyone should most definitely follow them online @fluxxwyldly.

I owe my agent Laura Williams for her input on the first draft of 'this serial killer book club novel thing'. Whilst the manuscript wasn't picked up for publication it was not due to lack of trying. Thank you for entertaining my weirder ideas and for giving such great feedback to bring them down to earth as gently as possible.

Thanks go to 'rebecacovers' on Fiverr for the amazing cover art and to 'cheymongeon' also on Fiverr, for their proofreading skills. Both offer a professional service at competitive rates and I definitely recommend them.

And as always a big thank you to everyone who has purchased, read and reviewed this book. It makes such a difference and I can honestly say I read every single one.